Also by Richard Wiley

Soldiers in Hiding

Fools' Gold

Festival for Three Thousand Maidens

Indigo

Ahmed's Revenge

RICHARD WILEY

Ahmed's Revenge

A NOVEL

RANDOM HOUSE NEW YORK

All rights reserved under International and Pan-American Copyright Con-
ventions. Published in the United States by Random House, Inc., New York,
and simultaneously in Canada by Random House of Canada Limited, Toronto.

A portion of this work was originally published in slightly different form in the
Colorado Review.

Library of Congress Cataloging-in-Publication Data

Wiley, Richard.
    Ahmed's revenge : a novel / Richard Wiley. — 1st ed.
       p.   cm.
    ISBN 0-679-45744-5 (acid-free paper)
    I. Title.
  PS3573.I433A74   1998
  813'.54—dc21   97-15374

Random House website address: www.randomhouse.com

Printed in the United States of America on acid-free paper

9   8   7   6   5   4   3   2

First Edition

Book design by Caroline Cunningham

For my family

Acknowledgments

The author wishes to thank, in the United States, the University of Nevada, Las Vegas, for partial funding of his research; Gail Hochman, for her belief all these years, and for her tenacity; and Richard Bausch for keeping the faith.

In Kenya, he wishes to thank Connie Buford for the use of her home in Nairobi; Ann and Ted Goss for answering his questions about animal behavior and poaching; and most especially David Bartholomew, for help and friendship on all kinds of levels.

Ahmed

This is a perfect fiberglass model of the famous elephant of Marsabit. In 1970, His Excellency President Jomo Kenyatta decreed that this elephant be placed under permanent 24-hour honour guard protecting him from poachers. He became a national symbol.

Ahmed died of natural causes in 1974 and was prepared for exhibition by Zimmermans of Nairobi. Normal taxidermy methods could not be applied in the mounting.

Hii ni sanamu dhabiti ya yule ndovu maarufu aliyeishi huko Marsabit. Hapo mwaka wa 1970, mtukufu rais Mzee Jomo Kenyatta alimpatia ndovu huyo ulinzi wa sheria ikalazimika alindwe usiku na mchana kutokana na wezi wa mawindo. Ahmed alifuka kutokana na uzee hapo mwaka wa 1974 na sanamu yake ikatengenezwa na kompani ya Zimmermans hapa Nairobi. Utengenezaji ya kawaida ngozi haukauwezekana.

STATISTICS

Age at death	55-62 years
Height at the shoulder	3 m (9'10")
Tusks: Right	3 m (9'9")
Left	2.8 m (9'4")
Weight of each tusk	67 kgs (148 lbs)

(The above appears on a sign situated in front of the life-size replica of Ahmed in the National Museum in Nairobi.)

Act One

1

Jules et Jim

I had a farm in Africa too. My farm was not in the Ngong Hills but on even richer land about eighty miles west of Nairobi. To get to my farm you drive down off what is called "the escarpment," into the Great Rift Valley and then up again, forty minutes or so north of the dusty Maasai town of Narok. My husband, Julius, and I bought the farm from an out-of-luck Kikuyu man in 1968, and when the rains came or when our evening reading didn't suit us, we would sometimes get out Julius's maps and notice that our farm, along with those of Isak Dinesen near the town of Karen, and Elspeth Huxley out Thika way, formed an obtuse triangle, with Julius and me at the pinnacle, which seemed right to us since we were alive and young and farming while those other two were not, one long gone and one buried, both of their lives mythologised in books and film and on the BBC.

We were lucky to have found such a good farm quickly and to buy it with so little trouble. The Kikuyu man was anxious, which should perhaps have warned us away, but Julius wanted to grow coffee, and though farmers in our region had always grown wheat, everyone assured us that coffee would grow just as well. We had a soil study done and an analysis of the annual rains, and we rented a big shed in Narok where we could do our own drying and processing. At 6,200 feet we were certainly high enough for coffee, but I think we'd have gone ahead even without the studies. Julius thought that the growing of coffee was a godly kind of enterprise, something he wanted to do, and I, because I loved and believed in Julius, thought so too.

It took a year for us to prepare the ground and hire a crew, to really get started with the work, but as anyone who has ever had a cup of our coffee can attest, it was worth the wait. Even from the very beginning, from that first harvest in December of '69, things were done right. Our coffee was rich and sure of itself, robust and flavourful. There were no tricks to our coffee, just as there were no tricks to our marriage. Julius said our processing foreman was a gift from God, but it was because of Julius that our coffee had none of that hickory-chicory nonsense that other growers sometimes tried to put in. I used to think that you could taste Julius's character in each cup, but alas, maybe I was wrong.

Here is the slogan Julius wrote for the sides of our first batch of burlap coffee bags: *"One sip and you will know, Grant's coffee is the kind to grow."* It was a little out of the way, as you can no doubt tell, but it was pure Julius, open arms to everyone, you too can grow your own. We actually argued about the slogan, and in the end I had a hand in calming it down. By the time we ordered the bags again we got rid of that senseless second clause. Strange to say, it has stuck in my head that maybe we shouldn't have, maybe I should have left things alone.

/   /   /

I like the story about Julius and the burlap bags because it helps me to remember his exuberance and his joy. The other story I want to tell is how his name stopped being Julius and became Jules.

We had gone into Nairobi one weekend, it was in May of 1974, to see a film at the French Cultural Centre. Julius and I both knew French, and since those films were our only chance to keep up with the language, we went every month or so.

The film we saw that particular weekend was François Truffaut's *Jules et Jim*, do you remember it? Well, it's a good film, very innocent and sweet, and to our great surprise, Julius looked like Oskar Werner, the actor who played Jules. I'm not talking about some slight resemblance here, but a dead-ringer kind of thing. Julius and that actor could have been brothers, they could have been the same man, and though Oskar Werner was not unknown, neither Julius nor I had ever seen him before. It was a silly thing, but, my God, Julius was proud. He'd had a couple of drinks before the film, and when it was over he was the cock of the walk, doing a rooster shuffle around the French Cultural Centre with his arms pulled back. Some of the French women in the audience started calling him Jules and flirting with him outrageously but in a funny kind of way. A few of them even asked him for his autograph, playing the whole thing out. Julius kept strutting, smiling till his mouth got tired, but all he would say was that Oskar Werner was too short, that it should be clear to anyone that he was taller and better-looking than the man on the screen.

We stayed in Nairobi that night, at the New Stanley Hotel. Down in the restaurant Julius kept on speaking French and he drank too much wine. He went around the room introducing himself as Jules, saying it the French way, which sounds like "jewel" but with a soft and runny *j*. He irritated the real French patrons who happened to be about, and after dinner, when the coffee came, he was so critical of it that for a while I thought he and the maître d' might actually get into a fight. In the end, however, the maître d' laughed and Julius went out to our lorry and brought the man a small bag of Grant's Coffee to make up for the scene he'd caused. I remember it all so well. That was one of the last bags of Grant's Coffee with the original slogan on the side. Julius had been saving it to send to his uncle in Canada, but the maître d' got it instead. And what Julius got was a different name. After that Julius was Jules, most of the time. Surprising to say, it was an easy change. And during our more intimate moments I was occasionally Jim, a situation that didn't make any more sense than that original coffee slogan did.

I think the night we saw *Jules et Jim* was the strangest night of our life together, though there were certainly more dramatic ones. I didn't think so then, but in retrospect, you know, it had to have been. Jules was drunk and he was in a randy mood, but he smelled too much like wine and his eyes were rheumy and his hair was standing up in a ridiculous cowlick. That was the first time he called me Jim, and I didn't like it at all. He crowed that he wanted to call me by the name of the female character in the film, but he couldn't remember what her name was, and I wouldn't tell him, so pretty soon he started calling me Jim over and over again. "I want you, Jimmy, I want you, Jim," he said, and I said back to him, spitting my irritation through a closed jaw, "If you want me call me Nora, that's my name."

I should say that Jules was still speaking French and I didn't like that very much either. I kept switching back to English. "Nora Grant," I said, "call me Nora Grant, say it right now. And stop speaking French, Julius, your accent's no good." That was weak since both of us knew his accent was better than mine, but all his earlier flirting came rushing back to me then, and I got madder than I was before. The more I thought about it the more my anger came. I was willing enough to call him Jules, since that's what he seemed to want, but what I wanted was my own true name, which I was happy with and loved. My name and the natural contours of my husband's voice, I'd always thought, went together like coffee and hot milk, and were the perfect aphrodisiac. "Not tonight, Julius," I shouted, "not on your life!"

Already, only a short time after he'd been christened Jules, "Julius" was sounding punitive on my tongue, but no matter how I shouted and raved, Jules just kept saying "Jim," and anyone who has ever been married knows what something like that can do.

"Stop it, Julius!" I screamed. "Stop it right now!"

"Jim, Jim, Jim," he said, "Jim, Jim, Jim."

I began flailing around the room, searching for something to throw, when suddenly Julius stormed out of the place, slamming the door behind him. It was absolutely and powerfully strange. He got into the lift, somehow slamming that door too, and soon I saw him from our window, down on Kenyatta Avenue, walking away from the hotel.

I sat on the windowsill and fumed, wondering how he could behave like that, but as is usual with me, no matter how I tried to hold on to it, my anger started leaving as soon as I was alone. Hadn't Julius been weaving more than the drink would make him weave, I asked myself, and where in the world would he go? As the anger went out of me worry came in, so though I normally wouldn't do such a thing, pretty soon I ran out of the room myself, leaving the lift and taking the stairs, reaching to the street in no time to follow my husband along.

•   /   /   /

I was thirty-one that year and Julius was thirty-five. We had been married for six years and we were happy, so when I trailed him down Kenyatta Avenue I swear it was as protector, not as detective, that I went. It wasn't very late, only a little after ten, but Nairobi could be dangerous to a man alone, especially if the man was weaving about as if he couldn't defend himself. I had a little trouble catching up with Jules, but when I finally did, I slowed down, staying a block or so behind. I was beginning to feel foolish and putridly wife-like, and of course I knew that if Jules was robbed I wouldn't be able to do much to stop it. I only worried about the reaction of Jules himself, to the robbers in my mind. My husband was tough, he had a low center of gravity, and he could box, so if a robber came out and told Jules to give up his wallet, the weaving might turn into bobbing, and Jules might knock the robber down. And if that happened Jules might really get hurt, for *pangas* and knives can beat boxing nearly every time.

I thought Jules was going to the bar in the Six Eighty

Hotel. He liked that bar with all its women of the night. We would, in fact, go there together sometimes, for a daytime bottle of beer when we were in Nairobi buying supplies. But when Jules turned across the street and up toward the central market I no longer had any idea where he was going. It occurred to me that he might just walk in a big loop, that he was cooling himself off and would come back to our room to call me Nora as I wanted him to, and when that thought got me I nearly turned around and ran back so that I could catch my breath and act languid when he stumbled through the door.

Jules slowed when he got near the market, which, of course, was closed at that time of night. He turned down Market Street and walked to a corner on which there was a nightclub upstairs over a petrol station. Market Street was dark but he kept going, past the nightclub and down toward Loita Street, which was pretty nearly out of the downtown. By this time Jules had speeded up and not only lost his weave but was walking so assuredly that I knew he'd known where he was going all along. Ah-ha, I thought, the bastard had it planned. Following him got harder since we were the only two people on the road. What is my husband up to? I kept asking myself, but all I knew for sure was that the idea of me as protector was totally gone. Now I was a detective all the way.

There was a small two-storey building at the end of the block, around the corner to the right. The building actually seemed like someone's home. It was separated from its neighbours on the street, standing alone and dark. A person could walk along narrow pathways on either side of the house, and that's what Jules did, choosing the pathway nearest him and entering a side door halfway down.

What was I supposed to do, what would anyone do in

circumstances such as these? Julius and I had a marriage that really was based on trust, that wasn't just a word in our case, but a kind of easy-to-handle general rule—the way a wedding ring binds a finger, that's the way trust bound Julius Grant and me. But this situation was beyond me. Not long ago we had been at the French Cultural Centre watching *Jules et Jim,* and a half a day before that we had been on our farm, overseeing our harvest and looking out at the Mara plains. And now I was at the dark end of Loita Street alone, and my husband was inside the building at my side. My normal frame of mind would have told me to go back to the hotel and wait, but try as I might, I couldn't find my normal frame of mind.

I had not thought so at first but there were, after all, lights on inside the house, turned down low. Seeing them gave me the idea to go up to the front door and knock and ask whoever answered if Julius Grant could come out and play. I thought such a tactic contained the proper lightness of touch and might even get me off the hook for following him when what-ever Jules was doing turned out to be fine. But as I got closer my courage left me, and I suddenly veered past the front of the house, following instead the path Jules had taken, the one that led to that ominous side door. Once I was on the path I walked quickly, in my usual no-nonsense kind of way, and by the time I got to the door, all my courage returned. I was prepared not only to knock on it but to turn the handle and go inside, just as Jules had done. Unlike the door in front, however, this side door had a window, and through a crack in its curtain I saw a scene that stayed my hand. My husband was there, standing by a table and drinking from a bottle of beer. I had expected a woman, I admit it now, but what I saw was stranger than that, both better and worse at the same time. I can hardly say the word, but what I saw was ivory, the raw material. My husband, Julius Grant, was standing in a room full of yanked-out elephant tusks.

Let me say right now that no one I knew was farther from the complicated world of poachers, no one was farther from Kenya's illegal ivory trade, than Julius Grant. Still, though that window didn't afford me more than a couple of seconds' worth of looking, I know what I saw. My husband was next to the table, a dark expression on his face, and all around him tusks were tied together in bunches, on top of the table and beside it and everywhere across the floor. They weren't long tusks, not three feet on the average, and they hadn't been cleaned. Jules's bottle of beer was before him, its liquid an unsettled sea. There was no one else in the room, but I caught sight of someone leaving through a doorway to my right. I saw the bottom half of a medium-brown jacket, and the black heel of a shoe. The room was a kitchen, I knew, because there was a sink and a refrigerator on the far side.

I jumped away from the window, but I didn't duck back the way I had come. Rather, I ran toward the rear of the house, where there was another low building of some kind. I did consider that the wearer of the jacket I'd seen might be back there too, but I also knew that a beeline in the general direction of the hotel would afford me the best chance of not being caught by Julius or someone else coming out of the front door. I ran quietly, but I didn't run slowly, and soon I discovered that the path led into someone's small *shamba*, a garden, believe it or not, which I immediately tumbled into, severely scratching my thigh. I shouted, but I got up before anyone could come and lurched onto another path that led to an adjoining street on the block's far side. Though I had a lot of trouble trying to think, I certainly knew enough to continue moving. I wanted to be back in our room at the New Stanley Hotel, feigning sleep, by the time Jules returned. So I let it all out, sprinting along Kenyatta Avenue like a schoolgirl, all the way down to Kimathi Street.

I was exhausted and sweating, and my thigh was bleeding a lot, so as soon as I got back to our room I jumped into the shower, stopping only to hide my filthy clothes. I found part of a large thorn in my thigh and pulled it out, and since neither Jules nor I had brought pyjamas with us, when I was done I crawled into the bed, naked but dry, a small towel wrapped around my thigh. I tried to calm myself, to regain my natural optimism and to make my heart-beat slow down. I tried to believe that Jules would tell me everything the moment he came in, but whatever I told myself, what I had seen made no sense at all. Julius Grant was a coffee-growing man, that was how he lived his life, and if I knew anything about him, it was that he did not suffer poachers. He hated the bastards, and he absolutely celebrated the wildlife on our farm, even the elephants who sometimes came crashing through. But it was also clear to me that Jules had started our fight, all that rubbish about calling me Jim, so that he could storm out of the hotel and get over to that kitchen on Loita Street without my knowing about it.

My mind was teeming with the images I had seen, I couldn't make it slow down, but by the time I heard the door open, I was nevertheless able to lie still. And sure enough, when Jules came in he was contrite. "Hello, Nora dear," he sang. "Nora Barnacle home from the sea." Nora Barnacle indeed. When Jules drank he liked to pretend that he was James Joyce, and it was all I could do to keep from sitting up and calling him Jim.

But Jules was a thick-bodied man and a good slow lover, I haven't said that yet. I also haven't said that I made love with Jules on the night we met. My father was staying in London and I was visiting him and Jules was a houseguest of the man next door. It was a hot summer night and I was sitting on my father's porch, watching people walk by and thinking vaguely of Kenya and England, of the vast differences between them, and the direction my life was taking, when Julius came out and told me his name and asked if I'd like to join him at the pub. He was polite and funny and I told him "Sure." I was twenty-four then, nearly twenty-five, and I remember feeling that there had already been too many men in my life. There had been five, and Jules, by the end of that night, was number six, making a neat half dozen, and ending my experimental period once and for all.

Jules believed I was asleep when he got back, but he was determined to awaken me by going down beneath the sheets and playing. And though I didn't forget about the house on Loita Street with all those horrible tusks, I soon enough put the image aside, since everything he did down there was an apology, everything for my pleasure, nothing for his, and I knew he would tell me about it anyway, in his own good time.

The next morning, however, neither of us said a word. Since I didn't ask him, Jules didn't have to lie, so oddly enough it was only I who lied that day. When we got out of bed there was blood on the sheets, and when Jules said he was surprised,

I turned my leg away, telling him only that several hours after all our ruckus my period had come. Then I sent him down to the chemist's for some sanitary pads, while I quickly went to work on the real wound I had.

By that I mean the tear in my thigh, not the larger wound, the one that neither Jules nor I, as it turned out, would ever be able to do anything to heal.

2

Farm Life Disrupted

When Jules and I got back home again we had the welcome prospect of hard work to keep conversation at bay. I decided that I wouldn't say anything about what I'd seen on Loita Street, that I'd wait for him to speak no matter how long it took. Still, a hundred times I was on the verge of ripping it out of him, and a hundred other times, I swear, I knew that full disclosure was on the tip of Jules's tongue, ready to step out and clear the air between us without me forcing it at all. But, alas, neither of us spoke. It was harvest time and we had people everywhere, crews to feed, sheds to tend to and equipment to repair, an endless array of lorries coming and going in the afternoon light, taking our coffee to the processing plant. It was a hard harvest that year, the hardest we had had, and it left no time for serious talk. We could eat and we could discuss what tomorrow might bring, but that was all. Sleep was third on our agenda and it was always the longest item.

During past harvests, I guess I am inclined to say, every little disturbance, even such a thing as a broken-down lorry on the road, seemed to define vitality for Jules and me. Every unexpected event, however awful at the time, was a lesson in what it meant to be alive and involved with something that we loved. We worked our farm together, and when we ate our evening meals, we sat on a porch that looked over miles and miles of the kind of land that God must have created first, if He created it at all. We had a small pond about eighty yards from our porch, and often at dusk, while we drank our coffee or finished a bottle of wine, animals would come out of the surrounding bush to drink, the way the biblical animals must have done, not quite the lion and the lamb together, maybe, but certainly the lion, and sometimes the leopard, and giraffes and impalas and warthogs. Since I am a daughter of Kenya it may seem strange that I find it thrilling still, and the truth is that when I was young and used to go on safaris with my dad, I didn't think nearly so much of it as I do now. But I was educated in England, and there I learned the lesson that I had started at the top, or conversely, that if there's a scale of beauty and wonder in the world, I had grown up on that scale's heavy end. And when I came back with Jules tagging along, anxious to start a new life with me, I never took it for granted again.

All of this is not to say that there weren't frustrations for Jules and me even before the thorn of his secret started festering in my thigh and in my heart. Working the land as we did was always hard. The Maasai were constantly coming around, once setting down a whole village on land that we intended for planting, and for a time we couldn't catch a leopard that killed the farm animals we used to keep, one or two a week, for an entire year. But, my God, the gifts of the planet were so abundantly laid at our door. Even when elephants trampled a coffee crop, wandering through like fat ladies in a seed store, as they did in '71, I could never quite summon the outrage that such an act deserved, though I had to stop Jules several times from running for his gun. Jules loved elephants, I've already said that, but he loved his coffee more, and he did everything he could think of to keep them off our land.

/   /   /

We had been back from seeing *Jules et Jim* for a fortnight when one evening there was a disturbance out by our pond. Jules was in the bathtub, washing the day's work away, and I was at our desk writing checks on our Kenyan shilling account so that Jules, who was going back into Nairobi the next morning, could visit the merchants and pay our bills. Our pond, of course, was only a convenient watering hole from the animals' point of view, so fights of one kind or another were a common affair out there. Elephants, however, because of all the fences we put up to keep them out, were not common at all, and I was moved quickly away from my bill paying by a single elephant trumpet, a weak kind of broken bugle call.

"Julius," I mildly said, but Jules had the water running and didn't hear.

I walked out onto our porch and listened again. There were some Maasai camped five miles or so on the other side of the pond, well down toward the Mara plains. Jules had told me they were there. I hadn't seen them yet, but the first thing I saw when I went outside were two young *morani* warriors standing there, close to the house, spears and bodies erect. I don't know much Maasai so I spoke in Kiswahili.

"Did you arrive just now?" I asked. "Did you see an elephant nearby? Was that an elephant that I heard, or was it some other sound?"

If elephants were going to run across our farm, this was about the best time for them to do it, because we'd just finished our harvest, but any farmer will tell you that no time is a good time for them to come. It would mean that our break was broken somewhere, our defenses down, and even if they stayed out of the coffee, our trees and outer buildings might get knocked around. Elephants on a Kenyan farm were the breathing equivalents of tornados in the American Midwest, and I knew that if they were there, we had to do something fast to get them turned around.

"There are too many elephants now," said one of the Maasai, "but this time only one small calf is at your pond. Tell Bwana to bring his gun."

Our pond had a spotlight next to it, but our generator wasn't switched on. Since I had a torch on a table just inside the door, however, I decided to ask the Maasai to walk me down to the pond and show me. A lost little elephant calf wasn't so bad. If we could scare it into moving off our land and back down toward the rest of the herd, we might still avoid damage.

"My husband is bathing," I said. "He'll be out when he's done."

I took the torch and came down off the porch and the three of us headed toward the pond. It could be a dangerous walk alone at night—even our African crew stayed pretty close to their dormitory—but with the *morani* there the animals would scatter, and I thought we'd be fine.

Our foreman had heard the elephant too and had pulled the cord to our generator, quickly lighting the pond. After that he came out to join us. Our foreman's name was Kamau and he had worked for the Kikuyu man before us, so he knew everything about the farm.

"They say there's only a single calf," I told him. "Let's just get it out the way it came in. You can take someone down to fix the break after it's gone."

At the pond, which we approached quietly and from the downwind side, there was indeed an elephant, a baby standing no more than three feet tall. Although this might seem like good news, it wasn't. Maybe such a small calf couldn't damage much, but I was sure it had been followed in by lions, that that was the reason for its pitiful sound, and with such an easy kill at hand, the lions might not be intimidated by the presence of myself and Kamau, or by the Maasai. Even if this baby's mother showed up it might be difficult to avoid a kill at our pond, and if that happened our routine would be disrupted, either by the unmovable carcass and the scavengers it would bring, or by the mother elephant's wrecking of our farm in her grief and rage, her desire for revenge.

The Maasai understood immediately what was going on and began producing noises that would make the lions think we were many and scare the little elephant away at the same time. The Maasai's trick was a good one but it worked too well.

The elephant calf jumped around in fear and, trying to run too quickly, fell to its knees in the mud.

After that things happened fast. A big female lion came out of the darkness very close to us. I had my torch on her and I saw her look our way even as she gained speed. The elephant calf was on its feet again. It trumpeted another small scream into the night just as the lion hit it, smashing into it with the force of a lorry accident on the road and flipping the elephant all the way over onto its back. The lion planted her claws deep into the baby elephant's head, and was biting the elephant deeply too, taking a large amount of the flesh of its neck between her jaws, puncturing the skin and holding on while the elephant wriggled around, still using all of its power but to no particular end, with no particular goal at all.

There was a single moment of relative quiet then, when we could hear the breaking of skin and bone, before three other lions, two smaller females and a cub, came from the other side of the pond. These females moved nearly as fast as the first one had, and though the urgency of the kill was gone, they tore into the elephant calf too, one of them pulling fiercely on a hind leg, the other pushing its teeth into the elephant's side. Even the cub, when it arrived, landed on the baby elephant's middle, then rolled off and began attacking the poor thing's trunk, which was coming off the ground haphazardly and waving at us in the savaged air.

Though I'd lived in Africa all of my life I had never seen anything like this before. I didn't feel very much personal danger, what with the two Maasai and Kamau standing near, but the kills I'd seen before had mostly been viewed through the safety glass of cars, and therefore were a bit like something I'd watched on TV. I knew that soon there would be other cats around, since these females, big as they were, couldn't drag the little elephant very far away. Either the males and other lions of the pride were on their way already or one of the females would soon go off to fetch them. In an hour there could be a dozen lions eating at our pond. Not only that, but there would be hyenas standing just away, vultures circling above, and who knew what else. We wouldn't be able to go anywhere near our pond for a day.

Jules had come out of the house and was standing close behind me when I turned around. He had his rifle with him, slung over a shoulder of his white terry-cloth robe, and his hair was wet.

"Oh shit," he said, "god damn it, fucking A," but he kept his rifle low. He had been in Africa long enough to know it was too late to do anything but swear.

It was right about then, with Jules's terry-cloth robe luminous in the moonlight, that we all seemed to get the idea of retreating at the same time. A lioness might be single-minded when stalking an elephant calf, but now there were three of them, not counting the cub, and one of them was beginning to look around. The Maasai started shouting again, an excited, high-up-in-the-throat chatter that sounded like a grazing-rights argument just before the spears come out, and Kamau took a step toward Jules, standing on the side of him where the rifle was still slung. And just at that instant the other elephants appeared across the pond. There had been a terrific amount of noise connected with the kill, so I wasn't surprised that we hadn't heard them. They came out of the dark like grey mountains out of a fog. There were two full-grown females, the one in the lead no doubt the baby calf's mother, and since they weren't wasting any time, the lions, though they roared like crazy for a brief second or two, turned toward us to go hide until things calmed down.

We had stood stupidly watching for so long that by then there wasn't a hell of a lot we could do. We were fifty yards from our house and, though I know I said I thought we'd be fine before, we had displayed a foolishness, an indifference to danger, not uncommon among people who have lived here for a long time. Still, the lions were running away from the elephants, not attacking us, so I thought that if we crowded together and stood still they might pass on by. Our house was off to the side of the way they wanted to go, and once the lions were past us, I believed, we could quickly run inside. The elephants would then either chase the lions beyond the workers' dormitory and into the coffee behind, or stop to mourn the calf. Either way they'd make a great mess of things, but right then that seemed like a fair exchange all around.

The two Maasai fell into a kind of kneeling crouch, their spears pointed up at forty-five-degree angles from the ground. This was a common warrior position, and was based on the perilous theory that an attacking lion would impale itself on the end of the spear before it actually got to the Maasai. I looked at their faces and they were calm, so since Kamau had immediately got down behind one of the Maasai, I got down behind the other. That left only Jules in a fully upright position, standing there shining in his terry-cloth robe. Jules took his rifle off his shoulder at about the time the first of the lions got near. She was still at least twenty feet away but she wasn't passing by fast enough. The elephants had stopped at the carcass of the calf, and the lions, who were still looking back, stopped too.

Because Jules was terrified, he wasn't very quick with his gun, even though the lead lioness was undecided about what to do next and thus had given him time. She first took a step toward the coffee, then turned back toward the elephants again and then turned to look at Jules. The Maasai and Kamau and I had pivoted in the lion's direction each time she moved. We were like human tank turrets, so she finally decided to run past us on Jules's side. Jules got his rifle up but the lioness was there instantly. She ran at him hard, then fell back suddenly and rose up above him, dancing in the dirt like a fish on a line, and swatting at Jules with the wide-open claw of what I thought of as her right hand. She immediately knocked the rifle away, into the dirt a few yards from Kamau and me, and then she backed up and began turning in circles, furious and completely unsure of what to do. The other two lions and the cub were gone now, so we all stood up, moving, again, toward the house, the Maasai spears pricking into the night air behind us. And I only realised that something was seriously wrong when Jules didn't come along. He had slumped to the ground and the white of his robe, from his shoulder to the cuff of his left arm, was turning slowly and deeply dark. I thought the lion had only knocked the rifle away, but now I imagined a shredded arm, though the terry-cloth didn't seem torn at all. "Julius!" I called. "Oh Christ, get up and come over here! Let's take care of it inside!"

The Maasai warriors took a couple of steps back toward Jules, and Kamau went over and quickly got the rifle. The lion was roaring again, still unsure, but when Kamau fired the gun,

Jules leapt off the ground, the lion disappeared, and so did the elephants, all of them running back around the pond. For a moment I thought that was the end of it but it was not. We all soon realised that Kamau's bullet, while it had successfully scared the animals away, had entered my husband's back just to the side of his right shoulder blade, first sending him after the animals, then plunging him into the dried-out dirt a half dozen yards from where I stood. His robe rode up above his waist in an undignified way, and the moonlight bathed his buttocks and legs and the horrible, filthy ground.

As soon as the shot was fired Kamau dropped the rifle and ran. One of the Maasai and I got to Jules at the same time, while the other hurried back toward the house, calling out for anyone.

I was afraid to turn Jules over or even to touch his arm, but when we got to him he let us know he was alive, at least, by trumpeting out his own harrowing sound. I grabbed the spear from the Maasai and used its sharp tip to tear the cloth at the bottom of Jules's robe. And once I had it started the Maasai and I pulled the robe apart quickly, making long thick strips of bandage.

"Hold on, Julius!" I said. "We'll just stop this bleeding and then I'll get on the radio. Looks like you'll be going back into Nairobi a day ahead of time."

I tried to keep calmness and order in my voice, but when we finally did turn Jules so that we could wrap the strips of bandage around his arm, calmness and order went away. What I supposed to be Jules's left bicep was flapping free of his bone, and though there had been a good deal of blood on the robe, the worst thing was that the bicep appeared to be bloodless now, like a piece of thick shoe leather or the lolling tongue of a dead cow. I could see the plain white expanse of my husband's humerus behind his bicep, desolate-looking and thin, like the handle of an unpainted hoe.

"Oh dear God!" I moaned, grabbing my own arm and turning my head away. But it was up to me to pick that bicep up and tuck it back in next to the bone. After that I took the cleanest piece of terry-cloth and wrapped everything tight, from my husband's shoulder to his elbow and below.

I think I forgot the hole in Jules's shoulder in order to deal with his arm, but once I got him turned over I could see that though the bullet had entered neatly, where it came out, the wound looked bad. Jules's right breast, the far right side of his chest, was like a crater on soft ground, so I simply placed layers of folded terry-cloth over it and pushed down.

"Can you help me now?" I shouted at the Maasai. "Can we carry him inside?"

I was speaking English but the Maasai came right away, and when we lifted Julius up he turned himself under my husband in such a way that Jules's chest bandage was pressed tightly between them, held in place by the warrior's back. And when I tried to help he motioned me away and carried my husband into the house, where the other Maasai or one of our field hands had made a makeshift bed on the floor.

/ / /

I am trying to let my telling of the story embrace all of the horror that the night contained, though when I remember it now, I think of myself as having been calm. I was doing my best to hold my emotions at bay until I had stopped the bleeding and done the work that needed to be done. Even inside the house with the door closed, I worked as I might had I been tending to a stranger or to a member of our crew. I found blankets to keep Jules warm, and I got on our radio, quickly calling the ranger in charge of the Narok branch of the Ministry of Wildlife and asking that he find a helicopter to send. For once the radio worked well, and in a matter of minutes I had everything arranged. I even went into the kitchen for a bottle of Irish whiskey, poured some of it into a tablespoon, and dripped it down over my husband's lips and tongue.

I had forgotten to ask where the helicopter was, whether it was in Narok or Nairobi, but it was too late to radio back by then, for I had begun to shake, I think because everything was done. I asked the Maasai to go out and look into the sky, to listen and watch for the helicopter, and then I got down next to Jules, laying myself along the length of him, so that he could make me stop shaking and I could make him warm. "Dear God, keep him alive!" I whispered. "Don't let him die!"

When I heard the helicopter not much time had passed, and when I'd collected myself, getting some money from our desk and calling a couple of the farm workers in from the porch, my shaking was gone. We had a stretcher on the farm, and after the helicopter landed, beating its blades frantically, like wings against our door, we moved Jules out and got him settled on a platform built for such things, on a pontoon just outside the cab.

The helicopter pilot was a man I knew, an old park ranger who had long ago worked for my father. "Francis," I said, "quick, get him to Nairobi Hospital. Please, Francis, make us get there now."

I got into the helicopter, taking the seat nearest Jules, and as we lifted off I saw my husband's hair move in the wind and I saw the two Maasai point their spears up and I saw the farm workers all standing together like a choir, their mouths forming zeros as they watched us fall upward into the sky. As we flew over the pond I saw the dead elephant calf, his trunk severed but beside him on the hideous ground, and when we banked into the somehow purple night, I looked down into the Great Rift Valley, then up toward Ethiopia and beyond it to the Middle East, to Jordan where the valley began, and where there was a river that Jules would surely be crossing, that he'd surely be crossing sometime that night or early the next day.

/   /   /

Things had worked better than I imagined they would—we got off the farm quickly and into the city in record time—but I hadn't thought to tell the people at Nairobi Hospital we were coming, and when we landed in the car park it took forever to get anyone at all to come outside, and to get them to call our own doctor, who lived out next to my father's house on Lower Kabete Road.

Jules's immediate problem was loss of blood. I told them his blood type was "O," and when they stuck needles in his arm, I swear I could see the colour coming back into his face right away. There was a certain articulation in his lips and a pinkness in the fingers at the end of his good right hand.

"Stay with us, Julius," I cried. "The worst is over. All you have to do now is hold on."

I was still acting, still trying for a light tone, for that can-do spirit that the relatives of dying people always seem to want to attain, so I was surprised when Jules opened his eyes and smiled. His lips moved, cracking the dried blood around them, and when I bent closer to hear what he would say, he growled, "Where is he? Find the little fucker, don't let him get away."

Since I'd bent over expecting words of love, I was surprised again, first because Jules seemed to know it was Kamau who shot him, and second because he didn't seem to understand what a horrible state he was in. All I could manage, however, was a smile and a nod before the attendants hurried over and rolled the stretcher away. After that I had hours and hours and hours to wait there in the hall, my mind moving like the helicopter, in and out of darkness, though I tried not to think of the darkest possibility at all.

/   /   /

In the morning I was pulled from a dream I was having by our family doctor, who had not awakened me when he'd come in sometime during the night. I was asleep on a bench outside the surgery door. I had actually been inside the surgery twice, but I hadn't gone too close to Jules, for I wasn't clean, and I was afraid to see that humerus again, evidence of a skeleton too willing to shed its encumbrance of flesh, far too willing to come all the way out.

"Nora, dear," said Dr Zir, "the operation is finished and our man is alive!"

Dr Zir, who is Indian, has been my doctor for all of my life. He is my father's age and he was my father's neighbour and best friend until my father moved to England. He was smiling as hard as he could when he woke me up, so I took it as a sign that maybe Jules was not only alive but out of danger too.

"May I see him?" I asked.

"We'll go in together," said Dr Zir. "We can see him if we like, but he won't be seeing us for a while. I'd say tonight or tomorrow in the A.M. He's lost a lot of blood, Nora girl, and though we've filled him up again, he won't be quite the same, I'm afraid."

We had been walking, while he talked, down two long hallways and up some stairs, and we had come to the door of a private room.

"But he's out of danger, is he not?" I asked. "Isn't that what you said?"

"Your husband is strong," Dr Zir told me, "a muscle man in spades, but he will need a different kind of strength when he wakes up."

Dr Zir paused briefly but he was extremely calm. "He's lost his left arm, Nora, and they've done a complete reconstruction of his right shoulder and chest. His right arm will surely be affected somewhat in its range of motion, maybe severely, maybe not, and there will be some nerve damage. Otherwise he's as good as new."

"Julius is left-handed," I said.

In my mind's eye I saw Jules unslinging that rifle, and I suddenly realised that that was what I had been dreaming about. Except in my dream the rifle was a fishing pole and the lion was a mangy barracuda, or some kind of junk fish dancing on the surface of a wild and frothy sea.

Dr Zir opened the door and we went into the room. Over the course of my life I have had a couple of stays in Nairobi Hospital myself, so I knew what I would find. The room was small and square, the walls a dirty white. The bed's headboard was against the cleanest wall, and to the right of the bed were a

couple of tall windows, with a view of the doctors' car park and
the helicopter pad down below. There was nothing on the
walls of this room and there were no chairs for guests to use.

Jules's left side was facing us, and sure enough, his arm was
gone. There wasn't the merest stub. His entire upper torso was
wrapped in white bandages, with tape running back and forth
across his chest in Xs and Zs. I shook my head and cried a little
but I could tell that Jules was breathing fine, and I had no
doubt that after the first day or two he'd take the challenge of
becoming right-handed more or less in stride. My husband was
tough in more ways than one. I told Dr Zir he had an opti-
mist's heart.

"He doesn't know, of course?" I said, pointing at the missing arm.

A young nurse came in just then, carrying a hard-backed
chair. "He does not," said Dr Zir, "and so we are going to station this girl here throughout the course of the day and night.
That way when he wakes up he will not be alone. When he
finds his body part gone, someone will be here to introduce
him to the trials that lie ahead."

"That someone should be me," I said, but Dr Zir told me
that there was no chance Jules would awaken before six o'clock
and very likely not for a number of hours after that. "This girl's
presence is only a precaution," he said, "a formality, if you
like."

I let him convince me that if I came back at four I'd still
have hours to wait for Jules to wake up. It was early in the
morning, after all, and the doctor told me that since he was
going home himself, he could drop me at my father's house,
where I could sleep away my weakness, prepare myself to be
strong.

So I went over to the bed and bent down and gave my husband a kiss. I kissed his lips, cleaned the dried blood away, licking the length of them with my tongue. Jules could always be counted on to lick back, but alas, his lips took my licking without comment, and I was undone by that.

"All right," I told Dr Zir, and when he offered me his arm I fell against it, coughing once from way deep down, belching in a vulgar and unseemly way.

We left the room after tucking Jules in and watching the nurse sit down, and in the hallway I had the worst premonition. Though I was filthy dirty and wearing farm clothes, for an instant I knew that if I glanced down at myself I would find that I was clean, that I was dressed formally and in black. I also knew that Dr Zir was my father beside me, walking carefully and holding me up.

When I actually looked at him, of course, it was Dr Zir that I found, and when I glanced down it was only a wrecked bush uniform that I wore. But I have wished many times since that day that I had let my premonition play, that I had tuned in to that part of me that smelled something rotten floating in the morning air. Had I done so maybe I could have saved him, that's a repeated refrain. Maybe, had I stayed in the hospital, I would have Julius Grant with me even today, and I would be telling the story of the extraordinary difficulties he overcame in order to continue his life, instead of the story that I have to tell.

3

Jules Sits Up

But I soon forgot my premonitions, and things went just as Dr Zir said they would during the rest of that day. Once inside my father's house I felt better, and once showered and in bed, I slept exactly as if I were exhausted by work and not by worry. I slept in my parents' bed, on what had been my mother's side, in the round-walled main bedroom of the house where I grew up, and when I awoke, at about two that afternoon, I looked out that bedroom window at the gladiolus and the bougainvillea, and at the avocado tree where, as a child, I had hidden to spy on my parents one time, watching while they made love.

At about two-thirty I called the hospital and was told that Jules was still out cold. There was no telephone in Jules's room, but I had the ward desk girl summon the nurse who was sitting with him, and she told me quite clearly that Jules had not yet shown any sign of waking. "I think six," she said. "If you get here by six you can watch him open his eyes."

If I have never had any regrets about purchasing the coffee farm, about moving into the deep country and working like mad every day of my life, it was Julius Grant who kept those regrets I've never had at bay. I would not have done such a thing on my own or with any of the men I had known before meeting Jules in London and bringing him home. What I'm saying is that before meeting Jules I was a city girl who thought a lot about her fingernails. I had a job at a local university and I had my chums and my rounds of restaurants and art exhibits, of dinner parties and the theatre and film. I had my own flat and my father's wonderful house to escape into whenever I liked. It was a romantic and a privileged life, living in Nairobi that way, going to London sometimes to see my dad. It had been, as a matter of fact, a great life, if a little empty on the inside, and it came very clearly back to me as I bathed again and dressed in clean clothing and looked out my father's bedroom window one more time, past the avocado tree and over the edge of the lush little valley that his property contained. Standing there, I could remember my past life perfectly, and I could, of course, remember the work of the farm, but I couldn't for a second imagine what kind of life I would lead from that day on. Jules couldn't farm, could he, with his left arm missing and his chest muscles torn away? Would we therefore become city people, would I become a city girl again, speaking city nonsense and driving Julius Grant around?

My father had an old Land Rover, a 1961, and I was

pleased to find that it started up quickly, though I hadn't done my job of coming to start it for a month or so. I asked the security guard, who, except for the housekeeper, was the only remaining member of my father's household staff, to open the gate, and I had driven out onto Lower Kabete Road when I saw Dr Zir standing in front of his own gate and waving, as if he had been waiting for me to come.

"I've just been on the horn with the hospital," he said. "What good news I've got—Julius Grant is sitting up in bed. His eyes are open and they say he's looking around."

I'd been on the telephone with the hospital myself not half an hour before, and I was surprised. "The nurse told me six," I said.

I did not feel happy, as the doctor clearly expected I would. I was angry with that nurse. I was to be there by six, I was to see him open his eyes. That's what she had said, and I had banked on it, letting it order my rest and my day. Because I loved my husband, and because any word of progress should have been lovely to hear, however, I looked at the doctor and smiled. I listened while he talked about how depressed Jules was likely to be, about the patience I would have to find in order to deal with his moods and help him with the rehabilitation of his remaining arm. But all the time I was thinking of that nurse with fury, just as Jules had thought of Kamau.

The traffic was light and we got as far as Haile Selassie Avenue without having to stop at all, but I was still absurdly angry, driving as if the Land Rover's steering wheel were the young girl's throat. When we arrived at the hospital proper, however, I quite suddenly let all that go. In the car park my hands fell loosely away from the wheel and the image of the nurse was replaced by one of Julius Grant sitting up, wide awake. And I made Dr Zir jump when I jerked around, fiercely staring into the back seat of the car.

I have been told many times over the years that people deal with grief in all sorts of ways, and I think it's true. Some feel it quickly, getting right to the point, whereas others have to dig for it, ferreting around. I think I fell somewhere in between. I had been tough and pragmatic all during the emergencies of the day before and I had got the job done, but now, after resting a little at my father's house, now that it appeared that Jules would live, I was realising the scope of what had happened and was having trouble getting out of the bloody car. First I'd been obsessed and raging at that unfortunate girl. Then I'd felt sure that Julius was in the Land Rover behind me, leering at me, laughing at the joke he had played.

Dr Zir came around and opened my door. He pulled me out and led me into the hospital and up the stairs to Jules's wing. The young nurse was actually the first person we saw as we turned down the hall, and she was smiling so sweetly that all I could do was smile back. When she opened her mouth, however, it was as if she knew what I had been thinking in the car. "He hasn't spoken," she assured me. "I think he's waiting for you to do that."

Dr Zir went to get Jules's chart and the nurse and I walked over to stand outside his room. The door was closed and its paint had peeled so much that the natural wood could be seen here and there. Jules was in Room 7, but the brass number was attached to the door by a single remaining nail and had swung around so that it looked like an italicised capital *L*.

When Dr Zir got back the young nurse opened the door.

Jules wasn't sitting up but was lying down flat, and when I saw him my anger immediately returned.

"Who put him down again?" I demanded. "Does he get up and down by himself already, can he move around?"

Someone had opened the window, which was the kind that swung out and away from the building like a cupboard door. I went over to close it and found a pillow from Jules's bed on a wide ledge that ran along the building's side. Immediately I imagined Jules, frustrated and alone, discovering his missing left arm. I imagined him taking the pillow in his sore right hand and throwing it. The window was only about three feet from the bed, but it wasn't such a bad throw, considering we didn't know whether or not he'd be able to use the arm at all, and somewhere in my mind I understood that this, at least, was a good sign.

I was only at the window for a second, but when I turned back toward the bed the nurse was gone and Dr Zir was facing me, an odd expression on his face.

"Something strange has happened here," he said. "This is unforeseen."

I was on Jules's good side, the side with an arm to teach, so I went over and took his hand, ready to shake him gently awake, and resigning myself to be calm. Jules's hand was not exactly cold, but it was cooling, like an ember pulled from a long dying fire. I had been avoiding his face, but when I looked at it then, it seemed at first to be awake. His eyes were open and staring, and his mouth was open too, as if he were about to say something important, or to commit something I had told him to memory before going on.

Dr Zir had apparently followed the young nurse out of the room, for when I said, "Look how bright his eyes are," there was no one there to reply. The only light in Jules's room was in the centre of the ceiling, and it was reflected in his eyes, making them look glassy and slightly teared. I remember thinking that they were the eyes of a bad actor, someone pretending emotion when none was truly there.

I was aware of small details and was in clear and sober control of myself as I watched my dead husband lying there. I felt a certain tenderness toward him, and a great desire to stay nearby, to prevent anyone else from getting near. There was something huge and dark coming into my consciousness too, like the bank of fog through which the *Titanic* must have sailed, or the darkness that had hidden those two grieving elephants so well, but as soon as I became aware of it I chased it away. I would, after all, be one of the slow ones, not plunging into misery and not in the middle, either, as I had thought before. I would step into grief little by little, I would take forever, like a bather at the edge of a cold sea.

Dr Zir was back with a whole lot of people who rushed into the room pulling a cart. The young nurse took me out of the way, and the other doctors, if that's what they were, stuck needles in Jules and then tried to shock him back to life by pounding on his chest with their hands and arms.

"I was at his bedside always," cried the nurse. "I left only when I saw you out the window, coming from the car park below."

She gestured toward the open window and then toward the chair where she'd sat, a chair that now contained Dr Zir, who was nearly as hollow-faced as Jules and was trying to catch his breath.

"He was sitting up tall!" the nurse said. "He wasn't happy but his eyes were open and he was calm!"

I didn't want to deal with such specifics, I didn't care about this girl's defence, but if she'd left the room only when she said she did, then even if Jules's heart had given out on him, as these furiously working people all seemed to think, he would have died sitting up, his head slumped forward on his chest.

"Stop talking!" I suddenly shouted. "Leave it alone!"

Poor Dr Zir was still sitting, teary-eyed and stunned, in the nurse's chair, and the nurse was crying, so when one of the other doctors pulled Jules's sheet up, covering his hollow face and eyes, I tried to cry too. I turned back toward the window and tried to enter that horrible darkness that I'd felt before. I would ride the *Titanic* or I would sink it with my iceberg heart. But search as I might, I couldn't even find the fog.

"Please," I finally said, "Dr Zir, take these people out of here, let me have a moment alone."

This somehow made the doctor jump, as if he should have thought of it himself, and in an instant everyone was gone.

I sat down on the edge of Jules's bed and pulled the sheet back from his face again. He had been staring up into whiteness, and I was irritated by that. Now was the time of Jules's greatest introspection, yet no one else had thought to make it easy for him by closing his eyes.

But though Jules's eyes closed easily, there was nothing I could do about his mouth. It was locked open, giving him a stupid, aged look. His skin was already waxy, already a lot cooler than it had been before. I could find the softness of him only in his hair, which I touched lightly, as I would have if he were a child and I were pushing it out of the way of his eyes.

I was alone with my dead husband in his hospital room, and what I wanted most to do was lock the door. I could feel that fog again, suddenly it was back, a great brooding mass of it, nudging up against the window, but I didn't want to face it with the door unlocked, and there was no lock on the door. For a moment I considered pulling the nurse's chair over and wedging it in under the knob, but all I did was stand and turn in circles in the centre of the room, staring up at the light.

The sheet was bunched under Jules's chin, so I went back over and pulled it up until only his hair was visible. After that I touched the hair again, drawing it out to its full length. I could see where his natural part was and I tried to arrange the hair so that the part was clean and sharp across his head, a straight little river with a dense forest on either side, like a tributary of the Zambezi or the Amazon.

"Hello, Julius Grant, are you there at all?" I peered at that hair as if I were a god watching a landscape through the clouds. Then I stood and went around to the other side of the room and pulled the nurse's chair closer to the bed and sat down.

"This is a vigil," I said. I think, as on the night before, I intended my words to sound only within my head, but they must have come out loud, for immediately the door opened and Dr Zir came in.

"Did you call, Nora?" he asked. "Did you want me with you, dear?"

The doctor came closer and behind him an empty stretcher nosed its way into the room.

"We should take him downstairs and find out what went wrong," said Dr Zir. "Do you want us to, or do you need more time?"

I looked up at him but I couldn't think of how to answer such a question, and I guess the doctor thought my silence meant he could let the attendants come all the way inside.

"Where will they take him?" I wanted to know.

The nurse had come back and had placed herself between me and the bed, so I couldn't see what was going on. And I guess I was finally in the outskirts of that fog, for I couldn't seem to concentrate anymore, could not decide to protest or to leave the room, to shout or to cry or to fall down.

"Nora," said Dr Zir, "the hospital staff has reported Julius's death to a policeman who incorporates the hospital in his round. Do you mind if that policeman steps inside, asks you a question or two?"

When the nurse moved out of the way I could see that the attendants had not yet done anything at all. They'd put the stretcher on the far side of Jules's bed, between the bed and the window, but they were waiting for a signal from Dr Zir, and Dr Zir was waiting for me to say it was okay for a policeman to come into the room.

"What does the policeman want?" I asked. "Have we broken any laws?"

"It is procedure," said Dr Zir. "Because his death was unforeseen." He paused a second and then added, "Besides that, he was on hand."

There was a man at the door, half his body bending through it, and when I let myself notice him, he came all the way inside.

"Good afternoon, dear Mama," he said. "How are you today?" He stood stiffly and then he bowed, as if he realised the impropriety of his words and wanted to take the last of them away.

"This is Detective Mubia," Dr Zir softly said. "We all know him here. He is a very nice man."

"May God bless you and keep you," said the detective. "May the angels loudly sing."

He was wearing a reddish corduroy suit, threadbare, with a white shirt and tie. He was a small man. He looked to be about my age but he had a severe face, a face chiselled or sculpted, perhaps by the awful things he had seen. He stepped past Dr Zir and stood where the nurse had been, right between Jules and me. I didn't want the attendants to move my husband when I couldn't see.

"If you please," said the detective, "tell me the particulars of your husband's demise."

"He was shot," I said, "and a lion tore his arm."

"Quite so, but I am referring to the particulars here at the hospital," he said, "the particulars of the last hour or so, from when you returned here until just now."

"We've only been here a few minutes," I told him. "The nurse said he was awake and sitting up." My answers were clear, my voice not unhinged at all. I wanted to wail now, I wanted to fall onto the floor and moan, but I just sat there like an expert witness, calmly giving the details.

The nurse spoke next, saying once again that Jules was alive only a minute or two before Dr Zir and I arrived. She swore that she had not left his side until she saw us get out of my father's Land Rover down in the car park. She was still crying. Someone might have thought it was her husband who'd died, the way she carried on.

"The window was open," I said. "Julius threw a pillow out and it landed on the ledge." I still somehow had the pillow in my hands, so I lifted it up for Detective Mubia to see.

"How do you know he threw this pillow?" the detective

asked, turning away from the nurse and back to me. "If you had just come into the room, how do you know what propelled this pillow outside?"

I shrugged. "He was alone," I said. "How else could it have got there?"

Detective Mubia took the pillow out of my hands. Turning with it he lightly pulled the sheet away from Jules's face again. He let the pillow rest on the edge of the bed and bent to look into Jules's mouth and nose. Finally I had had enough.

"Hold on!" I protested. "Leave him alone."

What a profound infringement this seemed to be! I wanted to hurt the man, to push my fingernails into the flesh at his throat, but when I got out of the chair he stood up straight immediately.

"I know it is difficult," he said, "but who would want to see your husband dead?"

Dr Zir stepped forward then, finally seeing the outrage in everything that was going on, but even to the doctor Detective Mubia held up his hand. He reached into the left pocket of his jacket and removed a key ring with no keys on it but a pair of tweezers and a pen-knife attached. He pulled the sleeves of his jacket up and very suddenly bent back over Jules, extended those tweezers into his open mouth, and, like a stage magician, quickly popped back up again.

"I have found a feather," Detective Mubia said. "It was stuck against the back of your husband's throat and it came from this pillow, the one you found resting on the ledge outside."

He gave the tweezers with that single feather in their grasp to Dr Zir and then he picked up the pillow again, smoothing the pillow case down and running his hands across it. "Here," he said. His hand had apparently run up against the pinprick of another feather, for he pulled one right through the pillow-case, holding it up for me to see.

"Someone else came into this room. And that someone else left through the window, dropping the pillow on his way out."

The nurse put her hands to her mouth, playing her part all the way, and Dr Zir started stammering, but I pushed them both aside and followed the detective back over to the window.

"Our someone else may have been waiting in a nearby room or he may have seen you arrive, just as the duty nurse did. He may have come into the room after she went out the door."

"That is not possible," said the nurse. "I was not out of the room long enough for someone else to come inside. And when we came back, the room did not look changed at all."

That seemed beside the point and the detective said so. "When you came back inside you were not searching for changes in the room but for changes in the man in the bed. You saw only his death. At a time like that small changes in the room would have been invisible to anyone."

We all somehow looked at Jules again then, at his dead face covered and uncovered so many times. At the doctor's bidding one of the attendants covered his face up once more, and then two of them lifted Jules off the bed, settled him on the stretcher, and rolled him quickly away. It was all too much, everything that had gone on, but though I wanted the private clarity of watching my husband go, Detective Mubia's words were so powerful that I could concentrate only on the scene he had created in my mind, of someone stealing into the room, drowning Jules in feathers, and then quietly slipping away.

"Do you know who our someone else might have been?" Detective Mubia softly asked when Jules was gone.

"I don't know," I said. "I have a thought but no good reason for having it."

That I would utter those words surprised me more than I can say. I hadn't intended them, and until the words came out I didn't have anyone in mind. But when I looked at the detective, hoping he wouldn't press me, I saw that he seemed to understand, and instead of asking me to give him a name, he removed a wallet full of business cards from his pocket and handed one to each of us in the room. It was far too late, but now he seemed to sense the violation, to know that he had interrupted my grieving time.

"I am sorry," he said. "Please contact me when you are able to talk again." Detective Mubia's first name was Frederic, and his telephone number was all twos.

The detective left the room, though by then I didn't want to see him go. The nurse left after him, her calm returned, and I was alone with my neighbour and my father's best friend, my childhood physician, who wanted so badly to console me but who couldn't console me at all. I was consoled by the detective, not by Dr Zir—does that seem strange? I could not find comfort in sympathy, but had found slight solace by engaging myself in the problem, by following the detective to the window and by listening to what he had to say.

As we went back down toward the car park Dr Zir tried to take my keys away, but I was too afraid of inactivity by then to allow him to drive my father's car. As we walked I held Detective Mubia's card in my hand, repeating to myself what the card said: Frederic Mubia 222-222, Frederic Mubia 222-222.

It was my mantra, the focus of my entire brain, but the inclusion of his name made the mantra too long, so by the time we reached the car I had distilled it until it went like this: 222-222, 222-222, 222-222. Pretty soon the numbers turned to letters, just as the one on Jules's door had done, and as they marched across my mind the letters were all Zs, a perfect symbol for the waking sleep that is grief and sorrow and loss. Julius Grant was dead. Good-bye, Julius Grant, 222-ZZZ. The letters gave me a second semblance of order, until I had driven Dr Zir to his gate and was mercifully and horribly alone.

4

A Conversation by the Church

But whether I felt grief or no grief, whether I was engaged in the mystery of my husband's death or in the grip of unyielding sorrow, there were many things to decide concerning Julius Grant, and though Dr Zir had done the job of calling my father in London, in the end I made each decision alone. I decided against cremation, against sending his body back to Canada, where he originally came from, and in favor of burying him on a small hill overlooking the Mara plains, at a peaceful little corner spot in the orchard section of our farm.

Dr Zir, bless his aging heart, supervised the embalming himself, very important in Kenya because inferior fluids were often used, and when my father arrived from London, Dr Zir picked him up at the airport.

I spent the first two days after Jules's death at my father's house alone. I played the piano a little, repeating Detective Mubia's telephone number over and over in my head, and I stared out at my father's valley in a cold and cataleptic way. My father's telephone rang often but I didn't answer it, and when cars occasionally stopped at the gate, I watched from the window while the gateman, following my instructions, turned the cars away. The six years of our life together had been private. Jules and I had dined and played in town sometimes, but Jules had always made it clear to me that he didn't want guests at the farm. So we had no real friends. We hadn't really seen anybody in a good long time.

/   /   /

It was on the morning of the third day that my father arrived. He was not terribly old, only seventy-two the previous autumn, but he had recently grown confused and was an unreliable witness for anything that had happened during the last three years or so. He'd had a series of mild strokes a few months before—I had been to London twice to see him—and since then, though his body wasn't affected, he'd developed a strange quality of mind, especially if the day grew long. I worried that it would be difficult for him to make the journey to the farm, and in fact I wanted to tell him that I preferred to go alone.

"The roads are terrible now," I said, almost before saying hello. "Stay here, Daddy, comfort me when I need it, after I come back to town. Why make the trip for fifteen minutes of silence at the side of a lonely grave? I'm telling you, Julius wouldn't mind at all."

"I'm going, Nora, and I'm staying afterwards," my father

said. He had just got off an all-night flight, but when he spoke there was no confusion, and when he smiled at me and took me in his arms, the father of my youth came out for a while, emerging from the wrinkles and the sunken chest like an actor taking a bow.

"We'll handle it," he said. "Put the two of us together and there's nothing we can't do."

I had planned on driving out to the farm in my father's Land Rover later that afternoon. I wanted to stay in town only long enough to greet my dad, and have lunch with him, maybe, but then I wanted to go. Dr Zir was bringing Jules's body out the next morning in a helicopter, so I tried a different tack, telling my father that he could more easily come then too. All he did, however, was turn me down again. He said, "I'll ride shotgun for you, Nora. The good doctor can come with Julius in the morning alone."

There was a lot of work to do once I got to the farm. There was the site of Jules's grave to prepare—I wanted to tell our crew to dig the grave deep—and a general clean-up to attend to, in order to rid the place of the havoc wreaked by those animals on that hateful night. I wanted Jules to be buried on an orderly farm, and come what may, I wanted furious work to occupy my time. That was how I would see myself through, and if my father came along he would be in the way, slowing everything down by insisting that the real wreckage of my life be examined in some immediate and impossible way. He'd be asking me every minute what I was thinking or how did I feel. I disliked such questions during the best of times, and they would be much harder on me now. But I also didn't have the energy to argue with my dad. So since he'd just come on that overnight flight, I decided that my best hope was that he would want to sleep after eating and I could use that opportunity to write him a note and slip away.

After lunch, however, far from wanting to sleep, my father suggested that we leave right away, before the afternoon traffic got too heavy on the escarpment road. I would drive, and he would ride quietly by my side. He would look forward to the sight of the Great Rift Valley again, but otherwise he would hold his tongue. Such was the nature of the promises he made. He didn't promise out loud, but they were everywhere in his eyes.

There was a vacant little church, the smallest I'd ever seen, sitting off the escarpment road, a mile or so past the area where all those baboons usually hang around and at just the point where the road finally turns and heads down into the Rift Valley proper. When my father saw the church he spoke for the first time, asking me to pull over. "For just one moment, Nora," he said, "so I can say a prayer. I haven't been here in years."

The church had been built in the 1940s by Italian prisoners of war, but it was empty now, broken down and dirty, a bad place to pray. Since it had been an occasional practice of Jules's and mine to rest here on our trips to town, however, I did what my father asked, stopping the Land Rover at the spot where Jules used to park our lorry, under the shade of a giant eucalyptus tree at the foot of the church's cracked front walk. The whole building was in utter disrepair, even the door didn't close properly anymore, and the floor of the church's only room was littered with rubbish.

"We came here sometimes when you were a child," said my

dad. "Do you remember? The place was clean then. Your mother thought it was bad luck to pass by without stopping."

We were inside the church, but everything felt damp. I remembered those times, but I wanted to leave again quickly, so I only said, "It's horrible now. Those days are over, Daddy. Mother's dead. The Italian prisoners would be appalled."

The curtness in my voice surprised me, even though anger had been my accomplice for three days now, but all my father did was push a bit of the debris around with the toe of his shoe. It wasn't the church's condition that occupied his mind, nor was he thinking of my mother. He wanted to say something else and his expression was pained. I tried to be patient, waiting for him to remember and speak, but he finally knelt at the ramshackle altar instead. And when he got up again he ushered me back outside and found a shady place for us to sit down.

"I would like to talk to you for just a moment," he finally said. "I have something unpleasant to discuss."

Ever since Jules's death, ever since the night of his wounding on the farm, I had been in a state of numb exhaustion, unable to sleep or to act in any animated way, and unable, as yet, to properly find that fog again and mourn. What I had been able to do, however, was focus on the tasks before me one at a time, to do what had to be done to clean up Jules's affairs and get him buried, and I didn't want that focus interrupted by my father's unhinged mind.

"I don't want to hear it, Daddy," I said. "I can't concentrate now." But my father had his right hand in the air, and he pushed my protest away.

"Julius telephoned me late last week," he said. "He called last Saturday night."

I admit I had expected platitudes, something about life being hard or learning to cope, but what was this? He was right, he did have something unpleasant to say, and it was that his senility had grown tricky and bold since last I'd met him.

"That's not possible," I said stiffly. "Julius was injured on Sunday. The Saturday night a week before that we went to bed early, I remember it because the harvest was still going on."

I didn't remember it because of the harvest but because it was the last time Jules and I had made love, Saturday night a week ago, at around nine P.M.

"His call came very late," said my father, "maybe three o'clock in the morning. He woke me up."

"He was asleep at three A.M.," I said. "We were both exhausted from our work. You know how it is when a harvest is not yet done."

"He called me, Nora," said my dad.

The place he had chosen to sit down wasn't peaceful. We were only a few feet off the road and a big lorry had just passed by fast, blowing dust around. These lorries always seemed to come in bunches, and because I didn't want to get behind too many of them I told him we should go. "Let's talk while we're driving," I said. "Let's hurry up."

I stood and reached back down to help my dad, but he wouldn't take my hand. "Never mind the traffic," he said. "I'm telling you that your husband was in serious trouble when he died. He was concerned for his safety and he was worried about yours as well. He called because he wanted me to come down and help straighten things out."

"He did not," I said. "What are you talking about, Dad? Try to think clearly. I don't have time for this nonsense right now."

I was suddenly furious and my father knew it, but I let my

words stand, only adding more softly, "I have to bury Julius to-morrow, you know. Can't it wait until after that?"

When my father didn't answer I sat back down.

"I was the Minister of Wildlife for many years," he said. "Before independence most of these decisions fell to me."

I put my face in my hands but then looked up again quickly, deciding to try to talk him around. "Now you're not making sense," I said. "What does that have to do with any-thing that's going on now? Did Julius call you up to remind you of what you had once been? If he called you, Daddy, tell me why. Otherwise let's go."

Even though I had braced myself against it before his ar-rival, what I'd wanted from my father was comfort and love, the safe harbour of his living breath and arms. I didn't want all this nonsense about what he had once been and I did not, right then, want any bad talk about Jules. Nevertheless I found my-self remembering that house on Loita Street and asking one more time, "Did Julius call you because he was in trouble, or are you mistaking the time of the call? Perhaps it was some other Saturday night, some past time when we both tele-phoned just to say hello."

"Before that night I had never talked to Julius on the tele-phone," my father said.

It was very hard to make international calls from the farm, and, indeed, I myself couldn't remember ever having called my father from there. We used to call once a month or so, but we always used the telephone at my father's own house, in town.

"If he called you on Saturday night I would have heard him," I said. "Using our telephone is a noisy exercise. He wouldn't have got through on the first try, he would have had to wait and raise his voice."

My father shrugged and said, "He called me and he told me that I should come." He paused a second and then said, "I had my tickets, Nora, before poor Julius got hurt."

I stood up again, but my father stubbornly remained on the ground. I turned and looked back down at him, and suddenly I found myself asking the strangest question I had ever asked my dad. "When mother died was there a part of you that felt glad? Did some part of you feel a certain sense of freedom, a release, maybe, in the fact that she was gone?"

"Certainly not!" my father said. "I cried like a baby when your mother died. I felt horrible, worse than you do now."

"When Julius died there was something in me that felt relieved," I said. "I'm ashamed to say it, but some small part of me grew lighter when I was with him in that hospital room. Maybe it was a sense of renewed possibility, I don't know, but it was a thought I'd had before. Listen, Daddy, in a way it was as if I was finally out from under him, as if my own real life had been on hold."

What I said was a deeper, or at least a more private, truth than I had ever told before. It had bothered me constantly while I'd been at my father's house. I considered it shameful and disloyal. I loved Julius Grant with all of the power that was in me and I would never have thought of leaving him. Our life together had been good, better, most of the time, than good could be, but there was an undeniable moment when I was captured by the idea of life without him, and no matter what I did, I couldn't make the memory of that moment go away. Even in the hospital room, even as I stood looking at his lifeless face and waited for that horrible dark fog to come near, even then there had been a small and terrible element of relief involved.

I felt a little better for having said it out loud, but my father didn't seem to have anything more to say about the truth I'd told, and I guessed that it was because I knew he wouldn't that I'd told him. It is easier to articulate the crimes of one's heart to a man who isn't really listening most of the time and who cannot remember very well when he is.

When I tried to get him on his feet for the third time, my father was looking high up into the branches of the eucalyptus tree. He had his hands clasped around his knees and the expression on his face was not deep.

"Come on, Daddy," I said. "It's time we got started again. There's work to do once we get to the farm and I want to have some daylight left to do it in."

He looked at me and I could see him coming back.

"Quite right," he muttered. "I only wanted to stop a minute. Your mother liked it here, did you know that? Did I tell you that before?"

My father stood up then and we were just walking down to the Land Rover when a dusty Toyota estate pulled in next to it. Detective Mubia was behind the wheel, the policeman from the hospital. He honked his horn and was waving at us as he got out of his car.

"Jambo Mama and Daddy!" he said. "I have come to search you out. Dr Zir told me you would be in Narok by now, but here you are, still on this escarpment road."

I was worried by then that we'd never get to the farm, but I introduced the detective to my father anyway, using my father's title: Nathan Hennessey, Minister of Wildlife, Retired. I had been Nora Hennessey before I was Nora Grant. The sound of my father's title seemed to bring him completely around.

"How do you do?" he said. He shook the detective's hand and then he struck a pose, something I hadn't seen him do in a decade or more, not since I was a child. My father looked like Mussolini when he did that, and I turned away, glancing back at the church and remembering my mother and the Italian prisoners of war.

"I know your name very well," the detective told him. "When I was a boy the Minister of Wildlife was often in the news."

It seemed clear to me that if Detective Mubia hadn't seen us he would have driven all the way to the farm, and though he was the last person I would have invited to Jules's funeral, his arrival didn't make me unhappy at all. I'd been thinking about what he'd said in that hospital room, and even if he didn't have news for me, I could use his appearance to dilute the strangeness of my dad.

"What do you want, Detective?" I asked. "Has something happened that made you drive all this way?"

There was something, but I got the idea the detective didn't want to say it straight out. Instead he said, "This little church is pleasant. I have never been here before."

My father jumped and went back over to the church's broken door. "Years ago it was delightful," he said. "My wife . . ." And then he turned and stepped back inside.

God, I thought, would I never get away from this place? If Jules were with us he'd have lost his mind, but since we could hear my father speaking in there, and we couldn't understand what he said, there was nothing to do but go in and get him one more time.

"Ah, but this is terrible," Detective Mubia said when we squeezed through the door. "No one has cared for this place.

This is the church of our dear Lord, Jesus Christ, a home for those who worship in His name. Let's clean it up."

I had gotten the idea earlier that Detective Mubia was a religious man, and he proved it now not only by what he said, but by furiously bending down and picking papers up off the floor. "Are there no people living near here?" he asked. "Surely someone should have seen to the maintenance of this place."

I didn't know whether or not people lived nearby, but the detective's energy instantly infected my father, who started cleaning up too, snatching food wrappers from the far side of the room.

"I'll bet there are still coffee bags in the back of the Land Rover, Nora," he said. "Run out and get a couple. This man is correct. Leaving this place filthy would be a crime!"

My first impulse was to argue again, to flat-out refuse to go, but I knew the act of arguing would take longer than just getting the bags and helping them clean up the floor. Once outside, however, I could see the Rift Valley in the afternoon sun, with the road leading into it, cutting its vast flatness in half. The day's quota of lorries seemed to have passed by, so it was quiet out there. A black-and-white colobus monkey, rare in these parts, played in the eucalyptus tree, but otherwise I was alone.

In the back of the Land Rover I found burlap bags all right, old ones with Jules's original slogan on their sides. These bags were made in England and had been a gift from my father several years before, at Christmas, I think, 1969.

Because the church was tiny, it was pretty clean by the time I went back inside. The debris was in a neat pile by the door, so my father took a burlap bag and began stuffing it full, sweets wrappers and bits of rotten food and empty booze bottles disappearing from the floor.

While my father worked I decided to ask the detective once again why he had come, but when I looked at him a different question came to mind.

"Are you a believer, Detective Mubia?" I asked. "Are you a religious man?"

It was an unnecessary question, even a stupid one, given what he'd just made us do, but if he was surprised by it he didn't let it show. He just took a long second to straighten his suit and stand a little formally before he replied.

"It is better to believe and know you are mistaken than to disbelieve and know you are correct," he said.

The detective looked pleased, though I didn't know whether it was with the job they'd done on the floor of the church or the comment he'd made. My father was standing at the top of the wooden ladder with his head in the belfry, but he came back down when I said we had to go.

It was then that I asked my original question one more time. "Why are you here, Detective? Why did you follow us all the way out from town?"

"It is embarrassing to say that I have invited myself along," he said, "but it has become clear that I must see how things stand on your farm, and if I wait any longer, things will stand differently than they do now."

My father had picked up the burlap bags, twisting their tops in his hands. "This is a family matter," he said. "We don't want the police involved."

I believed Detective Mubia would have turned around and driven back to town had I asked him to, but I held my tongue.

I liked the man and I trusted him, and I knew as well as he did that there really was something to be solved. Once Jules's funeral was over and I had endless amounts of time on my hands, I might even tell him about that night in Nairobi on Loita Street, after the French Cultural Centre film. Would it help his investigation for him to know about those torn-out tusks, ripped away like Jules's arm? Would it help me survive the weeks ahead if I told him?

Once outside the church again the detective got into his Toyota and sped on down the road. He turned toward Narok and was quickly out of sight.

And when my father asked me to let him drive the Land Rover I surprised us both by handing him the keys. We had hours to go yet before we'd reach the farm and had already taken far too long, but this was a day for contrary actions and questions I did not intend to ask. Is that what grief would do to me, I wondered, as I got into the passenger's seat on the car's left side. Would it turn me arbitrary since it couldn't make me cry?

5

Farm Life Further Disrupted

The road was badly potholed and my father's speed didn't pay the slightest homage to it, but miraculously I slept, until the outskirts of Narok forced even my father to slow down, and a sense of safety woke me up. There were Maasai cattle on the road and dust was in my nostrils, but this strange sleep had been the best I'd had in three days. I was rested, and being near the farm again gave me my first fleeting sense that maybe, someday, I would actually be able to go on.

"This is Narok," my father said. "I haven't been here in years." He seemed rested too, and happy to see the dusty little town.

There were more cattle than usual, and Maasai herders

were everywhere. I asked my father to pull in at a petrol station at the far end of town, across the street from the Spear Hotel, so we could fill the tank and get away from the cattle dust for a while. Detective Mubia's Toyota was already parked by a far-off pump.

"We've seen that man before," my father said. He was pointing out through the Land Rover's front window. The car park was packed, but when I followed my father's finger I saw a tall Maasai warrior, one of the two men who had tried to hold off the lions on the night of Jules's wounds. I wanted to talk to this man, to thank him and let him know that Jules had died, but just then I realised that my father wasn't pointing at the tall Maasai but at a shorter man, at Detective Mubia, who was walking our way.

"My God, Daddy, we were with him at the church," I said. "Don't you remember? You and that man were the clean-up crew just two short hours ago."

Detective Mubia was at my window before I could clear my thoughts of the new extent of my father's mental chaos, and by then the Maasai warrior was gone. Even so, I would have looked for him had the detective not opened my door, helped me out, and walked me a little away.

"I have something more to tell you," he said, "and something to give, which is in my car."

The detective was nervous now. He kept glancing over to make sure my father wasn't following us. "It is most strange," he said, "but the hospital personnel, the young nurse and some others, said you should have it before your husband's funeral. And the nurse said she was sorry again, she said it many times."

My father had got out of the Land Rover and was heading

toward the other side of the petrol station, where there were traders with beads and spears to sell, so I followed the detective over to his car, which was painted the same colour as his suit. The car's windows were all rolled down, but when I looked through them from the driver's side, I saw that the seats were empty, the entire car was clean. Detective Mubia took his keys out and opened the rear door. There was nothing in there either but a rectangular wooden box. I couldn't even see a tool kit, nothing to use to fix the Toyota when it broke down.

"I don't understand," I said.

Detective Mubia pointed at the box. "They insisted I bring it to you. I want you to take it out of my car, take it away now."

I was still confused, but when I picked up the box Detective Mubia stood back and said, "Don't open it here."

The box had Nairobi Hospital's logo on its side, and suddenly I did understand. That young nurse, the girl on whom I'd laid such blame, had sent me Jules's severed left arm, the only part of him that had died early enough for the rest of him to mourn! Good Mother of God, what a morbid remembrance! What kind of gift was this for a young nurse to insist upon?

"All right," I said, forcing my voice to remain even. "What the hell is happening? Who would do this? What's the meaning of it? What nurse would think to send a dead man's wife his missing arm?"

The detective didn't want to answer. He searched his pockets and looked at the ground as if he had dropped something, and when I turned from him, rigid of eyes and mouth, I felt the weight in the box shift, a quick imbalance that let me know the arm was loose in there, its fingers rapping on the walls.

I faced him again. "You better speak," I said. "You better

tell me now." But Detective Mubia shook his head and said only, "I didn't want to bring it but she placed it in my car."

I stepped away then, quick and angry. Maybe my sense of propriety was entirely gone, but didn't sending the arm have more of the feeling of a taunt than an apology? Wouldn't any-one think so? As I carried the box over to the Land Rover I felt such an alteration in the air that it was all I could do to keep from flinging the damned thing away, from smashing the box on the oily ground.

The detective had walked with me, but when I looked at him again all I could find in his face was the absolute fact that he was glad the box was gone.

I put the box in the back of the Land Rover, wedging it be-hind the jack and covering it with one of the remaining coffee bags. After that I called my father. And without further com-ment I told Detective Mubia to follow us up the Narok-Nakuru road to our turnoff and our farm. We were less than an hour away, but it seemed to me that the trip had taken days, and there'd be no time to do anything when we got there, since darkness was less than an hour away as well.

/   /   /

We arrived at the farm at six-thirty, with enough daylight left for us to see that the place had been ransacked, that the house and its nearby coffee fields had been torn apart, the latter by mourning elephants, maybe, but the former, without any ques-tion at all, by men. We parked in front of the workers' dormi-tory; those doors too were open wide, and all our farmhands were gone.

This was too much, the last straw, and though I had my fa-ther beside me, the detective in the car behind, I embarrassed and surprised myself by falling out of the Land Rover, going down on all fours, and crying out loud on the ground. Now I became the abject weeper that I'd wanted to be all along, a woman whose losses came to her at once, a woman whose control was gone. My husband was dead, his body given back to me in hideous parts, my farm was in ruin, my life undone. This is how I'd wanted to act in that hospital room—it was there that I wanted this torment, not now, not in front of the empty dormitory with Detective Mubia walking over from his car.

I tried getting up but could only rise far enough to place my cheek against the Land Rover. I was mortified and wretched and alone, and I would have stayed there if Detective Mubia hadn't knelt down beside me, taken hold of my hand, and helped me to stand. "You have informed me that the helicopter comes in the morning," he said, "and without your workers we must dig this grave ourselves. Show me the spot, I will begin right now."

Since there's a complicated mythology, a taboo of sorts, about Kenyans and graves, it was an extraordinary thing for him to have said, and it did the trick of bringing me around. "There's a place on a ridge over there," I told him, pointing, still weeping but keeping my filthy face down. "We call it the orchard. There are shovels in a shed at the orchard's near side."

"Do you have a generator?" the detective asked. "If you do, let's turn it on."

Enough light had already drained out of the sky so that the generator would soon be necessary even to see the house. "I'll take care of it and then I'll come out to mark the spot," I told him. As I spoke I could feel my voice growing stronger, an improving posture wriggling up my spine.

"There are paraffin camp lanterns in that shed too, and

there is extra paraffin in a can. Fill the lanterns and light them all—while we're digging they will keep the animals away."

Our generator was behind the workers' dormitory, so I got up and marched that way. And since my father decided to come with me, I asked him to hold the torch that I'd taken from the Land Rover's glove box. Even though it was darker behind the dormitory than it was in front, I was able to start the generator quickly, pushing all its levers into neutral in the weak torchlight.

While the generator was warming up my father swung the light, and I saw that even back behind the dormitory things had been disturbed while I was gone. Oil barrels had been wrenched out from against the building's wall, one of them turned on its side, its cap removed, and oil spilt everywhere. I pulled the hose from the turned-over barrel and placed it in one of the standing ones. If the intruders had smashed the lights, then having a working generator wouldn't mean much, so without waiting any longer I threw the switch that took it out of neutral, quickly supplying power to our house, the dormitory, and the pond. To my surprise the generator immediately bogged down with the size of its load. Not only had they not broken any lights, but every light we had was on.

I was about to tell my father that we should forget digging Jules's grave, that we should find Detective Mubia and regroup inside the house, when a sudden blast of sound filled the air, stopping me cold. It was music, I think, but it was incredibly loud. My father put his hands over his ears and shouted, but just as I reached to throw the switch, which would cut off everything and pitch us into darkness once more, the volume went down and I understood that I was hearing a Mozart piano sonata, a favourite of Jules's and mine and something from our record collection inside.

I was once again about to cast us into darkness, very worried now and sure that there were people in my house, when the music stopped and a human voice took its place.

"Mr Minister of Wildlife, Retired," the voice said. "We have been steadfast, we have kept our part of the bargain without fail. Now you must keep yours."

My poor father had taken his fingers from his ears and was looking through the light as if his time had come.

"What do you want?" he asked weakly. "Who is speaking to me? Who is there?" Then I did throw the switch, so that darkness and silence came back to us.

"Listen, Daddy," I whispered, "I think it's a recording. I think that voice is on a tape along with the Mozart."

I was pretty sure I was right, since we didn't have a microphone and since the voice had been amplified at the same level as the turned-down music. Also, Jules often used to complain that his speakers no longer had much clarity, and I could hear Jules's complaint in the reproduced quality of the sound.

"You wait here," I said. "I'll go see."

There was a bench behind the dormitory. I thought I knew that if anyone was intent on injuring us they would have done so when we arrived, but nonetheless I took a moment to pull the bench into a nearby thicket and place my father on it there. In the dark he was impossible to see. He stayed quiet when I told him to, and he didn't try to get up and follow me when I walked away.

Because our generator had failed many times before, I knew better than anyone how to approach our house in the dark. The house had many windows but only two doors, and if there were people inside, I was sure they'd be watching the doors. I was fit from all those years of working hard, so I chose an obscure window, one that let me fall silently to the floor of our bedroom cupboard. Once inside I couldn't see at all, but I could tell that things had been disrupted there too. I opened the door leading to our bedroom and quietly entered. Everything was completely black. Sometimes the evening sky lit this room pretty well, through the bigger window that was now on my left, but in the hours just after sunset, a time when Jules and I often went to bed, the room was usually dark. I opened the door to the main part of the house as quietly as I could, and then I waited a full minute, counting the actual seconds, before walking into the hall.

I could see at a glance that I wasn't alone. A man stood in the pale moonlight that pushed itself through the open front door. He was so intently watching the landscape before him that he hadn't heard me at all. I knew where Jules kept his guns, but everything was turned over in the living room too, and, frankly, I had been so sure that I'd find the house empty, so sure that the voice we'd heard had been a recorded one, that I hadn't thought what I would do if the opposite turned out to be true.

I could see our kitchen and the hallway leading to our office and the small guest bedroom that we had. I could also see a soapstone vase turned over on the coffee table between the man and me. If you know soapstone, then you know that though it's heavy, it's more fragile than glass, and I was surprised that this one hadn't broken when it fell over. It was a tall vase, meant for a single flower or two, and was shaped like a policeman's billy club. I picked it up, silently inching toward the man.

Clouds had reduced the moonlight by the time I got to him, but there was still enough of it, thank God, to save me from making a big mistake. The intruder was Detective Mubia. I recognised his posture and the altered hue of his suit even as I raised my weapon, but it took me a moment to change the course of the soapstone vase so that it came rushing past his ear rather than crashing down on the top of his head.

"Holy Mother in heaven! Jesus save me now!" said the detective. He had his police revolver in his hand but he used it only to shield himself, its barrel pointing up at the ceiling. Though I had clearly frightened him, he spoke softly and was quickly calm again. "I didn't hear you come," he said.

"Who did this?" I asked him. "Who wrecked my house?"

The detective pointed the tip of his pistol at Jules's tape recorder, out on the porch and facing the grounds. "It is a voice I think I know," he said. "If we could listen to it one more time perhaps I could be sure."

When I told him where I'd left my dad, the detective volunteered to bring him inside. He stepped off the front porch in an unstealthy way and walked toward the workers' dormitory. His pace was unhurried but I kept my eyes on him until he'd walked into the darkness behind the building. And just as I turned to survey the damage again, he threw the generator switch and the lights came back on. I went around quickly turning most of them off, to make me less visible and to lower the generator's load, and while I was doing so the detective returned alone.

"Would your father have walked away?" he asked. "Does

he know the area well? Is there someplace else he would have
gone?"

The detective tried to speak lightly, but he wasn't a naturally casual man. He had lifted me out of the dust and helped
to give me strength with his words before, but he couldn't do it
a second time, so instead he brought my husband's stereo
speakers back inside the living room and rewound the tape.
When he turned it on again, this is what we heard: "Mr Minister of Wildlife, Retired. We have been steadfast, we have kept
our part of the bargain without fail. Now you must keep yours.
We demand that you meet with us privately in order to give us
the details of your plan."

That was all, and there wasn't any Mozart at the end. I got
the feeling that the intruders had wanted to say more on the
tape, that they'd intended more, but that we had interrupted
them by our arrival at the farm. I also knew what I had done.
Though I hadn't even heard the demand they had made, I had
immediately acquiesced to it, putting my father on that bench
the way I had. But for a time I could barely register the fact
that he was gone.

"Do you have firearms in the house?" Detective Mubia
asked. "Are your husband's rifles still here?"

I was sure they would not be, but when I went into our office to look I discovered that the office was intact, that nothing
in there had been turned over or moved. I'd been right, then,
in my assumption—we had arrived when these men were in
the middle of their search. Jules's second hunting rifle was on
the wall, and it was loaded. The first rifle, the one Kamau had
shot Jules with, was not in the office, and I couldn't remember
what had happened to it on the night of the attack. In the desk

drawer I found our .380 automatic pistol, plus an eight-shot clip and a box of bullets. Jules's filing cabinet was locked against the wall and his photographs hung above it in an un-crooked way.

I called the detective, asking him to come in and see for himself, and when he didn't respond, I took the automatic pistol from its drawer and the rifle down from its place on the wall. I unloaded the rifle and pushed it down under Jules's desk, putting its cartridges in my pocket. After that I shoved the pistol clip home.

I was about to call again, but the image of myself, as vulnerable in our office as my poor father had been on that bench outside, made me listen and wait awhile. When I finally stepped into the hall again, however, the .380 ready, I could see the police detective right away. He was sitting on our couch, his own revolver still in his hand. He seemed to be staring out the front door.

"Detective?" I whispered.

He didn't look toward me as I came down the hall, but pretty soon he said, "My specialty is city crime, city crime is what I know, and it is my great misfortune that I also know the voice on your tape recorder too well. I do not agree that a city crime and a country crime should be connected in this way. A city policeman should never allow circumstances to bring him out of town. It would be best for a city policeman if he were to leave country crime alone."

He was quite oddly miserable, sorry instead of glad that he recognized the voice. And something about his sorrow kept me from asking him right away who the voice belonged to. It also seemed to be keeping me from worrying about my father.

When I told him that our office was untouched, however, he immediately revived, just as I had on the ground outside.

"So number one is that we interrupted these heinous men in their crime and number two is we seem to have given them your father without even knowing that is what they desired."

"Yes," I said, "and number three is they've taken my father away. Do you think they'll hurt him? You don't, do you? He is too old for this. He's just arrived from England and he's too tired."

The detective nodded, but instead of answering my question he said, "Number four is as follows: Your enemy is clever and he knows that you are vulnerable because sooner or later you must dig your husband's grave."

That didn't seem like number four to me, and I said so. "I think that if he had wanted to harm us he could have done it earlier, when we arrived. He only wants my father, who's involved in everything somehow. He tried to say as much earlier, he tried to tell me about it at the church, but I wouldn't listen."

The detective looked at me with an expression on his face that I couldn't read, but finally he asked, "What bad business could your father have had with such a dangerous man? What bad business did this man previously have with your husband, Julius Grant?"

"What man?" I asked, exasperated. "What do you know about it? Please, tell me what you think is going on?"

While I waited for the detective's response I wondered again whether or not I should tell him what I knew. Should I say I'd seen Jules in the house on Loita Street that night? So far as I could tell, Detective Mubia hadn't yet connected any of this with poaching, and I myself hadn't in the slightest degree yet come to terms with the new probability that my father was involved. But should I tell him everything, or should I not? It seemed that rather than answering my questions, he was looking at me strangely, as if waiting for me to decide.

"It is late and we are tired," he finally said. "If we search for your father now we will not find him, and if we dig your husband's grave we will be filthy and exhausted by the time we are done."

He was once again pragmatic and calm. No matter what danger my father was in, there was nothing I could do about it now, he was telling me, and I surprised myself again by admitting that it was true. I told him I would set my alarm for five, giving us time enough to dig Jules's grave with the morning light, time enough to wash ourselves before Dr Zir and the helicopter arrived.

I didn't ask again about the man whose voice he knew and Detective Mubia didn't offer to tell me his name. He only nodded one more time and said, "The unfortunate Minister of Wildlife, Retired."

After that, though the house was still turned over, I found towels for the detective and then went into the bedroom I had always shared with Jules, to latch the window I'd come through and to lie down. And in a little while, when I thought I heard the detective go into the bathroom and then come out again, I opened my door and saw him sitting on our front porch in the rocking chair that Jules had always loved. The front porch light was off, but the detective had found the switch and reilluminated our pond. He was rocking softly, his pistol out of sight, his eyes on a small giraffe that was standing at the water's far edge. Across the pond from the giraffe I could see the skin and bones of that elephant calf, and beside it, to the left-hand side, I could see the cool bright eyes of something else, some other animal hiding there. The entire picture, the living animals and the dead one and the expanse of land leading from them to the detective in our rocking chair, made me imagine my husband asleep on the ground, a lion gazing down at him with calm and curious eyes.

6

Two Queer Birds

Why was I so horrible about my father, who was too old to stay out all night long and who had been showing signs of increased senility ever since his arrival the day before? Why was I so unfeeling, so unkind? Detective Mubia had told me that looking for my father in the dark would be futile, but it wasn't like me to take my way of thinking from another person, from a recently met and out-of-place man.

As I lay on my bed I at first decided that I had acted that way because I had not yet found the grief and pain that had wanted to visit me when Jules died, that maybe some part of me hadn't been satisfied with my performance outside on the ground, and I was making worry over my father wait in line. I loved my husband, and I had always believed I loved my father too, but nesting with the misery I was keeping at bay were two queer and unexpected birds. The first one I've mentioned before: At Jules's death something in me began looking to the future with a sense of renewed possibility, a lightness in my broken heart that was brutalizing me nearly as much as losing Jules was. The second queer bird was this: With my father's disappearance, though his fate was far less sealed than Jules's, I was filled with such unfocused malaise that in my heart of hearts I didn't seem to care what happened to him at all.

I'd switched on my bedside lamp and was playing with my wristwatch while thinking about my dad. There had been a small mystery with my watch over the last three weeks or so. It would run fine all day but would stop every night at twenty minutes to twelve. Since Jules and I were always asleep by then, we never actually saw it stop, but we'd check it in the morning. The watch never stopped at twenty minutes to noon, it would only stop at night.

I was fingering the watch and asking myself why it stopped, and also what my father could have done to bring out such ambivalence in a daughter who'd never been ambivalent before, when suddenly answers to both questions came clear. My watch was stopping because its battery was low. It had enough power to move the hands around, but every twenty-four hours it had to turn the date as well, and it didn't have enough power for that. And when I understood the watch, *because* I understood the watch, I thought I understood my attitude toward my father too. During all of my life, when things were going fine, I had a full battery, enough power in me to love my father while never thinking critically about him at all.

But as soon as I heard the voice on that tape, as soon as things went wrong, I couldn't do it anymore. I had lost my power, my resources were just too low.

Does that make any sense? What I'm saying is that one moment I would have said that my father's career as Minister of Wildlife was unblemished, and the next I knew that it was not. We lie to ourselves in odd kinds of ways, especially as children, I suppose, but here and now, many years after his career was done, many years after he had lost his wife and I my mother, and as I lay observing the second hand sweep around the face of my watch, I understood that my father was finally caught in some kind of late-coming retribution, some wild and improper scheme. And I could not go outside and look for him, I think, because I knew that retribution was at hand.

Those were the two queer birds I slept with that night, a feeling of liberation at the death of someone I loved, and a feeling of anger at a father who had avoided my anger for too long.

/ / /

I had set my alarm clock for five A.M. but was up before it went off. I got shovels from our shed and collected all of the lanterns in the house, but I didn't wake Detective Mubia, for during my restive night I had come up with the idea that I would purge myself of queer bird number one, at least, by digging Jules's grave alone. After that I promised myself I would find a way to worry about my dad.

The beginning streaks of dawn had lit up the east but I still couldn't see very well when I finally went out and found the orchard earth where I wanted Jules's grave to be. This was our outside spot, the place where we occasionally slept and made love, our bodies blanketed by the endless array of stars. Jules loved this spot more than any other. It was here that he always kept a fresh campfire built, so he could light it with ease and lie beside it at a moment's notice, one or two nights a month.

The morning was clear when the sun came up, the view of the valley unsurpassed. I could see a thousand wildebeests and zebra down there, moving out across the Mara plains. I could see elephants, too, much closer, heading into another wind, camped against it with their heads bent down, and I wondered, was this the herd to which that calf had belonged? Would its mother come charging back through our land again, solitary like me and angry with herself for feeling some secret release in it all?

I had put on old work clothes and cinched my belt tight about my waist, and when I took the first shovelful of dirt I felt better. The ground was softer than I'd expected it to be. I moved down a foot without much trouble, and then down two. I wanted to dig the grave deep, eight feet was my goal, and by the time Detective Mubia came out I had already achieved a third of it, though the hole wasn't even, and not quite seven feet long.

"I will build a perimeter with string," the detective said, "I will make the borders square." He didn't know where things were, but he returned to the house and came back quickly, with twine and a few short stakes with dirt on them, from the *shamba* behind the workers' dormitory, where my father had been.

The detective was good with his hands, his work was quick and clean, and in a moment I was throwing earth up over a taut and definite outline, one that allowed me to make the grave sufficiently long even as I worked my way down. Detective Mubia had said several times the night before that he would help, but now he seemed to understand without my telling him that this work was mine to do alone, so instead of offering to relieve me he took another shovel and moved the displaced earth into orderly piles. Once he went back into the house to bring water, and another time he cut a piece of the string to eight feet, so that I could measure the depth of the work I'd done. Otherwise the detective stood by watching, and I took a kind of strength even from that.

I guess it should come as no surprise, since I haven't stinted in describing the abundance of game on our farm, to hear that during one of my breaks from digging, when the grave was at six feet but didn't want to go farther down, the detective noticed the patterned back of a giant python in the medium-tall grass a dozen yards away. This snake was one I knew, a kind of resident. It was eighteen or twenty feet long and usually spent its time closer to our pond, waiting for a dik-dik to come by or sleepily digesting the dik-dik that had come by the day before. I remembered a time when Jules and I were playing in the orchard and he actually pulled this snake's tail, laughing and then running away. When the detective and I walked a little nearer to the snake we could see a bulge in its middle, so I knew we'd be fine. It would neither come closer nor go farther away.

It may be hard to understand why, but seeing that snake, having it come very nearly to the edge of Jules's grave, put me in a peaceful frame of mind. I began to cry a little, this time soft and easy, and I began to remember what a good man Julius had been. Isn't that the purpose of funerals, after all, to remember such things? I knew, because my father was missing and I had seen Jules among the tusks, that I might not be able to think of him that way again, but for that moment I had his goodness firmly in my mind, and I didn't want to lose it until the funeral was done.

"Six feet is good enough," I told Detective Mubia. I'd been digging for about two hours, so I guessed it was close to eight A.M. Dr Zir had said he would leave Nairobi by nine, that we should be ready for his arrival here by nine-thirty or ten. Because the generator had been on all night, I knew there'd be hot water, so I asked the detective to stay outside, and I went in to take a shower. I haven't mentioned that I had it with me, but I picked up that .380 automatic pistol, which had been resting in the crook of a nearby thorn tree, and walked slowly back to the house.

I have never thought of myself as a vulnerable woman—I don't think anyone thinks of me that way. I'm fit and strong and during ordinary times I carry a certain self-assurance, a no-nonsense aura that I have fostered over the years. I am telling you this now because of what happened in the house shortly after I stepped out of my shower, hot and clean.

I was wrapped in a big towel, covering myself with it but also using one end to vigorously dry my hair, when I suddenly knew that I was not alone in the house. I picked up my pistol, pushed its barrel through the folds of the towel, and stepped down the hall.

"Hello," I said.

I think I had expected Detective Mubia but there were two other men standing at my open front door. Beyond them I could see the pond.

The men were staring at the tip of my pistol, which came

from the folds of my towel at a level just below my waist, but was aimed up. Of the two men I knew one. He was Kamau, our foreman, the man who'd shot Jules in the back. Kamau was carrying Jules's hunting rifle, slung over his shoulder the way Jules used to carry it, but I immediately understood that aiming it at me was the last thing on his mind. He was nodding gravely, his jaw and his anguished eyes moving wildly.

"What do you want?" I asked.

"We have your father outside," the other man said.

"What I want to know is what in the world are you going to do with him?"

I guess I had decided that a hard reply might give me more time to figure things out, but the one who'd spoken didn't like it. He hissed and said, "This is not a joking matter. Your father says that he remembers nothing and your husband is dead. Now we are turning to you."

"But I'm not in on it," I told him. "I never was. I really don't know a fraction of what my father does, even if his mind is gone."

This first man didn't seem to be armed. He was only a little older than me and he looked far more like a businessman than he did a poacher or a criminal. He was well-spoken and probably well-educated too. I had seen him before, I knew him, but I also knew that I wouldn't be able to remember how.

"When your father was Minister of Wildlife his memory was fine," said the man.

"That was before independence," I said, "a dozen years ago. If my father did something wrong back then, what took you so long? How can you hold him responsible now?"

Even as I spoke I knew I was on the wrong track, working only out of my own meandering thoughts of a few hours

before. But I had gained a little time, and maybe I had also
made the man believe I didn't know about the poaching, that I
thought everything was political, that it was all about settling
some old score.

The man didn't answer, so since I was the one with the pistol, I spoke again.

"I need to get dressed," I said. "Tell me what you want and
get out of my house. Let me get on with my day."

"I want only what is mine," said the man. "Ask that fool
policeman. Your father owes me money, too, but I am willing
to forget about that. All I want now is my property back.
There is no other way."

He had kept his voice calm, so I spoke calmly too, asking
"How much time do I have to sort things out, to find your
property and give it back to you? Do I have a week? Do I have
a fortnight? Do I have a month?"

The man looked at me carefully but ignored my tone.
"Very well, you may have a week," he said.

"Will you contact me?" I asked. "How shall I find you
again?" But he said only, "Arrange everything by the end of
next week." He then turned and walked out the door. Kamau
was right behind him, never having spoken at all.

I had dried inside my towel so I went back into the bedroom and jumped into clean clothes, a black dress with a low-
cut front, over which I wrapped a black *kikoi*. This time I left
the silver pistol in a hat box on my closet shelf. I combed my
hair in a stroke or two and went outside to stare into the blue
morning sky, off toward Nairobi, for the dot that would become the helicopter that was bringing Julius home. The sky
was empty but when I looked back down again, there was my
father, midway between the dormitory and the house, still

perched on that old bench. He looked small and pitiful. He was sitting on his hands.

I ran toward my father, full of guilt, but just at that moment the helicopter was there, rising up out of the Great Rift Valley, coming over the orchard hill. I stopped in my tracks, black *kikoi* pulled tight around my shoulders, and when my father stood up, Detective Mubia joined us, running over from the orchard as if the helicopter were herding him, nudging him our way. The detective helped my father follow me over to a flat patch of earth next to the pond and we all waved, showing the best place for a helicopter to land.

It had been a calm morning but the helicopter reminded me of uncalm ones, of the days Jules and I liked so much when storms rattled our windows and made our farm stand up, turning everything alive. I could see Dr Zir in the front seat next to the pilot, and I could see a plain wooden coffin strapped beside him, outside, exposed to elements that could no longer move its occupant at all. When the helicopter settled and the noise went away, Detective Mubia stepped in under its blades and opened Dr Zir's door. My father, who had taken my arm, and whose hand I now tightly pressed to my side, said, "I've known that fellow for years, Nora. His name is Zir."

When the pilot got out and unstrapped the coffin, he and Detective Mubia lifted it up and carried it slightly off to the side. And though Dr Zir and my father were old, they rushed to help too, everyone following the detective's lead, carrying Jules all the way over to the edge of his grave. A slight wind had come up by then, as if brought by the helicopter blades.

I had dug Jules's grave in a diligent and single-minded way, purging myself of anger and doing my duty at the same time, but I realised just then that I hadn't planned a service for him. I guess I thought I'd simply bury him without words, since adequate words would be impossible to find.

"I want to go into the house for a book," I said. "Something to read from while we lower him down."

"Me too," said my dad.

I would have asked Detective Mubia to come so I could tell him about my encounter with our foreman and make him tell me about the other man, but when my father came with me, the detective held back. My dad kept pace beside me, hands behind him, clothing all a mess. He not only didn't seem offended by my indifference to his last night's plight, he didn't seem to have noticed it.

"Did they let you get any sleep, Daddy?" I asked. "Do you want to try wearing something of Julius's when we get inside?"

"I slept like the dead," said my father, but after a moment he remembered to add, "Nora, those men asked me questions all night long."

Our small library, the one Jules and I kept in bookcases on either side of our fireplace, had been scattered by the intruders. I think I intended to give Jules a secular send-off, I don't know, perhaps reading a passage from some favourite book of his, but among the pile on the floor I saw our Bible first, and my father immediately found a book that he himself had written and published in 1956, a book entitled *Elephants of Tsavo and Other Lands.* Daddy had worked in Tsavo Game Park when he was a young warden, and this book had helped him move up through the ranks. I'd read the book a hundred times as a girl, but it was not a serious work, and I kept it now only because he'd written it. The book was lean on writing but full of black-and-white photographs, like *Who's Who in the Zoo.*

"You read from that and I'll read from this," said my dad.

His eyes had light in them again so I asked one more time if he wanted to clean up, but I couldn't interest him in that. I think he'd have been content, as a matter of fact, just to pull up a chair and read from his book right there in the living room, amid all the clutter. He came along readily, however, when I reminded him that Dr Zir and the others were waiting outside.

During the time we were gone, Dr Zir and Detective Mubia had walked around to the back of the house and found flowers, roses mostly, but lilies and hibiscus and a long and viney strand of bougainvillea from the plant that grew up our bedroom wall. They had laid some of the flowers on top of the coffin, but each of the men also held something colourful in his hand. It was a nice gesture, awkward and touching. Dr Zir was crying and Detective Mubia was looking down.

I had somehow imagined that more people would turn up, one or two of Jules's friends from Narok, perhaps, and surely most of our field hands. But it was just the five of us, so when I got to the side of the grave I opened my Bible and started to read. Ever since I was a child, however close or far I might have been from religious faith, I have believed, just like Saint Augustine, that a random reading from the Bible would point the way, would give its reader a message, so I placed Jules's face firmly in my mind and read the following passage: "Nevertheless let every one of you in particular so love his wife even as himself; and the wife see that she reverence her husband." That made me stop. Random readings had never before worked so well. But by the time I looked at the Bible again, it was too late to continue, for my father had taken my pause as his cue.

"In its rush through the jungle a herd of African elephants makes the ground tremble," he read. "They are the largest and heaviest animals of the dark continent. Forty or fifty of them in a herd may blacken the landscape for a wide area with their shadows."

My father had a rich voice, far more appropriate than mine, and oddly enough, the sound of it invested his words with greater meaning than my own.

When he looked at me and nodded, I read again, from somewhere near the same spot. "So ought men to love their wives as their own bodies. He that loveth his wife loveth himself."

"Praise Jesus, praise Jesus Christ and praise God," said the detective, but I thought my passages were getting pretty self-serving, so I quickly found another page. Too late; my father took over again.

"Elephant herds stampede when alarmed at the approach of ivory hunters with their high-calibre rifles or the native who attacks them with arrows for their meat. But as a rule they shuffle along slowly and silently in search of a good grazing spot, stopping to coil their flexible trunks around roots and tree branches, which they eat in great quantities."

I guess I thought that if I stopped reading my father would too, so I said, "My husband, Julius Grant, was an admirer of the peculiar. He was drawn to the absurd." I don't know why I said that. I hadn't meant to insult my father, and I looked quickly at him to make sure I had not. I could see, however, that if I didn't continue he soon would, so I read again, from the new place I'd found. "For God commanded, saying, Honour thy father and mother: and, He that curseth father or mother, let him die the death."

There it was again, and I thought, How could I have acted

so heartlessly last night? Never mind all that idiocy about the battery in my watch, my father had really done nothing except come down from England to console me, so how could I treat him like that? I put my Bible away, trying simply to hold my sorrow in and think about Julius at the same time.

"Herds retain their members for many years," read my father, "and the individual elephants are loyal to the community." He was crying by then, but though his voice shook, he read on, braving his own internal storm. "Led by the cow elephant they travel single file, keeping careful watch over the young and the sick. They step in the leader's tracks, and when the last elephant has passed, the tracks are deep pits, making it dangerous for men to follow. Often they risk their lives to save a wounded companion too weak to fight or run away."

Now I was crying too. While listening to my dad I had recaptured the night of Jules's wounding, could see it all so well. I saw that elephant calf again, mortally hurt, and I saw the other elephants, coming too late to rescue it and trumpeting their despair into the sky. I saw myself kneeling down, and I saw the steady eyes of the Maasai, crouched behind their spears like turret gunners. I understood that the calf's mother would have tried to kill those lions had the lions not run away and I thought, How was my own behaviour in comparison with the mother elephant's that night?

My father stopped reading and closed his book. He had written those words in 1956, but though they'd had no impact on the zoological world, they were somehow essential to everything now, not only to Jules's death, but to whatever my father was going to have to tell me about his relationship to that man. I watched him for a long time, wondering if what he'd read had been chosen at random also, or whether he was being tricky. Had he opened his book and let his fingers wander wherever they might, or was he trying to tell me something even now, as he stood there watching me cry?

When the silence grew too long I asked Detective Mubia to help me lift Jules's coffin down into the grave, but the helicopter pilot right away offered to take my part. We hadn't rigged anything like lowering straps, and I hadn't dug the grave with any extra room for standing, so the two men had to lean precariously over either end of the hole to lower the coffin to ground level, and then drop to their knees so they could take it most of the rest of the way down; they let it fall the last two feet or so.

The coffin had been lowered with flowers on top. I threw in the ones I'd been holding, watched them land where Jules's heart should be, then stepped aside so that the others, first my father, then Dr Zir, then Detective Mubia and the pilot, could throw their flowers in also. It had been too quick, but the end of my husband's funeral was at hand. I reached back and got a shovel and rained earth down on Jules without saying anything more. I put my earth on his chest first, over the flowers we had thrown, then on his legs and across where I supposed his genitals might be. I saved my husband's face for last, but when I got to it I covered it quickly, without any further delay. After that Detective Mubia took the shovel and the grave filled up fast.

That was all. Inside the house we washed our hands and my father found Jules's bottle of Bushmill's and Dr Zir got five glasses from the kitchen. Detective Mubia and I picked up the living room, setting things straight, ordering the chairs and putting the books back on the shelves. If filling Jules's grave took twenty minutes, cleaning my living room took ten.

Though the house had looked trashed last night, it really hadn't been. Nothing much was broken—half a dozen items from the kitchen, perhaps, and a lamp in the hallway.

The whiskey glasses were filled and waiting. I thought the helicopter pilot, since he was working, would refuse a drink, but I was wrong. We held our glasses up. Julius Grant and I had been married for six years, we had broken our backs putting our farm together and building our life, and now I was toasting his trip to the other side with my confused father and his oldest friend, and with two strangers as well.

The helicopter pilot flew off alone that afternoon. I expected Dr Zir to go with him, but he stayed behind. We put chairs out on our porch and drank tea until the sun went down, washing the feeling of the whiskey away. When the first animals arrived at our pond Detective Mubia sat up, pleased at their closeness and their variety. A warthog was there, and a dik-dik came right past us, from the coffee plants at the back of the house.

"Let's count them," said Dr Zir. "Not the individuals, but the species, let's keep track."

"Three," said my father, though there had been only two so far.

I went into our office for a pad and pencil and when I handed it to the detective, we all made guesses; before we knew it all of us were involved in the animal game, nodding quietly whenever a new species came to the pond. I looked at my father once and he smiled, saying, "Noah's ark."

After the sun went down I stepped in and switched on the pond light. We had been in the dark only a few minutes, talking and looking at each other for a change, but when the light came on everyone focused on the pond again. On its far side

now was a single male lion, small and young. The other animals had gone back into the darkness to wait.

My father took my hand and squeezed it and I said, "Oh
dear God, no."

"What's wrong?" he asked. "What's happened now?"

Since I was looking across at the Land Rover I didn't have
to answer, for the detective remembered it too.

"Ah," he said, "the dead man's arm. We forgot to bury it
with the rest of him."

"Oh my," said Dr Zir.

"Forget it," my father said. "We can bury it easily enough
in the morning. We can dig another grave an arm's length
deep."

"Right-o," said Dr Zir. "We will plant it next to the rest of
him. Perhaps we will get a palm tree."

There was a moment of profound silence. It was impossible
to laugh, but that's what they all wanted to do. Dr Zir was
looking down, utterly shocked and furious with himself, and
my father had his mouth clamped shut and Detective Mubia
was looking fiercely away. No one meant to be frivolous, least
of all poor Dr Zir, and I remember thinking that the next day,
when I went out to bury my husband's arm, this moment on
the porch would come back to me.

I reached across the small expanse of porch and touched
Dr Zir's shoulder until we all settled down. Another species
had come, a Grant's gazelle, as if specially to honour the
memory of Jules's name.

7

Interrogating My Father

The house was small, but no one suggested that any-one go out to the dormitory to sleep. My father and Dr Zir slept together in the little guest room that the detective had used before, and Detective Mubia, who spent most of the night watching animals from the porch, took charge of the living-room couch.

In the morning I was awakened by the sounds of breakfast being made, and when I dressed and came out of my room I saw that both my father and Dr Zir were wearing aprons and cracking eggs into a big bowl. They'd cracked a dozen eggs for the four of us, and there was a raft of crisp bacon already on the kitchen table, a stack of toast so high that I thought it would surely fall over. I could see that Detective Mubia was still on the living-room couch, his red suit still on his body, his shoes beside him on the floor.

My father and Dr Zir had been arguing about the eggs, but when I came out they turned and presented a unified smile. Detective Mubia moved his feet out of sight, then came up standing, slipping into his shoes and pressing down the sides of his suit as he walked across the floor.

"Did our leopard appear?" I asked. "Did you see him last night?"

"He came like a ghost," the detective said. "He had a pure white front and a tail that bobbed in back of him as if it was held up by a wire."

I didn't remember cleaning up very well, but my kitchen looked orderly again, and I asked Dr Zir how long they'd been awake.

"With the sun, dear," he said, "with the cock's crow, but quiet as mice until just now."

It was hard to guess from his appearance that Dr Zir was a medical man. He had a naturally sympathetic face, but otherwise he was ugly. He had small eyes with dark circles under them, and a big nose, a narrow mouth, and a weak jaw. He had incongruous features but they somehow worked to form a congruous whole.

"After breakfast we need to settle down and discover a few things," I said. I was speaking to my father, but he was putting plates on the table and didn't hear, so I went into the office and looked at the desk and files, all of them still locked and undisturbed. Through the window I could see the Land Rover, and when I remembered that another burial duty remained, I went back through the living room and walked outside, past the car and onto the porch of the workers' dormitory. This building was larger than our house and contained eight rooms, four to each side of a single hallway. It was a dreary place, dark at any time of day, but since we never had more than eight regular farmhands, it was decent housing, usually one person to a room. There was a shower in the building and a toilet out back. Some of our workers did occasionally bring their families to live with them in these rooms, but for the most part they lived alone. We paid them well, and when we needed extra pickers we hired them from the pool of men and women who were always available, down at the petrol station in Narok.

The first room to the right of the main dormitory door was Kamau's. It was dreadful to realize that Kamau had been working against us for who knows how long, that he no doubt shot Jules on purpose that night. When I tried the door to his room I assumed it would be locked, but it swung open quickly, startling me.

"Hello," I said.

Kamau's room hadn't been cleaned out. His bed still had blankets on it, and his table, which he'd placed below the room's only window, held a stack of letters, Nairobi postmarks on most of them, the rest from western Kenya. The letters appeared to be personal. The one I opened was written in Kiswahili and asked Kamau for money, saying that the money should come more regularly, as it always had before. Kamau had his responsibilities, the letter said, and he wasn't meeting them. It was a stern letter, unfriendly and unsigned, and written in what I took to be a woman's hand.

I put the letter back in its envelope and was about to open another when the gleaming edge of Kamau's *panga* caught my eye. This *panga* was Kamau's baton, his swagger stick; he was never without it when he walked around the farm. It had a well-cared-for blade, and I remembered that Jules used to tease him by saying that though Kamau's *panga* was the best and the sharpest on our land, no one had ever seen it do any work. It struck me as strange, then, even under circumstances such as these, that Kamau would go off and leave the *panga* behind. I checked his closet and his trunk, but besides the letters and the *panga*, his clothing and other personal possessions were gone. There was a small photograph of a woman and three children hanging next to the *panga* from a nail on the wall.

I took the *panga* down, ran my thumb lightly across its blade, and kept it with me when I stepped back out of Kamau's room. I was as sure as I could be that none of our other workers were involved with Kamau, for as I checked their rooms I noticed that they had been vacated in a much more orderly way. Even their crucifixes were gone from the walls, leaving shadows of crosses in the permanent dust. It was as if they had been ordered out but had been given time to pack. Kamau's room, on the other hand, contained the disorder of a man who was lost, the disorder of hasty flight and chaos.

As I was coming out of the farthest room I heard Detective Mubia calling me from the porch. "Mama," he said, "the gentlemen have prepared our meal." I tried to call him into the dormitory, to show him what I'd found, but when he didn't come I took the *panga* and stepped outside again, the blade flashing in the morning light. I told the detective about Kamau's room and then about the visit I had had nearly twenty-four hours before, from Kamau and his new boss, that hateful man in the business suit. I told him that the man had mentioned him, going so far as to call him a fool.

"That is the man whose voice I know," the detective said.

"I knew it yesterday, but I could not speak his name. It is a city name, an unspeakable name, and one he has taken to make his own father angry."

Yesterday when I asked Detective Mubia to tell me what he knew he had ignored me, but I felt sure he'd tell me everything now. When I asked him, however, he would only say, "Come, let us go inside and eat. The key to everything is not out here."

There was a sense of forced heartiness at breakfast. My father was expansive, uninterested in talking about his night with the bandits but wanting to tell stories of the old days, about the Tsavo game reserve and the years when he was a warden there. The rest of us listened politely. Detective Mubia, who hadn't heard the stories before, really did seem engaged, and since I couldn't get the detective to tell me anything, I found myself trying to gain some sense of what was going on now by what my father said about the past.

"Daddy's real love was elephants, as you no doubt gathered from his book," I said. "He had a dedicated concern for their well-being, he always tried to keep them out of harm's way."

It was a blatant comment, but no matter how I hinted, I couldn't move my father to mention poaching, nor could I make Detective Mubia say that other man's name. So when Dr Zir started to clear the table, I stared into my father's sallow eyes. If he knew what was going on, I wanted him to tell me now, but I was also strangely reluctant to ask. It seemed oddly necessary that my father volunteer the information, that the words come freely without my insisting on them. It was as if only that could save the relationship between us once the truth was known. I sat a little farther back and looked at the detective too. The answers I wanted were brewing inside both these men, but they wouldn't come out until the brewing was done.

I'd intended to use the time after breakfast to go out and bury Jules's arm, but we all somehow went back into the office instead. The office was small, intended by the original owner to be another bedroom, I think, and since Jules and I often used it together, there were two desks in there. There was a couch under the window, and Dr Zir and Detective Mubia sat on that. My father stayed in the hallway outside. I opened the file cabinet next to the desk, pulling both drawers all the way out.

"Julius was fastidious," I said. "If he has anything written down, anything that will help us, it will be here."

I bent over the drawer and began looking through the files. Everything before me seemed to start with the letter C. There were notes on coffee sales, notes on wages paid and owed, receipts from a dozen Nairobi businesses for supplies, and lists of orders made.

I slammed the first drawer shut and began taking files out of the second, but this drawer contained coffee files too, and where the files ended, Jules's collection of maps began. Jules had been a superb and enthusiastic cartographer, it was his hobby, and so we had hand-made maps for much of the country, everywhere we had ever gone. Jules's maps were drawn with such detail that they always included the smallest roads. I pulled out the first map, of the Samburu region to the north and of the Rendille area around Marsabit. Jules often drew animals on his maps, small depictions of the game that was there, and at Marsabit he had drawn a wonderful likeness of Ahmed, the government-protected tusker who was always in the news these days. "Look," I told the two men, "Jules was an artist. See what he could draw."

I had begun to cry again, they could hear it in my voice, but neither man said anything. Detective Mubia was examining the frayed front of his lapel, and when I looked at Dr Zir he went out of the office and came back with his doctor's bag. "Let me give you something, Nora dear," he said. "Something mild will help to get you through the rest of today, something for tomorrow too."

Dr Zir's watery eyes were shining at me. He held a pill box, no doubt containing sedatives, which would let me understand my father better if I took them, but I grabbed the doctor's hand and firmly pushed the pill box away. He had a glass of water with him, and he surprised me by shrugging and taking a pill himself, quickly washing it down. And after that we all felt calm.

I was putting Jules's map back in the file cabinet when another file, behind where the maps were, drew my attention. It was an ordinary manila folder with a clipped-on label. "Elephants of Tsavo and Other Lands" is what the label said.

"Hold on. What's this?"

"Elephants of Tsavo," Dr Zir read. "How nice. He's managed to remember his father-in-law."

Inside the file were three thin sheets of paper, each with lists of numbers on them. There was nothing about elephants in the file, and there were no hints as to what the numbers meant. Everything was in Jules's hand, but other than that, nothing meant a thing to me. I showed the file to Detective Mubia, but he couldn't make anything of it either. Dr Zir was starting to stare at us with my father's unfocused eyes when my father himself appeared at the door.

"That would be our code," he calmly said. "No one knows it but Julius and me."

Detective Mubia got up and my father sat down, taking the three sheets of paper from my hand. "We were in very deep, Nora," he said, "over our heads by a mile."

I had the file folder on my lap and I gave it to him quickly. "Look, Daddy," I said. "What do these numbers mean? Nothing matters except that you tell me what's happening now. That way we can find our way out."

My father's face was smooth, making me fear he might leave us again, so I tried to speak firmly. "Tell me now, Daddy, and try to be clear."

Detective Mubia leaned forward.

"I was never a crooked man," my father said. "I never took a bribe and I never stood still for poachers. I was the guardian of the elephants, all during those years."

"I know you were, Daddy," I said, "but what do the numbers signify?"

I knew I was pushing too hard when my father turned around in his seat, looking at the office door. Detective Mubia, however, helped me by reaching over and putting a thin finger on the first number on page one. "What does this one mean?" he asked. "Only this one, nothing more."

The number was 8773-3-1-211ka, and my father hardly glanced at it before saying, "That was our first shipment. Eight July 1973."

"What does the second three mean?" Detective Mubia asked.

"That's the number," said my father. "That first time there were only three."

I hated to interrupt, but asked the question anyway. "Three what, Daddy? Three tusks? Does it mean you smuggled only three tusks that time?"

To impeach my father so readily and in front of the others was exactly what, at breakfast, I had told myself I wouldn't do, but that was what he was saying, wasn't it, that he and Jules had been smuggling ivory out of the country for over a year by that time?

My father was quiet for a moment but then he said, "Yes, three tusks," and when Detective Mubia asked him about the number one he said that it meant England. Three tusks were shipped from Kenya to England on the eighth of July, last year.

I was sick at heart but made him say that what remained was a flight number and an airline. And after we understood that, their rudimentary code was so easy to break that it made me even madder. Any fool could figure it out. Dr Zir very smartly took my father back into the other room, and Detective Mubia and I pored over the lists, failing to understand almost nothing, and discovering that my husband and father, no doubt in connection with the man who had come to my house with Kamau, had smuggled nearly one thousand elephant tusks out of Kenya, all on commercial airlines, to a half dozen cities around the world. By cross-checking the lists with another that we found in the coffee files we discovered that the tusks had left the country in burlap bags of beans. *One sip and you will know.* And the date of the last entry was a month before the date of Jules's death, or only a fortnight before I saw him sitting in that Loita Street room.

I was seething with anger, furious with both men, but since

Jules was already dead, it was my father that I wanted to kill. And he was in the other room, with the doped-up Dr Zir, having another cup of coffee, sitting among the stacks of cold toast and the dried-out eggs.

"What a couple of bastards," I told Detective Mubia. "What consummate shits both those men are!"

The detective's face got stiff at the language I used, and for a moment I was mad at him, too. Everyone was cryptic, even this odd man. But though I have said I was furious with my father, that was wrong. Furious is hot, and what I felt was cold at its heart, something solid, like a cancer unveiled in a routine exam, and the fact that he volunteered the information, an act that I had thought would save us, meant nothing. This is why I had let my father stay out all night long, without once going into the coffee to call his name. My analogy with the watch battery had been right! Think of it, both of the men in my life weren't what they had appeared to be. And it was too late for me to deal with it in any redeeming way at all.

/   /   /

My father and Dr Zir were waiting in the living room. My father was sitting on the couch where Detective Mubia had slept, and Dr Zir was pacing back and forth past the open front door. My father had his hand up, and when I came in he began talking right away. "It isn't what you think, Nora, Julius and I weren't really smuggling elephant tusks. It was all a joke, don't you see. It only got a little out of hand."

I still had the file with me so I opened it again and pointed at the final entry. "Don't lie, Dad," I said. "I saw him. In a house on Loita Street. There were tusks all around him on the fucking floor."

Jules had taught me the power of such adjectives as "fucking," but I had never used them in my father's presence before. All he could manage to say, however, was "Why didn't you tell me?" and that made me shout.

"Don't be such a coward, Dad! Who's the man behind Julius's murder? Who kept you out all night? Who came here yesterday with Kamau, all dressed up in his London suit? I want the bastard's name!"

If my father had answered stupidly again I might have struck him, but my fury seemed to bring him back to life. His adrenaline was up too, giving him an odd kind of lucidity.

"Did he threaten you?" he wanted to know.

"He was businesslike," I answered. "What is his name?"

"I don't know," he said, and then he said, "If Kamau was with him, it was probably Mr Smith."

"Mr Smith? He was Kenyan, Daddy, he was Kikuyu, I'm sure."

My father didn't answer that but Detective Mubia said, "You are right, he is Kikuyu. Mr Smith is the awful name. When his activities put him on the criminal side he is called Smith because it creates a distance from his family and because his crimes are often committed abroad."

"That's him," said my father. "He's the devil responsible for everything, the rat. It wasn't Julius and it wasn't me. We didn't do anything wrong."

"He says he wants his property back. He's giving me a week. After the week is up I think he'll try to harm us." This time I spoke slowly, using my coldest voice, but I couldn't make it last.

"I'm going outside now, Daddy," I said. "And I want you and Dr Zir to get ready to travel back to town. When we get to Nairobi we'll iron everything out and get you back to England, where you belong."

I thanked Detective Mubia for what he had done, for bringing Jules's arm, macabre as it was, but particularly for sticking around to help, and for finally telling me that the voice on the tape recorder was that of a known criminal man. And after that I went out to the Land Rover and collected the wooden box. It was bigger than Jules's arm, twice as wide and nearly half again as long.

We had left two shovels out overnight, so when I got to the grave I put the box down on top of it and began to dig again, a short distance away. I think I intended to dig this second hole so that it would do justice to the first, but as I began to sweat I let my anger rise again. I had loved Julius Grant better than he had loved me, that was the truth of the matter, though I would never have believed it when he was alive. When he was alive I would have bet my whole life on the proposition of Julius Grant's love. When he was alive I knew that he would not forsake me, that betrayal was impossible, that he would always be by my side. I had been fierce in my love, I was its defender and protector. And now I was discovering the hollowness of what I'd been protecting, too late to do anything but bury my husband.

I wept as I dug, and slowly, instead of digging well, I began to dig a grave that went straight down, a grave that was narrow and deep and that echoed Dr Zir's joke of the night before. I dug the grave as deep as I could, and as I pulled the shovel out, dry soil flying away, I let my anger boil until soon I was stabbing the earth, plunging that shovel into the heart of it, exhausting myself. I tried four or five times for a last good stab, a last bit of earth lifted from that hole, but finally I collapsed onto the ground, too tired to dig anymore, too tired to feel anything at all.

I stayed that way for a time, numbed by everything, but work on the farm had accustomed me to recover quickly from physical exhaustion, and I got my wind back sooner than I wanted to. I opened my eyes and looked along the ground. As it happened, I was facing the edge of the hill, and as it happened also, I could see the body of that lethargic snake again, that unhungry python, the sight of which yesterday's digging was preventing from being a surprise.

I sat up slowly, raising myself to my knees and then, with the help of my shovel, all the way to my feet again. I raised my shovel, at first, I think, to clean up the edges of the hole, to make it better, but with my regained wind my anger came back, and I suddenly turned the shovel around, aimed it at that other grave, and let it come slamming down on the top of the wooden box, easily splitting its lid and exposing Jules's arm.

I was appalled at what I had done, but not enough to keep my shovel from hitting the box twice again, one time coming in from the left side, next time coming in from the right. This box was padded, built to withstand temperature variations, maybe, but it couldn't withstand my shovel, and by the time I was done, Jules's arm had rolled free of the box and was lying next to the freshly dug grave, palm down, fingers curled over the edge of the hole, as if they'd just finished the digging themselves. It was bizarre, and what made me angrier still was that Jules's wedding ring was there, his fingers fat around it, as if yeast had been used in the embalming, making them rise.

"God damn you, Julius Grant," I said. This was no

automatic expletive like the one I'd used in the house with my
dad, but a genuine heartfelt curse. I wanted God to damn him,
to send him down through the hole where his arm was already
headed and to let him burn in hell.

Insanity sometimes comes in momentary doses, I had
learned from observing my father's wandering mind, and what
I did next was along those hereditary lines. I picked up Jules's
arm at the place where his bicep had previously been, and I
held it above my head like a hatchet. Then I walked the
twenty paces or so over to the lip of the hill and swung his arm
down, letting his fat fingers slap that sleeping snake. The snake
moved in the grass, turning its head and tail both at the same
time, as if it were about to twist around whatever it was that
was bothering its middle. The snake's head was the same size
as Jules's hand, and when it opened its mouth and reached
back, I introduced the two of them by casting Jules's whole
arm in the snake's direction and then leaping out of the way.
The snake struck then, catching Jules's arm above the wrist,
and rising up high enough into the air to look for an instant
like a cross marking the spot of Jules's grave, like those shadows in the dust on the dormitory wall. And then the snake was
down and gone. Not quickly, the way a smaller snake would
go, but not slowly either. It slipped over the edge of the hill
and down toward the Great Rift Valley with my husband's
arm. I could see it going, but I didn't follow it with anything
but my eyes.

I was spent by the time I returned to the house. My father
was still actively contrite and waiting on the porch with his
travelling clothes on. Dr Zir and Detective Mubia had locked
all my windows and had shut down the generator and closed

the door to the workers' dormitory. The detective offered to take one of them back to town in his car, but both men said they would go with me in the Land Rover.

I watched the detective leave, knowing I'd see him again, knowing now that he had a great deal more to tell. In Narok I stopped at the petrol station and asked the proprietor to hire security guards on my behalf, stationing them strategically around my farm, twenty-four hours a day. It was a service that the proprietor had performed for us before.

/   /   /

That's it, the beginning of my story, told with as much skill as I can muster. Maybe it's been a long beginning, but it hasn't been a bit longer than it needed to be, considering that it relates not only the events that led to the loss of my husband but those that led to my loss of innocence and the beginning of my interest in revenge as well.

In the next part of the story you'll find a slightly altered me, one with a clear purpose and a definite agenda in mind. That's what coming of age will do to you, it will make you sober, it will make you think and grow, it will make you plan.

If you don't believe me, turn the page.

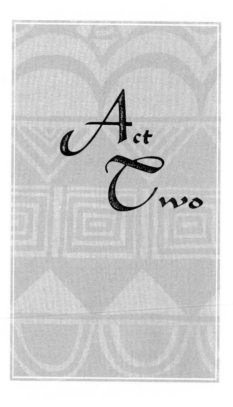

Act Two

8

The House on Loita Street

We rode back into Nairobi in utter silence, the two old men together in the back seat, three hours with no one speaking, me speeding over potholes, banging into some of them as if I wanted to break the Land Rover's tyres. When we got to Lower Kabete Road I dropped Dr Zir at the top of his drive, not even saying good-bye.

The security guard opened the gate to my father's house, and only after I'd driven through and parked down under the avocado tree did I notice that my father was asleep in the back seat, slumped over into the space that Dr Zir had occupied a moment before. His mouth was open wider than Julius Grant's had been, and with the engine off, I could hear the troubled rasping of his breath.

I got out of the car and slammed the door, but since my father still didn't wake up, I left him there, opening the door again only to push the window a little aside so he'd have fresh air.

At first to be back inside my father's house was a relief. I washed my face and arms, removing the dirt of the road, and then I sat at the piano in the living room, letting the fingers of my right hand remember the first four measures of the Mozart sonata that Mr Smith had recorded on our farm, a perfect melodic line used in perfidy, to introduce a further madness into my life. I thought, What is it about living that makes it so impossible to keep the lines straight, to keep order and intimacy among humankind? I had been a happy child, quick and easy under the avocado boughs and at home among the animals of the African plain. I'd had a thirsty intellect from the very start, with the unfettered energy to let it drink. At home I was everyone's joy, and at school I was at the centre still, though of a wider world, with friends gathered around. By the time I went away to Oxford I was not only terrific at learning, but I could speak Swahili perfectly, and decent French as well. At Oxford I was owlishly aware of the world of books and short with those who weren't. I gave myself away there, first in the name of Karl Marx—I hate to say so but it's true—and twice more after that, once in honour of Dylan Thomas, as you may already have guessed, and twice again for Keats and Shelley, in a kind of photo finish. That made four men in my life, plus one more, all before returning to London to visit my still-sane father and to meet my truest love. And now my truest love was gone, dead because of some stupid plan, and I was alone, and I could only think, What's a woman's life but a series of encounters such as these? Is there any real work for a woman to do, any real life for her to live, if she is thirty-one and still naïve and already widowed and alone? What is there for her to do if she has lived her life, thus far, in juxtaposition to the lives of all these unreliable men?

/ / /

My father stayed in the Land Rover until sundown, and when I heard him coming through the front door of the house, I went out the side, circling around and getting into the Land Rover again. While he'd been sleeping I'd slept too, a little, and then I'd bathed and found clean clothes to wear. It was my intention to go out and discover as much as I could on my own before questioning my father again. Since the housekeeper was off, I left food in the kitchen, and I knew that soon Dr Zir would come, renewing the habit he'd formed, over years of being my father's neighbour and friend, of walking through the valley and coming in to drink a glass of port and play a game of chess.

But whatever my intention, as I drove out the gate and down Lower Kabete Road toward Westlands and town, I had no clear idea what I would actually do. I'd left food for my father but I hadn't eaten myself, so at Westlands I searched around a little bit, trying to find a bakery or a restaurant that would serve me something at such an odd time of day. I used to know this part of town well, but it had changed over the years, and I hadn't paid attention to the changes. There had been a restaurant and I had known where it was, but now it was gone, and the other restaurants I passed were either not open yet or were in some other way wrong—too expensive or presenting the wrong kind of food or impossible to enter alone. I circled the area twice, then gave up and drove downtown the back way, toward the National Museum, down the Parklands Sports Club Road.

Now I was driving alone through the only part of Nairobi I had ever lived in as an adult. I saw the building where I'd had my flat, and when I passed the sports club where I had exercised my young girl's body playing squash and running around, I nearly turned in, to experience myself as I had once been. Could I walk as a single woman across the club's creaking wooden floor? Could I do that? Though I tried, I couldn't even summon the faces of those I'd played squash with in that other life of mine, but could I walk in there now, renewing my membership to eat a solitary meal on the patio or in the darkest corner of the club's main bar?

It was already eight o'clock and I was still hungry when it suddenly came to me what I was doing and where I would go. On the streets of East African cities a strange quiet takes over in the early hours of the night, that's what Jules always used to say. Restaurants and bars and nightclubs dot the towns, of course, but the actual streets are nearly deserted. I've seen it in Harare and Mbabane and Addis and Dar. Nairobi's no exception, and as I drove into the main part of town I could see that all over the business district, even on the streets around the big hotels, things were by and large calm. I cruised the length of Kenyatta Avenue, then turned in front of the New Stanley and doubled back to park beside the bar of the Six Eighty Hotel, the one I thought Jules was headed for on that fateful night, and only a short walk from Loita Street. I was going back to the scene of the crime, the place where I had first understood that there was anything amiss at all.

I got out and locked the Land Rover's doors, but I had two things inside it that I didn't want stolen—that automatic pistol, which was lodged up in the springs under the driver's seat, and the file I had found in our office on the farm—so I asked the bar's security guard to watch the car while I was gone. After that I took a direct little road that led up beside the central post office, crossing Kenyatta Avenue in the dark.

The first time I saw the building, on the night I followed Jules around, I had approached it from the Market Street side, and it was harder than I expected it would be to find again now. And once I did find it, it looked less dilapidated, far less like a poacher's den. It had shingled sides, not the flaking brown paint that I'd have sworn it had before, and its front-room windows were large. All in all, in fact, it wasn't a place that had the guarded appearance that I'd seen with my foolish, wifely eyes, but, rather, one that seemed open and fine. It still had the residential aura that I'd felt before, and I still thought that was odd, on a street that otherwise contained businesses and vacant lots. There was no security guard in front, and there was no fence, but though it was well past business hours, the windows of the place were lit, as if reading lamps were on.

I had no idea what I was going to do at this place now. Could I follow the inclination I'd had on the only other night I had been here, nearly a month before? Could I knock on the door and ask whoever answered, not whether Jules could come out and play, but why they'd had to see him dead? Since my father and Detective Mubia wouldn't tell me, could I see if some stranger might?

I looked at my watch. It was already later than I wanted it to be, nearly eight-thirty on a never-ending day, but I stepped onto the porch of the house and tried to look through the

small windows that fanned across the upper portion of the
door. I had to stand on tiptoes, and the glass was bevelled, ob-
scuring my view and fracturing the internal light, but I could
see there was a man standing there. He wasn't looking at me
but seemed to be cleaning something, rubbing a cloth against
an object that he held in his hands. I stepped back a foot or
two and knocked firmly on the door.

"*Hodi?*" I called. "Is anyone home?"

I could see from the way the shadows moved on the glass
that the man on the inside was standing against it now, but he
didn't answer my call.

"I have business here," I said, "a question to ask of the
owner or the resident, whichever the case may be."

I'd been sure that the man was standing still, listening from
the other side of the door, but suddenly I saw his face, peering
out at me from the lower and larger window to my left.

"Mr N'chele is not at home," the man said. "He is never
here at this time of night. He is at the New Florida Nightclub,
taking his evening meal."

"What?" I asked. "What did you say?" I had heard the
man's words perfectly well, but I had no idea how else I could
reply. My God, was this Mr N'chele's house? Mr N'chele was a
famous man whom I had met once or twice as a girl. He'd been
in the papers every day at the time of Kenya's independence a
dozen years before. He was a fervent nationalist and a political
candidate back then, but I hadn't heard his name in years. I
guess I had supposed that he was dead. But if this was Mr
N'chele's house, whatever my husband had been doing here
became an even larger question than it had been before.

After the servant told me what street the New Florida
Nightclub was on, I thanked him and stepped off the porch

again, walking quickly away. The New Florida was nearby; it
was the nightclub I'd seen above the petrol station on my original walk down here. But how could I approach a man like Mr
N'chele in a bar? What could I possibly say?

I went back toward the end of the block again and was
soon out of sight of the house. Walking straight would take me
to my father's Land Rover and home, but the New Florida
Nightclub was to my left and I somehow turned that way, not
exactly deciding to go into the bar, but only intending to walk
for a while, to amble forlornly along. And it was just then, just
after I made my turn, that a kind of dizziness set in, a vertigo
that made me put my hand against the nearest wall. I could already see the top of the New Florida Nightclub, but the street
where I stood quite suddenly seemed changed, familiar to me,
but in the oddest of ways. I felt as I had at that petrol station in
Narok when I finally understood that what the hospital box
contained was Jules's severed arm. The building I leaned
against, which I'd barely noticed before, became one that I
recognised from years and years ago. When I stood away from
it, putting my hands to my head to rub my eyes, I could see the
building as it had been, with a different coat of paint on it,
with a newer and stronger look. And its juxtaposition with Mr
N'chele's place, whence I'd just come, made me see everything
else on the street as it had been when I was a child as well.

I went up to the front door and looked at the listing of
businesses that currently rented space there. There were den-
tists and doctors and trading companies of various kinds, but
there were also several names that I immediately remembered
from when I was a child, from a time when I had to look up at
the listing that I now looked down upon.

It was a profound and troubling moment. I was on Market

Street, as I had been scores of times during my adult life, but this time I had entered it with an altered perspective, from the Loita Street side, having just heard Mr N'chele's name for the first time in a decade, and with my mind searching everywhere, open to a range of possibilities concerning Jules.

I had known Market Street intimately as a child, but during recent years I hadn't once remembered that this was where my father's offices had been. With my child's perspective unexpectedly returned, however, I was not only able to remember precisely how the street had looked back then, but I was beginning to remember something else as well. I closed my eyes and touched the building one more time, and the scene that came into my mind was this: I was holding on to my father's hand. We had walked out of this building, back the way I'd just come. It was a clear day and I was skipping to keep up with my dad. When we got to Loita Street we turned right, stopping at the door of the place I had just walked away from now. What I am saying is that I had been to Mr N'chele's house with my father, so very many years before.

/ / /

The New Florida Nightclub was accessible only by climbing up several switch-back flights of stairs. I must have stayed outside on Market Street a long time, for when I entered the nightclub it was nearly ten, and the place was packed. The area around the two bars was filled with young Kenyan girls standing three deep and dressed to kill. A small orchestra played in the club, and I was beginning to remember that there were dancers and other acts too, that this was a nightclub with an entire floor show.

A few tables in the room were free-standing, but there were many more booths, crescent-shaped things with slick black vinyl coverings and too much stuffing in their seats. These booths were elevated and somehow more prestigious than the tables, so I scanned them for Mr N'chele, hoping to recognise him in the crowd.

All of the booths were occupied, but a waiter soon found me a small table at the edge of the dance floor, and I sat down and ordered a drink. I then tried to look into each of the booths in turn, taking my time. Some were occupied by tourists, either alone or with Kenyan guides. All of the booths together formed a larger half-moon around the room, and in the booth that was precisely in the middle, staring into the mid-distance the way my father always did, I found the man I was looking for. He was old and thin. He wasn't alone in the booth—two young men sat at its outer sides—but he was clearly alone in his evening, vaguely scanning the bar and taking an occasional bite from the food on his plate.

I found a note-pad in my bag. The paper wasn't plain, as I would have preferred, but was pale pink and had a cute slogan across its top: *Mary, Mary, Quite Contrary*. The words were highlighted by pencil-thin drawings of vegetables, suitable, perhaps, for a little girl to own, but pretty odd for me to be using under the circumstances at hand. I looked at the note-paper for a while, but since my only immediate alternative was to write my message on a cocktail napkin, I drew a dark line through the vegetables, and wrote the following note below it:

Dear Mr N'chele:

My name is Nora Hennessey Grant, daughter of Nathan

Hennessey and widow of Julius Grant. Do you remember me? I believe we met nearly twenty years ago when my father had his offices on Market Street nearby.

I read the note over and was not very happy with it. I should have written only, "My name is Nora Hennessey Grant. May I have a moment of your time?" The recent revelations, the things I had discovered while walking over here from his house, were far too new for me to be writing them down. Instead of starting over, however, I simply added, "May I have a moment of your time?" at the bottom, signed the note, and had a passing waiter take it away.

The orchestra had started to play and my drink had come when the waiter returned with Mr N'chele's reply. "Of course I remember you, Nora," it said. "When you are free, come, let us chat about days gone by."

Mr N'chele's note was written on the back of my own, in an equally informal hand. People were on the dance floor, but I could nevertheless see Mr N'chele rather better now that my eyes had adjusted to the room's dim light. He was younger than my father but had a bald head, balanced on top of a neck no thicker at its middle than my husband's abused arm. His head even seemed to shake a little because of the difficulty that neck was having in holding it up.

I had expected someone healthier, I'd expected vitality, a certain aggressive posture that I could oppose, but I'd already stood up and I was approaching Mr N'chele's table too quickly for any kind of tension to build. When Mr N'chele saw me coming he tried to slide out of the booth so that he too would be standing up when I arrived.

"Miss Nora Hennessey Grant," he said. He was slightly out of breath but he extended his hand, letting it sway in the air until I caught it and shook it, calming it down.

"I have come to ask some questions about my husband," I said. I wanted to be direct, to ask my questions and then go home, but I'd spoken too soon, for Mr N'chele was sliding back into his booth again, and my comment was swallowed by the noise.

Once he was seated he told me to sit on his left side. His two young men tried to sit down beside us, hemming us in, but he ordered them away, telling them to wait at the bar.

Mr N'chele's table seemed to have its own waiter, and when the man came over, Mr N'chele ordered a steak dinner for me, one just like his own. After that he looked at me and said, "Nora Hennessey Grant. Tell me how we can settle things down."

Mr N'chele spoke to the point, which was what I wanted, but his head was shaking so much that the words seemed to lurch out of his mouth. I was sure that this wasn't the man I had seen leaving my husband alone in his kitchen that night.

"Nathan Hennessey is your father," he said. Now his head stopped shaking and his words had an apologetic tone, as if he were telling me something that was horrible to know.

"Yes," I said. "My father moved to London several years ago but he's here now, in Nairobi. He returned for the funeral of my husband, who was recently killed."

I was careful to speak without accusation in my voice, but my words had struck home. I could see Mr N'chele thinking things out, the picture of my father replaced by one of my dead husband in his mind's eye. I watched him for a long time, completely calm, and finally I began to see something else moving in to cloud his face.

"Really," he said, "a lady should not be coming out so very soon after her husband has died. What possessed you to come here? This is a nightclub, my dear. You should be staying home, remembering your husband and preparing yourself for your difficult time."

There was a moment just then when I realised I was probably strong enough to take this man's neck in my hands and twist until his head fell permanently down to one side, but soon after that I began to smile. How absurd it had all so quickly become. Here I was confronting the man who might be responsible for Jules's death, who might actually have ordered him killed, and he was scolding me over a failure of decorum, a social impropriety.

Mr N'chele didn't like my smile, but though his face got tight again, the shaking of his head was still controlled. The steak he had ordered for me had come on a trolley and the waiter was standing a little back, waiting to set it down.

"Do you know Mr Smith?" I asked. "Is someone by that name working for you?"

I had stopped smiling and had kept my pleasant tone, so Mr N'chele relented a little too. This time he looked at me and sighed.

"His name is not Smith," he said. "Please don't call him that. His name is N'chele. I have asked him to stop using that ridiculous and offensive name a hundred times, but he continues to let it stand. Really, that name represents the trouble I have had with him over the years, ever since he was a child."

The room seemed very still. "Mr Smith is your son?" I

slowly asked. As my mouth came open, Mr N'chele regained his previous calm.

"But it will not help you to ask the father about the business of the son," he said. "In your note you remembered accompanying your father to my home all those years ago, but do you also remember that my son was your playmate during that time? Do you understand that my son's introduction to your father was something he never forgot?"

"Did you ever meet Julius Grant?" I asked. "Did you ever see my husband, who has died?"

I was beginning to believe that Mr N'chele wanted to tell a truth of some kind. Of course he couldn't know that I'd seen Jules sitting among the tusks at his kitchen table that awful night. He probably hadn't even been at home.

"I knew his face when I saw it," Mr N'chele said, "but I only saw it once or twice." His voice grew soft and he dropped his eyes to the plate that the waiter had placed before me. "Eat your steak," he said, "it might get cold." And then he said, "Your husband didn't know it but he interfered wrongly, he kept my son from doing right."

Something seemed to happen between us then. I wanted to ask him to explain but I knew I couldn't force it, so for a few minutes Mr N'chele ate his steak and I ate mine. We ate slowly, chewing each piece and passing the salt between us and sharing a salad that had come. A sense of community was forming, and when Mr N'chele spoke again he was careful and kind.

"But I am so sorry," he said. "About your husband's demise. It is unforgivable of me not to have said so by now. It was not you but mention of your father that caused my insensitive nature to come out. Now, however, let us talk about this awful business at hand. Let us try to stop it if we can."

I moved a little closer to him on the seat. "Tell me what they were doing," I asked quietly. "Were my husband and father in league with your son to smuggle ivory out of the country? Is that what it was?"

Since I had that cryptic list of flights and destinations in my car, and since my father had told me so, I already knew the answer, but I wanted to hear another confirmation of it, affirmation coming from this man's mouth.

"Absolutely not," he said.

"But I have evidence," I let him know.

Right away I worried that I had said too much. However truthful he seemed to want to be, it wasn't through his son's kitchen window but through his own that I had seen Jules among the contraband. Mr N'chele went right on. "I have not seen much of my son since all this began," he said. "In recent years, in fact, we have been estranged. But they were not smuggling ivory, of course they were not. I have my spies. There are many activities that I might wink at, but my son knows where I will draw the line. I was trying to draw it, don't you see, when your husband got involved."

I knew he was lying, he had to be, but the mood we'd established was so conspiratorial that I asked another question anyway. "If they were not smuggling ivory, then what were they doing that was so much against the law?"

"Nothing whatsoever," Mr N'chele said. "In this case everything they did was legal. On that you have my word."

Though I had sparred well enough thus far, I certainly wasn't gaining much ground. If I spoke pointedly, this man danced away, and if I seemed unsure, he came back slowly, like my partner in a minuet. Should I go ahead and say it all? Should I tell him that I'd seen my husband standing in his house, hefting a beer bottle among the phallic disarray? Should I tell him that his son had kidnapped my father and threatened me in my own home? Mr N'chele was lying to me now, so what did I have to lose by speaking out?

But all I did was look at him silently. Was it also possible that he simply didn't know, that his blindness as a father was equal to mine as a wife?

"Maybe I'm mistaken," I said, "but if so, then what business did they have together, my husband and your son?"

It was Mr N'chele's turn to give me a long look then. Finally, however, he seemed to decide. "My son's business, such as it was, was with your father. He wanted to trick your father, to cause him pain. It was a bad idea, it was too complicated, and it came far too late in the day, but your husband's involvement was accidental. He was brought in by your father in order to give him a hand."

I think Mr N'chele wanted me to ask what my father had done, why his son wanted to cause him pain, but I had something else in mind.

"Our foreman shot my husband in the back," I said, "using his own rifle. He was trying to shoot a lion but he shot my husband instead. Our foreman was working for your son."

"That man will not be found anywhere for a good long while," Mr N'chele said, "and I doubt if he will ever visit your farm again." He spoke as if it was Kamau's welfare I was worried about, but I kept my neutral tone.

"As a matter of fact I did see him there," I let him know.

"He came back only yesterday. He was with your son when he paid a visit to my father and me."

Even as I spoke I was deciding against saying more, but just that much made Mr N'chele sigh. He reached across the table and took my right hand in both of his own. I was still holding my steak knife but he encompassed that too, touching its serrated edge with his thumb.

"They were dealing in plastics, my dear," he said, "not ivory. More precisely, I guess, it's acrylics. My son learned the technique in London in a dental laboratory where they make false teeth. Perhaps it was not an absolutely honest plan, but it was not criminal under Kenyan law, and it certainly should not have ended this way, but your husband's injuries were accidental, surely you know that is true. No one could have planned such a death as he had."

"Plastics," I said, "acrylics, you say?"

Kind as he seemed to be trying to be, Mr N'chele nevertheless did not seem to have a comfortable relationship with specific speech. He was doling out what he knew, handing me these tidbits reluctantly.

"Were they selling plastics or buying them?" I asked. "Tell me the rest, let me leave here tonight with more than I brought in."

"But I've just told you," he said. "Think about it for a while. They were exporting *artificial* elephant tusks to Europe and selling them there as real. They were selling fakes, tusks made of an acrylic combination, quite ingenious. I don't doubt that the Europeans have laws against what they did—it was my son's plan, in fact, that your father would get caught on that end—but in Kenya they were simply making wonderful replicas and fooling everyone with what they made. I was fooled, your husband was no doubt fooled. Everyone thought it was a joke worth playing. My son said your husband believed that anyone who would buy such things was getting what he deserved."

"But if all that is true, why didn't he tell me?" I asked. "I admit it sounds like something Julius might do, but he wouldn't keep it from me. If it was a joke he'd want to share it, to include me in it all."

That was the heart of the matter for me—why I had been left out—but I also understood that it was stupid to ask Mr N'chele, and that I had probably let the heart of the matter for him go for too long.

"Tell me why your son hates my father so," I said. "What did my father ever do to him?"

Mr N'chele stared at me so hard that I took my hand away and cut another piece of steak. I ate it and pushed my plate aside.

Finally he said, "You were present that day, my dear, and you were not so young. Is it possible that you remember nothing, while my son remembers it all? He was a good son when he was small, but what your father did festered in him, first turning him bitter and then turning him around. For a while he wouldn't speak to me or let me tell him what I thought about it. And when he did finally speak, the nature of his speech had changed."

Mr N'chele was by then looking at me as if he was waiting for an apology, as if my ignorance of whatever had happened was an ill-mannered pretense. But what could I say? My father could be blamed for a lot of things, no doubt, but could he be blamed for the fact that this man's son had turned out bad? It was a preposterous suggestion and it made me angry. Jules was dead, but instead of finding solace in trying to discover why, I was sitting here talking with this old man. I looked at my watch and moved on the seat.

"It's late," I said, "and I've left my father alone." But Mr N'chele didn't hear me. His mind was running along channels of its own.

"It was an uneventful day," he said, "and it promised to remain so. Otherwise I would not have taken my son along."

"What day?" I asked. "Tell me what year it was, at least."

This time he heard the sharpness in my voice and responded with true surprise. "Why, 1956, of course. Do you mean to tell me you've been serious all along, you really don't remember? It was the year before your father got the wildlife job. I had gone to his office to complain about his elephant book, about what the book implied."

My father's book? What the hell was he talking about?

"*Elephants of Tsavo and Other Lands?*" I asked, as if it could have been another.

As soon as I spoke the words I felt something unhinging slightly, far back in my brain. But I also felt my energy flag. Things were getting too far afield, the day had gone on for too long. I wasn't paying attention to business anymore.

"I really must go," I said.

"How old were you in 1956?" Mr N'chele asked. "Were you ten that year, were you twelve? How is it that you don't remember? My son remembers everything and he was only fourteen."

I was trying to stay calm, to keep something in reserve for the long drive home, but this conversation was really dragging me down. It wasn't 1956 but 1974.

"I was twelve," I said. "I've got to go home now." But Mr N'chele took hold of my arm.

"I will tell you why you remember nothing and my son re- members almost nothing else," he hissed. "Though you were twelve years old, your father's life, the examples he set, taught you not to care, that's all. He taught you not to notice ordinary Africans. Who knows, maybe you thought it was a joke, but if the roles had been reversed, your father's and mine, believe me, you would have remembered it well."

"What would I have remembered well, Mr N'chele?" I asked, stammering a little as I spoke. "Jesus Christ, what do you want me to know?"

Mr N'chele stiffened, as Detective Mubia had when I'd sworn earlier, and said he wouldn't tell. He said telling would be easy and I should remember it on my own.

If there was a time in my life when I might have sought the kind of ministry this man wanted to provide, now was not that time. I was exhausted from digging graves and cleaning house and rolling around on the ground.

I thanked Mr N'chele for the dinner, and when I slid out of the booth, the nightclub came alive. All during the time I'd sat there I'd had the sense that we were alone in the room, alone in a world of our making, a manufactured realm, but now the crowd surged up to meet me, pulling me away. Was it a week- end or a weekday? Was it a Saturday night? African girls were swirling around the dance floor and pushed up against the bar, the moon-faced white men among them like planets among the stars.

On the stairway going down, Mr N'chele's private waiter caught me and handed me a folded cocktail napkin with an- other message inside. "Give my son what he wants," said the note. "After that everything will turn out fine."

I nearly went back up the stairs when I read that note. I

turned and then I turned again and then I turned once more, as that lioness had done in our yard. It was there for me if I wanted it—all I had to do was dig. It was not, after all, something I had forgotten so much as something I had long ago decided not to know. There was a moment when I could have reached it right there on the stairs, I think, but in the end I lurched out of the nightclub and went directly back to my car.

At home, if my father was asleep, though I was as tired as I had ever been in my life, I wouldn't go directly to bed, I knew. Rather I'd find a chair on my father's verandah and sit overlooking his valley, watching for monkeys coming up from below. The monkeys would come slowly if they came, and when they got to the edge of our yard they would stop, they would see me and be afraid.

This is what I would do late on the night of the fifth day after my husband's death, late on the day I had dug his second grave, an arm's length deep, before striking the side of a snake with the open palm of his dead and detached left hand.

9

A Message from
Julius Grant

When I got back to my father's house he was indeed asleep, but I didn't go out onto the verandah. I went straight to my bedroom and got on top of my bed, and the next thing I knew it was well past noon on the following day. I awoke with my father's knock at my door, and with the idea that the events of the night before hadn't really taken place, but had been an odd dream, Mr N'chele an invention of my growing obsession, my decision to focus all of my energies on figuring things out.

"Nora," said my father, "are you quite all right?"

"Are you alone?" I answered back.

"Beatrice is cooking. Come and eat some food."

Beatrice had been my father's housekeeper for fifteen years.

She lived in the servants' quarters out back and kept the place clean and ready, even when my father was gone. When Jules and I occasionally slept at the house, Beatrice came in to cook for us, but she and I had never been on overly friendly terms. There had been another housekeeper when I was a child, an ayah, and I had missed her for a decade after she'd gone.

I opened my bedroom door and asked, "Where is Dr Zir?"

My father was dressed in a dark-green safari suit with boots and a rumpled light-green hat. He struck a pose again, waiting for a compliment.

"If the suit fits . . . ," I said.

"Oh, Nora, be kind. Julius and I would never do anything bad. You should know that about both of us by now. We thought it was a lark, a swindle of those who needed swindling, nothing more than that."

"Fraud's illegal, Dad," I said. "So is smuggling, last I heard."

But since the night's rest seemed to have given my father his lucidity back, I stopped, fearing too much serious talk would use it up. Instead I spoke lightly, asking him what he wanted to do with his day.

"It's bacon and eggs for breakfast," he said, "and then I want to go down to the post office to check my mail."

By the time we got to the kitchen Beatrice was ready to leave for church. She would not have worked at all on a Sunday if it hadn't been my father's first real day at home. Beatrice was wearing her church uniform, a light-blue dress with a white head-wrap, and she looked fine. She was a member of a charismatic Christian sect and liked to spend all of Sunday standing in a field, dancing and playing her drum. My father had told Beatrice that we were going into Westlands after breakfast and that we would give her a ride. Her church didn't have a building but met in the center of one of the Westlands roundabouts.

There was a lot of food on the table and when I saw it I sat down. My father loaded his plate and I loaded mine. There was fresh milk and mangoes, and after we finished the food Beatrice had prepared, I got half a cooked chicken from the fridge and we ate that as well, arms moving out and back, the tension between us somehow lessened.

Beatrice was in the back seat of the Land Rover when we went outside. She seemed impatient, but when we pulled through the gate her mood brightened. It was a glorious day, the sky was clear, and the deep purple of the jacaranda trees was all along the road. Since this road led directly into Westlands, we would drop Beatrice at the roundabout and then go to the post office, where my father could unlock his mail box and peer inside. When my father was younger his mail box was always full, but not anymore. I had a key to the box and used to check it whenever Jules and I were in town, but only a half dozen times since he'd lived in London did I find anything that actually needed forwarding to my dad. Now that he was back, however, I knew we would have to go to the post office every day.

When we stopped at the edge of the roundabout Beatrice jumped out of the car. We could see that her congregation was already there, singing and warming things up. Beatrice was the last to arrive, and that made her run.

"If we're going to stay in the house we need to get some food," I said. "We ate everything just now that we could have saved for tonight."

"Dr Zir is coming to dinner," my father said. "Or I am going to his house, I don't remember which anymore."

It was Sunday but there was one market open, so I told my father I'd drop him at the post office, do the shopping, and pick him up in a half hour's time. It would take him about a second to check his mail box, but he loved walking the streets, looking in the shop windows and stopping at a bakery for coffee and a roll.

I waited until my father crossed the street, then searched around for a place to park. Though my life was in turmoil, shopping had always been a favorite activity of mine. When the farmwork overwhelmed us, Jules and I would often make plans to move back into town someday, either into my father's house or into one of our own, and whenever we made such plans I always got the most pleasure from thinking about going out alone and shopping, buying everything that such a house would need.

After I parked the car I took the empty baskets that Beatrice had put in the back seat, and saw that I'd left Jules's file folder in the Land Rover overnight. I didn't think that what was written in the folder was important anymore, but it was all I had, so I shoved it down into the empty shopping basket. After that I remembered the pistol, and reached under the seat and pulled it loose too, putting it in the bottom of the basket and covering it with the file.

So here I was, early on a Sunday afternoon, the sky high and clear and the vegetable market before me, and I had an automatic pistol at my side. When I got out of the car three boys ran over, one carrying roses and the other two each holding a bag of apples that they wanted me to buy. The roses were red and perfect, held together by rubber bands, and the apples were green. "I'll take them all," I said. When I spoke Swahili the price went down, and when I asked the boys to put them in the back of the car they all hung around, leaning against the Land Rover like security guards.

I started to browse the tomatoes and fruits, started, against my conscious will, to picture eating with my father again, revisiting my earlier life but with the added routine of tracking the fault lines of his mind. I would question him during meal times, I decided, unravelling everything while he ate.

I bought more mangoes and passion-fruit and sweet-looking onions for a salad I know, and when I picked up the coconut and radishes and plantain I imagined curries and stews, vegetarian *masalas* and a Yorkshire pudding that my mother used to make. The butchers were all closed, but I would come in the morning again, or send Beatrice to buy roast beef and ground pork, silverside or topside, for other half-remembered recipes that were tucked away somewhere in my mind. In this way I resolved to try to engage the rest of the hour, the rest of the day. I filled two baskets and had to call one of the boys from the car to help me carry them while I carried what remained. Until further notice I'd approach my problems with a shopper's mind, listing things and checking them off, consuming them and throwing them away.

But I had spent too much time, I had shopped in too leisurely a way. I tipped the boys and locked the Land Rover. Jules's file folder and that automatic pistol of mine were now beneath the fruits and vegetables at the bottom of the basket, so I left them there, and walked off toward the bakery that my father always chose. This bakery had outside tables, and from way down the road I could see my father sitting there. What I saw, however, wasn't a lonely old man with a roll in his mouth, but an engaged old man who was reading his mail. Surely not, I thought, surely he'd picked up a flyer or an ad, but as I got closer I could see that it was a real letter that my father had, and next to the roll on his plate was a small package as well.

"What's this?" I said. "You've just returned and someone is letting you know how they are? I like that. I'm always around and I don't get three letters a year."

The tone and energy of my comment pleased me, but when my father looked up he didn't smile.

"I'm sorry, Nora," he said. "I shouldn't have opened it. It is addressed to you, and I can't understand what it says."

I never used my father's post office box so the letter couldn't be for me—Jules and I had a box of our own at the downtown post office I'd passed the evening before—but to please my father I took the letter from his hands. He was holding only a single sheet, yet on the table before him there were perhaps a half dozen more. It was a long letter, and in order to open it my father had had to tear the envelope in a wide and circular way.

"Don't worry," I said. "Anything in your mail box ought to be opened by you." But when I looked at the first page of the letter I lost my cheery tone. The letter was from Jules. This is what it said:

My dearest old Nora:

If you're reading this then things are in a muddle for my idea was to take it from your father's P.O. box myself, once things settled down. I was going to get your father's key, retrieve the package I've sent along, and then stand where you're standing now and burn this letter, all the while swearing to myself that I'd never do anything so stupid or dangerous again. I've even placed a match down inside the envelope to start the fire.

Ah well. Nora, you are no doubt wanting to know why I didn't have the guts or whatever to let you know about everything in person, and I swear I don't know the answer to that one myself, except to say that I was too embarrassed, and that until just about now I thought that the story would go better as an anecdote, something to talk about after the fact, don't you see, once it was over.

Listen, Nora, everything started as a lark. One night, well over a year ago now, your father was visiting from England, and he invited me out on the town. Do you remember that night? We were staying at his house and I told you we would be back shortly but it was very nearly dawn before you saw us again. When we left the house I thought we'd get a beer at the Parklands Club and then maybe stop at one other place and then come home, but your father said he had arranged for me to meet some special man.

He was acting very odd, your father, and would only give me directions, turn here, turn there, until he had me way down in the industrial district, you know, nearly past the game park and then in there somewhere on the other side. When I say that your father was acting odd I mean in a cheerful way, like the cat who ate the canary, so I was inclined to humor him, since I had never seen him that way before. Though I was driving it was quite like I was blindfolded, quite like after we arrived wherever we were going I'd find you there ahead of us and that some kind of surprise party had been arranged. The day, as it happened, was very close to my birthday, and that is actually what I thought.

He wouldn't talk except to give me directions, but

finally we came to a warehouse, and your father actually told me to honk on the horn, three times short and one time long, like the beginning of Beethoven's Fifth. Imagine my state of mind, Nora. He was happily mysterious and I was ready to feign polite surprise, and completely ready to engage myself in whatever it was your father had in mind. After all, this was the first time since I'd met him that he'd ever invited me out for a drink, and because I wanted him to like me a lot better than I thought he did, I was ready for anything, come what may.

The warehouse was brightly lit, but once inside I could see only one man standing there.

I didn't want to stop reading, but when my father stood up to call for more coffee he bumped the table, sending the package and the other pages of the letter flying to the ground. Over the last half hour a breeze had come up and right away the pages started to blow away from the tables and down the empty road.

"Oh, grab them!" I shouted. "Don't let them get away!"

I really screamed, so four or five people helped us chase after the stationery, which was scattering all about.

"Oh, Father, damn it, damn it!" I cried.

My father was the slowest of the pursuers, but he nabbed the closest page and picked the package up, holding both of them above his head. I got a second sheet just at the edge of an open sewer, but a thin man dressed in a black business suit seemed to have the best luck in getting the rest. He was everywhere—each time he got a page he took off after another. He was so fast that I calmed down, sure he'd safely catch them all.

"Oh, thank you, sir," I said. "I never would have got them back. Thank you very much."

I noticed, as the man smoothed the sheets out and handed them to me, that Jules had numbered each page, so I tried to put them in order again. I had pages two, three, four, five, and seven.

"Daddy, do you have page six?" I asked, but my father's hands held only the box and the first page.

"No page six?" the man said. "Let's have another look around."

He left me with the pages he'd rescued and went off again, in the direction the wind was going, away from the bakery and toward the place where Beatrice and her churchmates were singing their songs.

"I'll be right back," I told my dad, but my father wasn't listening anymore. He'd sat back down again and was staring at his reclaimed roll.

I took my letter and the little package and went the way the man had gone, toward the singing, which was hard to hear because of the steadily rising wind. I wanted page six, but I'd been so involved in the first part of Jules's letter that I wanted to continue reading as well, so I stopped again, leaning against a rail. Rather than read the letter, however, I opened the little box. It was thin and cylindrical, and when I first saw what was inside I must still have been under the influence of the shopping, for I thought it was a naked ear of corn, or a thin cucumber, maybe, that someone had peeled and put away. It was harder than any vegetable, though, and when I picked it up, prepared to let it go again should its hard exterior suddenly give way, its surprising weight made no further guessing necessary. It was a tiny elephant tusk, about seven inches long but with a big tusk's curvature and with a surface that was marked and scarred. Its point was chiselled flat as if by use, and there was a slight chip on the tip's inside. At its base the tusk was finer, the ivory thinner, and it had a more polished look. I leaned on the railing and rocked back and forth, clutching the tusk to me as though I could dig with it into Jules's mind. At that point I saw the thin man crossing the road and searching around the edges of Beatrice's crowd, so I stuck the tusk down into my belt and hurried after him. The little tusk immediately slipped down and was poking at my inner thigh, at the spot where that thorn had torn it nearly a month before.

When I got to the man, he was creeping along behind the drummers and singers and had stopped behind a woman who, from the back at least, looked a lot like Beatrice. All these women were wearing blue, so it was easy to see that a square of white paper was stuck to the back of this woman's gown.

"Grab it," I said, "take it down."

I'd just reached him and we were both sort of crouched behind the congregation.

"You grab it," he said, "you take it down."

The woman had a big rear end and the paper was riding it well, conforming to its contours, and was even tucked into the folds of her gown. I handed the man the other pages of Jules's letter and reached up, trying to find a loose end on page number six.

The etiquette of Beatrice's church service seemed to be that each time the preacher said something the women would beat their drums and sway. I'd heard these drums all of my life but I had never come close enough to figure out their method before. When the preacher said, "Our Lord Jesus shows Himself in many ways," I took hold of the paper and pulled.

"Ouch!" the woman said. She missed the beat of her drum and jumped around quickly, her drumstick raised in the air.

The woman's shout drew everyone's attention. The configuration of their circle didn't break, but no one played her drum and everyone looked our way. Even the preacher was watching.

"I'm sorry," I said. "I dropped my letter and a page of it blew against the back of your dress."

"That's true," the man said. "We both chased it over here just now."

When the woman turned to look at us page number six stayed attached to her.

"Excuse, please," she said, "but it is only that I have mended my gown."

As she spoke it was suddenly easy to see that the square on her bottom wasn't paper, but material. I could even see the stitching at its edge.

"Oh, my God," said the thin man.

"He is everyone's God," said the woman. "Let's praise Him."

Jules had used good stationery for his letter, and this woman's material was poor, so they met at that place where paper and cloth are cousins and they looked almost the same. I took my letter back from the man and held a page up so the woman could see that it was true. I was about to beg her pardon again, but the preacher took over and when he spoke everyone turned back to face him, once more banging their drums. It was only then that I actually did spot Beatrice, way across the circle, staring at me coldly from the other side.

"Let's get out of here," the man said. "Your page six must have gone a different way."

He took my hand and led me back, helping me to cross the roundabout, where we ducked behind a building before either of us dared stand straight again.

"That was terrible," I said, "and to lose a page of my letter is worse."

"In that case let's continue looking until we find it," said the man. "We should split up. If you like I'll take the farther reaches. It is also possible that the page is staying near your father, so perhaps you should look there."

I was about to thank him again, and to ask how he knew my dad was my dad, when it became clear that this man knew me, that he was someone I had known before.

"Very well," I said, but he saw my hesitation.

"I am Ralph Bunche N'deru," he said. "I was your classmate at school. You and your girlfriends used to tease me by calling me Ralph Bunche Road."

I remembered Ralph Bunche Road, one of the few black Kenyan boys in our school, but this man wasn't him. Ralph Bunche Road had been skinny and quiet with his ears sticking out, and this man was handsome and tall. This man seemed self-assured, whereas Ralph Bunche Road had always looked to me as if he was about to break down and cry.

"I've changed," he said.

He was off then, darting out from the protection of the building and over to the sewer so quickly that I thought he was going to leap it, the old schoolboy inside him showing off. When he got there, however, Ralph slowed and began searching among the grass, so I took the territory he'd assigned me,

looking everywhere as I limped back toward my dad. I had
been desperate to find page six just a few moments before—it
was Jules's last letter, after all—but now I had that tusk, and I
began to think that I would likely be able to piece things together using the pages that remained. By the time I reached my
father I was a lot calmer than I'd been before. My father's roll
was gone, but his coffee cup was full again.

"Do you know who that was?" I asked. "Did you recognise
the man who tried to help me just now?"

"Ralph Bunche Road," said my dad. "I knew his father well."

"You recognised him! I wouldn't have known him in a mil-
lion years."

"He's a travel agent now, a safari man. His father was a
travel agent too. I was Minister of Wildlife when he was setting up and I helped him out. I'm surprised you haven't seen
Ralph in Narok. He used to take tourists out your way."

Jules and I were too far off of the Narok-Nakuru road to
get tourists, but in Narok, and when we went out toward the
Maasai Mara, we did see them all the time. I was trying to
think back to Ralph in school, but it was no longer clear to me
whether I was remembering him or one of the other African
boys. They were all running together in my mind.

"What's the name of his company?" I asked, but my father
didn't know.

When I looked for him I couldn't see Ralph anymore, so I
pulled the tusk up into my belt again and sat down next to my
father to wait, opening Jules's letter once more.

The warehouse was brightly lit, but once inside I could
see only one man standing there.

"You are late," the man said. Your father had been excited when telling me he wanted me to meet this man, but now he was all business.

"Show my son-in-law what you showed me before," he said. I think the man had intended conviviality. Behind him there was a table with three chairs and some peanuts and beer. But when he heard your father's tone the muscles of his face hardened and he led us to the back of the warehouse, not talking again until we were standing beside a row of odd-looking machines, burners and an acetylene torch and ceramic ovens and boiling vats. It looked like a laboratory of some kind with broken molds all over the floor. "Here it is," he said. "Look what it can do."

"It makes tusks that look like real ones," your father told me. He was suddenly excited again. "You won't believe it, Julius," he said. "No expense to the elephants and a great expense to the buyers! Ha-ha!"

The man poked a button and there was a racket and pretty soon he poked another button. The machine stopped and he unlocked its middle and opened the whole thing up. There was a tusk inside and the man asked my help in lifting it out. . . .

This was not the kind of letter I could easily stop reading, but Ralph was back and I had to look up. He was empty-handed, but I thanked him anyway and then introduced my father, who smiled and said, "Ralph Bunche Road."

"Do you remember me, Mr Minister?" asked Ralph. "It is nice to see you again."

My father called the bakery girl, told me to pay his bill, and then asked Ralph to walk with him for a while. He grabbed Ralph's sleeve as he stood, and when Ralph turned to him he said, "What's new with you, Ralph? And how is your father getting along?"

"My father passed on," Ralph said. "Three years now. As for me, I am still running Wildebeest Road—our small business has grown since my father's days."

"Good for you," said my dad. He turned to me and said, "The name of his company is Wildebeest Road."

To be sure, I'd seen Wildebeest Road vans out in the Rift Valley, but I had never connected the company with Ralph. And since I couldn't think of anything to say, I asked stupidly, "Did you name it Wildebeest Road because we used to call you Ralph Bunche Road?"

It was an idiotic question but it made Ralph stop. "Maybe," he said, "though I hadn't thought about it until now. I just imagined it was a comfortable-sounding name and since we had to call it something, I suggested it to my dad."

"You would have done better to name it Rhinoceros Road or Leopard Road," my father said. "These tourists want assurances that they'll see something grand. One of the big five. Wildebeests are a dime a dozen. They all want to see cats."

Ralph smiled and I looked at him carefully, trying to find the boy I had known. I looked at his haircut, but though it was short, his ears didn't stick out. The more I looked at him the more I wasn't sure, though I clearly remembered the name, whether I remembered Ralph Bunche Road at all. Kenyan boys had been a long way from the forefront of my thoughts back then—was that what Mr N'chele had been trying to say?

We were at the car, and I unlocked my father's side. Ralph helped him climb in and then walked me to the driver's side.

"Do you have a family, Ralph? Do you have a wife, do you have children of your own?"

"Alas," he said.

"Are you happy, then," I asked, "without them?" It was an unexpected question, the kind of thing I would never have asked anyone before, and related, somehow, to what I had tried to tell my father back at the church. But I let it stand, keeping my look steady so that he might think I'd intended the question all along. What I really wanted to know, of course, had nothing to do with Ralph's life, but whether or not he knew of the recent events in my own, and while I waited for him to answer I began to cry. Tears ran from my eyes with a kind of consideration for the rest of me. That is, they rolled down freely, leaving my composure otherwise intact.

I expected Ralph to be embarrassed but he wasn't. He didn't touch me, but he also didn't look away. What he did do was reach into his pocket and bring out a pressed and folded handkerchief for me to hold.

"I heard about it, Nora," he said. "It was in the newspaper the other day. Also, a few of us meet for drinks at the Norfolk on Friday afternoons and we talked of almost nothing else last time."

"A few of you?"

"Oh, still the Hillcrest boys, and one or two others we've picked up along the way."

What he meant, I understood, was that the African boys who had gone to Hillcrest School had kept in touch all these years. I knew they'd been close, but I hadn't given them any thought since my school days, and the idea that they had spent last Friday discussing me made me stop crying and stand up tall.

"If I come next Friday, will I know any of them?" I asked.

Ralph shrugged as if irritated and said, "How should I know?"

I got into the Land Rover, pushing the window open.

"When you get home you will be able to read your letter in peace," Ralph said. "No more interruptions from various winds."

"I'm sorry, Ralph," I said, but I was not sure why.

When I started the car my father jumped. "Say good-bye to Ralph, Dad," I said. My father, however, was looking out the wrong side of the car and couldn't find him.

/ / /

When we got home it was after four. My father went to his room to rest and I sat on our verandah alone. Seeing Ralph had been as strangely unsettling as seeing Mr N'chele had been, so I didn't turn to Jules's letter immediately but waited for a calm within me, a debris-free sea on which to sail my husband's paper boat. And while I waited I looked at the tiny tusk again. It really did look scarred, as if it had been a well-used tool during the entirety of an adult elephant's life, and it still seemed absolutely real. I knew nothing of acrylics, but if this was put together by a man, then it really was a perfect job. There was no seam, and the jagged edges of the tusk's hollow end were unsightly in places, I could see that now, as if living tissue had once been there and had dried.

Previously, when I tried to imagine what had attracted Jules to such an unlikely scheme, I'd come up with nothing, but with this tusk in my hand I was beginning to see the draw. Maybe there was a certain justice in selling phony tusks to the ivory hoarders of the world, a certain pleasure in making them think they were real. Maybe Jules really had understood it as an ironic joke. Wasn't that like him? I asked myself.

Indeed it was, so I took a breath and asked myself that other question one more time. Even if all that was true, why hadn't he told me about it? We had shared the work of our farm. We had shared our bed and our journeys to town and our films and our illnesses and our food. Jules and I had shared all of our lives, so why hadn't he shared this with me? Did Jules think I wouldn't understand?

I fell asleep on the verandah with this question lodged in my mind and when I awoke it was nearly dark. Jules's letter was still in my lap, the tiny tusk weighing it down. When I raised it up my eyes knew exactly where they had left off.

My God, Nora, the thing was heavy and it had the col-oration and markings appropriate to age. When I asked how he did it the man told me he had dyes that would vary the colors quite as much as nature did, and when I asked him how he got the thing so heavy he said it was a secret and he wouldn't tell.

We saw tusks of various sizes, the tiny to the huge, proof positive in the accompanying box I have sent, and when we got back to the front of the warehouse your father was in a state. Now he wanted to sit at the man's table and drink the man's beer.

"I will sell them in Europe," he said. "Think what a joke it will be. I am the Minister of Wildlife, Retired! All those would-be hunters will be standing in line!"

I understood right then, Nora, that what your father was about to ask me to do could get us in trouble, but I liked the idea too, I have to admit it, and with the beer and the man's talk and your father's compelling joy, before I knew it I had agreed to ship these things to Europe for him, to smuggle them out of Kenya in our coffee bags. Your father's job was to be sales and distribution which, don't you see, was actually the most dangerous part. If I got caught smuggling the things I would only need to prove that they weren't real and it wouldn't be smuggling!

Ah, but why didn't I tell you about it, Nora, as soon as I got home? I guess it's because there was money in what we were doing, and by the end of that first night we had all agreed that no one else should know. So for all this time, Nora, since shortly after the evening I've described, whenever I went to town I would pick up some of these artificial tusks and arrange one way or another to get them out of the country, the smaller ones stuck down inside bags of coffee beans, the larger ones in boxes marked machinery and the like.

Oh, Nora, you married such a fool. The longer things went on, though no one at the airport ever looked inside our coffee bags, the more I began to understand what . . .

I turned the page, furious with Jules again, but hooked anyway. That was the end of page five, however, and page six was gone, the crux of the matter nowhere to be found. I read page seven, but it contained only the following lines:

So now you know the extent of my idiocy, the full damage that a truly stupid man can do. While you are reading this letter, who knows, I could very well be in jail. But at least

I've done some serious harm to the man who has most harmed me, though if you know me at all you'll know that is small satisfaction at this late stage. After reading this letter you alone have the key to what I have done. Now promise me, Nora, that if I can't do it you will do it for me. No matter what people say, revenge is sweet, I know it is true.

Promise also that you will try to visit me wherever I am. Now that I have, at least, committed my secret to paper I feel better. Memorize my message, Nora, then use the match in the envelope. Burn what you have read and go on.

Your illegitimate husband,

Jules

Beatrice came to the kitchen door and called me. The friendly quality of her voice seemed to retain nothing bad, no hint of the embarrassment I had caused her earlier in the day.

"Dinner, please!" she yelled.

When I got to the dining room my father was at the table, a big cloth napkin tucked into his shirt, second button down. Dr Zir, whom I had hoped was preparing a meal for my father at his house, was in the guest's chair, his own napkin precisely where my father's was. The doctor stood when I came in. "Nora, darling! Nora, dear!" he said.

"I've had a message from Julius," I said, "a letter."

Dr Zir cocked an eyebrow, looking quickly from me to my father, as if some flawed genetic imprint might be visible in the air.

"It's true," said my dad. "When she opened the envelope there was a dove inside but it quickly flew away."

"Page six," I told the doctor, "that was the dove's name."

Beatrice served us, putting platters of food on the table, and giving the doctor a moment to calm down. There was no music playing, so my father asked Beatrice to put the Mozart on.

Dinner was pork chops and boiled potatoes and gravy and rolls. My mangoes were there, and there were thick slices of the big tomatoes I had bought as well.

10

Chess

My father's disease, his condition, his progressive dementia or whatever it was, didn't seem to hinder his ability to play the game of chess. Since I hadn't gotten nearly enough information from what Jules's letter said, what with that missing page, I wanted to question my father again that night at dinner, but I didn't want to do so while the doctor was there. And because of chess, Dr Zir simply would not go home.

The chess-board was set up in the living room, and by the time I'd made coffee and brought it in to them, Dr Zir had already resigned the first game.

"Don't fool with me, Zir," I heard my father say. "Play the game correctly or don't play at all."

Because it seemed clear that Dr Zir had thrown the first game, they had to play a half dozen more, all but the last one to a draw. And once the doctor was gone it was midnight and my father was droop-mouthed again, too tired to begin to answer any of the questions that I had.

"Help me put away the chess set, Nora," he said. "Help me get on to bed. We can talk tomorrow."

My father's chess pieces, ironically, I suppose, were made of old ivory and had smoothed out nicely over time. They were lovely to hold. This was not the kind of chess set with a folding board that you could put away quickly, not the kind, in fact, that you could put away at all, but my father and I had formed a ritual years ago of wiping each piece with a chamois and placing it back in its original position on the board. We called what we did "putting the pieces away." It had long been my privilege to put away the big pieces while my father put away the pawns, and I was holding one of his queens when I suddenly reached into the pocket of the apron I wore and brought out the tiny ivory tusk.

"Where did this come from, Dad?" I asked.

My father took the tusk from me, holding it up to the light. I could see him working at it, trying to say something clear about the mess he was in, but in the end all he said was "This isn't a chess piece. What are you talking about?"

"What do you suppose it is then?"

"It is the tusk from a little elephant, the smallest I have ever seen."

"Where did I get it? Where did it come from, Dad?"

My father had a couple of pawns in his other hand, and I could hear the sound of them as they played against each other. Once when I was about eight I had somehow lost a pawn. After that day my father gave me the job of putting the important pieces away. For a number of years I thought he'd done so in order to let me know that my losing the pawn meant nothing to him, but he had really done it because the important pieces were larger and harder to lose.

"It is the raw material for a fine chess piece," said my father. "But look how scarred it is. It has been very well used, as if the little elephant who owned it was old."

"Can we burn it, Dad? Can we light this little tusk on fire? Can we do it right now?"

"We cannot," he said. "Whatever gave you that idea?"

I pulled out Jules's letter then. There was only about a third of the envelope left, but I took out the stick-match Jules had so dramatically included. I held the match up so that my father could see it, and then I asked him to give me the little tusk back.

"You know, I've never actually done this," I said. "I tried it once on an elephant-hair bracelet, but I've never actually tried to see if a tusk will burn."

"It won't," said my father, "unless the fire is very big and hot. A petrol fire might do it but a match will not."

My father gave me the tusk, but when he put the pawns down he made sure that they were considerably away from me. "It won't burn, but it will discolour," he said. "Wouldn't that be a pity. I'm not sure how easy it will be to get it clean again."

I struck the match on the bottom of my shoe. I had never done that before either, but there was a small nail protruding there, and the match surged immediately into flame. "I'm going to burn the tip off," I said. "I'm going to watch the easy deformity of it and then let you tell me how such a thing could be."

Since the little tusk had taken on a crude kind of significance to me, I didn't really want to burn its tip, but my father was not relenting. He wasn't going to tell me it was acrylic, if, indeed, he could remember that it was, until I proved it, so I put the hottest part of the flame right on the tusk's tip, where it was only about a quarter of an inch thick. The match Jules had left me, however, was a poor one, and the flame wouldn't stay. It licked at the tusk, but it was too democratic, bouncing around too much and licking at the surrounding air as well.

"That's enough," said my dad. "You'll burn your fingers next."

He was right about that, but I held the match longer anyway, only my fingernails touching the wood. There was a strong sense of authenticity about the tusk, a firm refusal on the part of this excellent material to burn.

"Ouch!" I finally said. I dropped the match onto the chess-board, then swept it away with my hand.

"Is it discoloured?" my father asked. "Get a sponge and try to wipe it clean."

There was a smoky kind of stain on the tusk. I took the chamois from the chess-board and was able to wipe much of it away using that. "Wow," I said.

"Wow, my backside," said my dad. "What did you expect? After living your whole life in Africa, did you think an elephant tusk would easily burn?"

"I thought it was fake," I told him. "Small as it is, I thought this was one of the tusks that Mr Smith made, for Julius to smuggle and for you to sell to the outside world."

My father looked at me for a long time. Since I'd let the whole thing out, I was sure he was about to tell me everything now, forgetting to use, for a moment, the excuse of a weakened mind. In the end, however, all he said was "Well, I guess it wasn't." And then he placed the rest of the pawns on the board and went off to his room to bed.

Had I had another match I might have tried again; had I several I would have taken my father's prize queen, who had watched everything from the palm of my other hand, and put her face in the fire. But Jules's one match was gone and I was alone and nothing was burned, not the tusk I now held in the hand with the queen, nor my husband's letter, which would have done the match's bidding quickly and without complaint.

I put the tusk in the chamois next to the queen. The tusk was longer than the queen was tall, but not by much, by less than an inch, I'd say, and it was lighter in colour. I put the chamois in my apron pocket and went out onto the verandah again, to look at the stars. On our farm, with no city lights to bother us, the stars would come down close. Indeed, when Jules and I slept outside they would sometimes lose their timidity altogether, settling around us so snugly that they seemed like sequins on our dressing gowns. I remember that I used to want to make love when we slept outside but that Jules usually did not. He told me once that it was because he didn't like to expose the pinkness of his bottom to the hands of the night, but in truth I knew it was because the grandeur of the world made him feel too insignificant, too small. He wanted to breathe the night air and he wanted to listen, to aim himself outward, and to pray.

This is what I was thinking about on my father's verandah as I took the tusk out again, as I clutched the antique queen in my left hand, and let the tip of the tusk travel south to nose its way under the apron and the loosely belted pants that I wore. The stars above me were nearly as fine as they were on the

farm, with only the dim kitchen light to bother them, and the
tusk and the queen had grown warm together inside the folds
of their chamois and while I let the tusk work its way through
the forest that it found down there I kept my eyes on the
queen's carved face and thought I could see that it was as
flushed as my own.

Could I remember Julius Grant while acting in such a sad
and solitary way? While that tusk was meeting a tiny replica of
itself and getting that replica to behave, I stared so hard into
the queen's face that rather than making the world expand,
which is what always happened when it was Jules and the stars
and the farm, now everything wanted to contract, the entire
universe rushing in. I could see the queen's cheek-bones and
how her jaw was firmly set and how her lips were pursed in a
tight and pleasurable sort of way, as if her hand, too, was busy
somewhere, down underneath her gown.

Is it too much to admit, too much to write down, that so
shortly after the dawn of my widowhood I did this, forcing a
release that I couldn't find in my heart or in my mind? For a
long time I thought I would leave this part of my story out, but
here it is, and as I exercised the wrist and fingers of my right
hand, as the face of the queen seemed to let her lips part too, I
tried to purge myself of the pain that Jules had caused me with
his death and his deceit and his lack of faith. I tried to find my
love for him again by concentrating on its physical aspect and
ignoring all the rest. It was a poor idea, I suppose, for in the
end I was ecstatic and embarrassed and trying to be quiet all at
the same time. And when I finished and the thrill was gone, I
wasn't truly satisfied, I was simply outside in my father's lawn-
chair, all alone.

I languished on the verandah until the muscles in my

thighs calmed. Then I got up and faced the house, its lit kitchen door reminiscent of Mr N'chele's, but quiet and welcoming just the same. And though the person who entered the house was the same person who'd left it, when I walked down my father's shadowy hall, I somehow came to feel different about Jules's death and the mystery of the tusks and my husband's unlikely decision not to tell. My change in mood wasn't forged from further knowledge of the facts, or from the simple passage of time, which dulls even the most grievous insults. Rather, it was based on the idea that Jules had placed that little tusk in the box and mailed it to me not only as proof of what Mr Smith had been up to, but also so that I could have something to hold on to, something to remember him by.

11

Madama Butterfly

It was not a Friday, but because I didn't know what to do next, at five o'clock the following afternoon I found myself sitting in the café of the Norfolk Hotel, sipping a shandy and looking around for Ralph. I had telephoned Detective Mubia, but he was out, so I left word that I would be at the Norfolk and then went there to sit and wait. Since Mr N'chele had talked to me only in mysterious little doses of a line or two, I would try to make the detective be more forthright, hoping his natural tendency toward full disclosure would get the better of him over a glass of whiskey or a cup of tea.

Across the street from the Norfolk was the National Theatre, where I'd had tap and ballet lessons as a child and where, during the fullness of my merry youth—until I went to London and met up with Jules—I would occasionally audition for plays. I knew, since I had called him, that the detective might come, but as I sat there I decided to finish my drink and go over to the National Theatre anyway, to try for a different kind of reconnection with my past.

The dusty centre of Harry Thuku Road was easy to cross, considering it was past quitting time on a Monday afternoon, but the car park of the National Theatre, where I'd left the Land Rover only half an hour before, was now busy, and there were people waiting at the theatre's front door. I edged my way by the people, past the ticket seller in his ungilded cage, and into the foyer, where I immediately heard singing, a woman's voice, coming from the stage. There was an audition or a rehearsal going on, so though I kept my body in the foyer, I parted the curtains to watch.

The woman was African and she was superb. She was singing something from *Madama Butterfly*, that opera's one truly memorable song, and as I stood there listening I realised that I knew the singer, or had known her during years gone by. When I'd worked at the university she had been the friend of a physics teacher there, but shortly after I left the university I heard that she'd gone away, to London or New York or maybe Milano, making her way in the outside world. I hadn't known her as well as I'd known Ralph, but now, in the course of two days, if I include the awful fact that Mr Smith had been part of my childhood too, I'd seen four people that I had known before. Such a thing is not unusual, I suppose, but in six years of living on our farm I'd hardly seen anyone at all.

The woman's voice went right to my heart. I could have

stood listening to her for the rest of the night, but I'd only been there a minute when the director stopped her, thanked her, and told her she could go. So when she left the stage, I went outside again and walked around the side of the building, trying to find the doors to the rooms where I had learned to tap and studied ballet.

There was a time in my life when my mother, not my father, was central to my swelling self, when my mother was the pivot on which my young life turned, and this ballet studio reminded me of that time. My mother had been a dancer, and for a few short months she brought me here twice a week, sitting down on the floor at the back to watch. That is the strongest memory I have of my mother, seeing her sitting there. Often, when I try to think of her, all I can conjure is a sense of thick curtains and the medicinal odour of the room in which she died, but for those few months at least, my memory wants to tell me, it was my mother who taught me how to dance.

I expected the back studio door to be locked, but it wasn't, and when I stepped through it I found the opera singer there, staring into a mirror and stretching her mouth in unattractive ways. The door hadn't been quiet, but she was concentrating, and didn't let my presence improve the expression on her face at all.

I was about to leave, since I was interrupting and since I could tell in an instant that the studio didn't look the same, but the singer suddenly looked up at me in the mirror and said, "I think a beautiful sound should come out of a beautiful face, don't you?"

She had a most beautiful face, so I was a little irritated by the comment. Though hearing her sing had made me want to cry, I didn't want any more contrivance, and I wasn't about to assure her that her face could equal the music she made. But instead of leaving I shrugged and gave a weak reply. "I don't suppose it would do for the face to be absolutely horrible," I said.

This made her shut her mouth and turn. Her eyes were wide-set and honest, her forehead high, and the mouth she had been stretching was a no-nonsense kind of mouth.

"I remember you," I said.

It was clear that she didn't remember me, but she came closer, peering at me with those eyes. "You don't work here?" she asked. "You're not on the theatre board, I hope."

"I was only peeking in to marvel at how my old ballet studio had shrunk. I'm Nora Hennessey. We met years ago when you used to come around the university. You had a physics teacher friend who was musical too."

I was sounding terrible, overly urbane and glib, with a lilt to my voice. I had sometimes been possessed by the unfortunate desire to impress people in the past, but it hadn't appeared in years, and I was surprised by its sudden emergence now, when I had so many other things to worry about.

The woman looked at me hard, and suddenly I found myself thinking of what had happened on my father's verandah the night before. I put my hand in my pocket, closing it down on the tusk.

"Of course," she said. "You worked there somehow, didn't you? And you were in a few plays. An Ibsen or an O'Neill. You played strong women and after that you married someone and bought a farm."

We both laughed at her tidy and accurate summation of my life. I told her that luckily enough for the local audiences, I

hadn't auditioned for a play in seven years, and then I somehow asked her if she wanted to walk back to the Norfolk with
me, to join me for a drink. To spend time with someone who
knew nothing of my recent problems seemed a proper tonic,
and I hoped that she would come. Her name, I remembered,
was Miro.

/   /   /

I sometimes fear there's too much randomness in my story, too
many of the arbitrary activities of everyday life. This Miro, for
example, had stayed out of my mind for years. She had nothing to do with Jules or the problems I was having now. She had
nothing to do with anything, yet because I felt self-conscious
sitting at the Norfolk bar alone, because, in fact, I'd gone there
on a Monday looking for a Friday man, I now have a vaguely
remembered acquaintance coming into my story like a regular
player with a regular part to play. And though my impulse to
invite her for a drink had everything to do with the fact that
she didn't know what had happened to me, what else would I
do with her once we were settled in our chairs but tell her?
How could I relate to her, except as a kindred spirit and a sympathetic female ear?

I stood in the car park while she changed into street
clothes, but when I looked toward the front door of the National Theatre again Miro was there, and I understood that the
small crowd I'd passed before weren't ticket purchasers but
fans. Miro took all the time she needed to sign her name on
old programmes and to chat. As I watched her I imagined her
solitary exits in London or New York, the loneliness she'd encountered wherever it was that she had gone.

When she broke away we walked across the street quickly and without speaking, until the dust of the car park and road no longer had much chance to invade her nose and mouth. "I get hoarse so easily," she explained.

In the bar my original table was taken so we had to sit in the back. We were against a wrought-iron railing that looked toward the National Theatre car park and separated the bar from the sidewalk and street below.

"Now," said Miro, "tell me about this farm of yours. Don't tell me about all the hard work. I want to hear about the satisfaction that comes at the end of the day."

The question was humourous and seemed entirely sincere, but the expression on Miro's face told me also that she expected stories of a special kind. She wanted a success story that was entirely contrary to whatever had happened to her in the singing world. Maybe that had been her own motivation for coming along.

"It still exists," I said carefully. "But a week ago my husband died, so I've been spending most of my time in town."

"Good sweet Lord," said Miro, "dear Jesus, no!"

I hadn't planned on making such a dramatic announcement, but I did get authentic pleasure from her reaction. Her look contained focussed shock, and seeing someone else struck by the enormity of what had happened was a large part of realising that enormity myself. I'd been surrounded by clowns with vendettas or slip-knot minds: the Mad Hatter and his doctor, a religious policeman in a red suit, and the father of my enemy showing partial scenes from a distant day. It may not seem like it from the story I've told so far, but before my life with Jules began I'd had a penchant for best friends. In school there was always one girl or another whom I kept right by my side. Now I was alone with Miro, and I understood that what I'd been trying to do all week was to connect with someone, to find just one person who could help me see this through, whose spirit would be willing to mingle with my own. That is why I'd been taken with Detective Mubia, and that, believe it or not, is what I had tried to feel with Mr N'chele as well. I wanted connection, I wanted a confidant.

"It's a horrible way to tell you," I said. "I should find an old friend to burden with such terrible news."

Our drinks arrived, and Miro, who had ordered whiskey, tossed half of hers down and told the waiter to bring another. "But we are old friends," she said. "We just weren't very close ones."

After that I told her everything, from seeing *Jules et Jim* to the night at Mr N'chele's house the first time and the night at Mr N'chele's house the second. I gave as clear a description as I could of the hospital on the afternoon of Jules's death, I told her about Mr Smith and Kamau, and about my visit to the New Florida Nightclub two days before. I even showed her the note Mr N'chele had given me on the paper napkin. When I told her about the tiny tusk and the letter that my father had found in his post office box, and when I mentioned Ralph chasing after its pages on the road, I slowed the story down, letting Miro ask questions, of which she had more than one or two.

"How well do you know this character Ralph?" she asked. "And don't you think it's odd that he should show up just then?"

I hadn't thought about that but I didn't think it was odd

and I told her so. Miro, however, gave me a sage nod. "No doubt he isn't involved, but you must think about everything, my dear. If you fail in your battle with these men it will be the casual elimination of such possibilities that does you in."

"But I knew Ralph all the way back in school," I said. "For as long as I can remember he sat in the back of the room."

As I spoke Ralph's name his adult face was clear enough in my mind, but I still couldn't remember what he'd looked like as a boy.

"Tell me," asked Miro, "did I find you today or did you find me? At the National Theatre, I mean."

"You found me," I said. "You were hiding out in my old ballet room."

"Ah-ha," she said, "then you do see my point. Though I was hiding out in your ballet room, you found me, you can't deny it. And I'll bet Ralph came along in some sort of helpful way. I'll bet he found you, am I right? If not, say so and we can go on."

"The wind blew my husband's letter away and Ralph was there to pick it up," I said, "but he didn't supply the wind, and he didn't insist that I take my father to the post office. His safari company is in Westlands and he was just walking by."

Miro's eyes lit up and when the waiter took that moment to put her second whiskey down, she pushed it aside. "Maybe so," she said, "but if it wasn't he who supplied the wind, it was nevertheless the wind that gave him his opportunity. It's a possibility, that's all I want you to admit."

I didn't think it was a possibility, not in the slightest, but Miro was so engaged by the idea and I loved sitting with her so much that I went ahead and said it was.

After that we both seemed to decide that we were hungry. Our lurking waiter brought menus and while we examined them I felt the kinship again, the closeness that I'd just begun to understand I wanted and needed so much. My God, Jules had wrapped me up so thoroughly, had covered me so completely with his own sense of the world, that my life had been his while he was alive, simple as that. I hate to say it, but his view of things had been my own.

My eyes rested on the menu while I thought those thoughts, but I hadn't really been reading it, so when the waiter came back again I ordered a chicken salad. Miro said, "What the hell," and ordered ham and eggs. She had tossed down her first whiskey in nothing flat, but the second one remained untouched, and when I finished my shandy and ordered another, she told the waiter to bring some mineral water. Whenever we wanted something our waiter was right there. Such attention was not a part of the Norfolk's reputation, so I teased Miro, saying that he hovered in order to be near her. When our food came we laughed at the waiter, and when we finished eating and the after-work crowd thinned out, we moved to a better table, one closer to the front. This new table was out of our original waiter's section, so Miro went back to get our bill. While she was gone I ordered tea and put my elbows on the table, resting my chin in my hands. I felt something like contentment, I was sure I did, and I felt something like guilt for feeling that way.

When Miro was seated beside me again I asked, "How long have you been back?"

"Why I only just this second got here," she said.

"I mean to Nairobi. How long have you been back in

Kenya? When did you give up your attack on the serious opera world?"

"Ah," said Miro, "when did I give that up? Let's see . . ."

She didn't like the question, so I said, "When I was at Oxford I assumed I'd never come back to Kenya to live. I told everyone it was beautiful but that it wasn't connected with the real world. Does that make sense to you? To have the feeling that the real world is somewhere else all the time?"

"It does make sense and it doesn't," she said, "but I don't like talking about the real world. When it comes to singing, such a world simply means all those northern countries, and they are very cold."

"Oxford was cold too," I said.

Miro pushed her hands into the air, brushing my words away. "You don't know it," she said, "but my ambitions were large. I had the voice and I had the energy and the discipline and training. I also had the stage presence and the guts or whatever to stick with it, come what may. When I left I was truly leaving, I had truly said good-bye."

"So what happened?" I asked. "Why didn't you stay? What are you doing back here, singing at the National Theatre again?"

Our tea had come. Our old waiter had somehow got his station changed and when he brought the tea there was a note tucked between Miro's cup and saucer. Since the cup wasn't riding well, some of her tea had spilled, wetting the edges of the note, so the waiter lifted the note and set it beside the saucer on the table.

"I had no intention of coming back," she said. "I was living in New York at the end. I was singing every day and was finding a foothold. I had found the ladder, at least, and was ready to step up onto that ladder's first rung. I knew people at the Met, and I was getting a reputation, those people were telling others I was there."

"But you did come back?" I said. I knew little about opera and a lot less about whatever it took to become a star, but everything I did know told me that this girl could make it anywhere. She had everything she said she had and she was charismatic. In the short time we had been together she had made me want to stay by her side. I was both comfortable with her and glad that she wanted to be my friend, and our waiter, whose infatuation clearly surpassed my own, was nearly at the point of approaching our table on his knees. It wasn't that she was so beautiful, but she was magnetic, and as likable as anyone I had ever known.

"It was my father," she finally said. "He got sick. Word came that he was dying, so of course I flew home."

"My father's still alive," I said, "but I know what you mean."

"Ah, but my father is alive too," said Miro. "God forgive me, but that's the problem. He keeps insisting that he won't last long, that death is calling to him from the next room over. He actually says things like that. He's past sixty now, but whatever he says, I don't think that death is anywhere near the next room, I don't think it's even in the house. He's an assistant curator at the National Museum and believe it or not, he's gone back to work, he goes almost every day."

"So why don't you leave again? Go back and find that ladder in New York, climb it all the way."

Miro shrugged. "My father is as strong-willed as I and I love him very much," she said. "He gave me his blessing when I left the first time, but now he is lonely and wants me to stay."

She laughed and then cast a thumb over her shoulder

toward the National Theatre. "And now there's *Butterfly* and I do love the part. Since its run is short, I thought it wouldn't hurt to see it through."

Miro had taken up the waiter's note and was turning it in her hands, absently testing the sharpness of the three corners unaffected by the tea.

My God, how our fathers invade us, I thought. I was about to say it out loud, but just then a shadow fell across our table and made us both look up. I expected the waiter, but Detective Mubia was standing there.

"Godspeed, Mrs Grant," he said.

Since Miro already knew about the detective, and since I'd described him pretty well, she smiled when I introduced them, demurely looking down. I called the waiter over and ordered another cup of tea, but I had been prizing my time with Miro so much that I could no longer remember why I'd wanted the detective and I wished he'd go away. When his tea came I said, "I know I shouldn't be telephoning you like this. It was kind of you to come."

Miro heard the artifice in my voice, and she'd have none of it. "Nonsense," she said. "Sit down, Detective, and tell us what you know. So far no one will speak plainly to this girl. She's getting pieces of the story, but she doesn't know how to make the pieces whole."

Detective Mubia sat down slowly and then slightly bowed. "It is good to call," he said, "but there is nothing new that I can say. It isn't really a case, you know. There are irregularities, but my superiors have not yet given it a case number. Everything is supposition, even until today, and we are too understaffed for that."

The detective had been speaking to Miro, and when he

finished she asked, "What about the feather in her husband's mouth, what about the pillow on the ledge outside his room? Surely that alone is enough for you to assign such a thing as a case number. Do your superiors suppose that there isn't anything to it, that there's nothing for her to worry about? Do they suppose that nothing more will happen if you leave it alone?"

Detective Mubia nodded, and for a moment seemed to be a nearly social man. His face was kind of bemused, as if he was pleased to be taking up the question he'd been asked. He waited and then he said, "I am not a supposer. If I were a supposer my supposes would be suppositions, don't you see, and we are too understaffed for that."

There was a second or two of odd silence before Miro started to laugh. Detective Mubia had made a joke, if that was his intention, but he had kept his face so completely straight that both of us felt left behind.

"Very good," said Miro, "but I have asked the wrong question, I can see that now. Tell us what you know about Mr Smith instead. What does he want Nora to give him that he thinks of as his property? Surely not just another elephant tusk or two." Miro looked at him, and while she waited she picked up the waiter's note.

Detective Mubia had paused again, but this time I knew he wasn't trying to think of something clever. "Mr Smith is evil but his father is good," he said. "When good and evil are brothers, when they are father and son, we cannot destroy one without destroying the other. Were the father out of the picture, then I could tell you everything you want to know about the son."

His speech was impassioned, for a man with such a narrow

emotional range, but his words were just as ambiguous as those of the good and evil men he spoke of.

The detective sat forward to drink his tea, and Miro still had her second whiskey next to her, in a shot glass that she now covered with the waiter's folded note. She had been looking at her watch for a short while, so I soon called for the second part of our check and pushed my chair away. It was nearly eight o'clock and the after-work crowd was gone.

When Miro and I stood to leave, Detective Mubia bid us good night, saying he would order more hot water for his tea and stick around. Miro would have left the waiter's note where it was, resting over her whiskey glass, had I not touched her arm and pointed at it. The waiter was watching from his station by the kitchen door, so Miro took the note, held it up to him briefly, then unfolded it and leaned under the nearest light to read. She read quickly, with a serious expression in her eyes, and when she finished she folded the note again and tucked it into a pocket somewhere.

"Which way are you going?" I asked. "In what part of town do you live?"

Miro laughed, taking hold of my arm. "Like you, I am staying with my father," she said, "but we are going opposite ways."

There were taxis waiting across the street by the entrance to the National Theatre car park. "I don't mind driving you," I said, but she waved my offer away, and just then a driver got out of his cab and opened the back door.

"I didn't say so earlier," Miro said, "but one coincidence in all of this is that my father's house is out on Ralph Bunche Road."

Miro got into the taxi and rolled the window down. She

had my phone number and I had hers. "From this evening we will be friends," she said, but the driver wouldn't wait for my reply, and since the cab threw dust into the road, I didn't stand there watching her go.

Over in the theatre car park my father's Land Rover was safely standing by. There was little traffic on Harry Thuku Road by then, but I had to pause for another taxi, which had blocked the car park entrance to let its occupants down. It was then, as I waited for the road to clear, that I happened to glance over the top of the taxi and into the bar. Detective Mubia was still at our table, but he wasn't alone. Our waiter stood above him, and the seat I had occupied, the one facing me now, contained another Kenyan man. He was very dark and wore a black suit with a white shirt and tie. At first I thought this man was Detective Mubia's superior and that the detective was being scolded in some way, I suppose because the man was sitting up straight and poking his finger into the intervening air. I considered parking the Land Rover again and going back inside to try to explain, but when the taxi moved and I could see the table better, I realised that the man sitting there was not Detective Mubia's boss, at least I hoped he wasn't. This was a man I had seen before, and though his father didn't like the name, I said it anyway, sitting alone in my own father's old car: "Mr Smith."

And just then a tall lorry pulled up, blocking my vision but letting me use its cover to turn onto the road and drive away.

It wasn't a long drive from the Norfolk to my father's house, but by the time I got there I had put myself at sea again. After all his talk of good and evil, could Detective Mubia be working for Mr Smith? Was that also possible in this colliding world? And since the waiter was standing with them, what was the nature of the note he had given to Miro? Perhaps it wasn't infatuation that made him write the note, perhaps it wasn't he who had written it at all. And if all that was possible, then what about Ralph, and why shouldn't I worry about Miro herself? Could Mr Smith have everyone on his side? What about Beatrice, what about Dr Zir?

I parked the Land Rover in the drive and was walking into the house, feeling desperate and sorry for myself and tossing it all over in my mind, when something suddenly shot past my ear and something else slammed into my back, knocking me down. Oh God, Jules, I thought, here I come!

My right shoulder was hit at just the place where Kamau had shot Jules, and though I tried to crawl forward, I couldn't seem to move. I screamed, I think, and while I waited for the blood to come, other objects slammed in around me, bullets thudding into the ground. Let it end now, I prayed, let my father find me, let me ask my questions on the other side. I closed my eyes and was about to turn toward the onslaught, letting the bullets tear into my unloved breasts, but to my great surprise my father's security guard came over and took hold of my arms, utterly fearless, and helped me stand. "Oh Mama!" he screamed. "Those filthy buggers! I didn't see them come!"

I was sure I was dying, since now there was pain and I could also feel an ooze. The back of my shirt was clammy, and I thought the wound might be larger than the one Jules had. The guard was brave. He dragged me onto the porch, all the while screaming in Swahili, "I did not know they had come!"

Then, instead of applying first aid, he seemed to forget my wounds as soon as he got me settled. He ran back outside again, turned on the garden hose, and sprinted with it across our yard.

I thought the security guard was gallant, but I also thought he'd gone mad, so instead of staying where he'd put me I crawled over to the edge of the porch to watch. The guard had aimed the hose up into our avocado tree, and dozens of monkeys were now streaming out of it, throwing an occasional avocado at him, but pretty much giving up the battle, heading back down into the valley from whence they'd come. When they were gone the guard came back slowly, looking worried and winding up the hose.

"They sneaked in behind me while I was watching the road," he explained.

He was sure I'd be furious, since watching out for marauding monkeys was a big part of his job, but I only asked that he scrape the mess off the back of my shirt and then help me inside. There was half an avocado on my shoulder blade, and when the guard tried to take hold of it his fingers and thumb burst through its skin, like five skaters going through the ice. "It's a rotten one," he said.

"Just turn the hose on again. Just let me step back outside."

We had had dozens of security guards over the years, and this man wasn't someone I knew well, so when I asked him to hose me off, he was chagrined.

"Only go and remove the shirt for Beatrice," he said.

"It's too awful," I told him. "The smell will be horrid and it will mess up the house."

The security guard's hands were covered with the pulpy avocado, so when he turned the hose back on he washed them first, then lifted up a paltry stream.

"Give it some power," I said. "Put your thumb into it."

He did as I asked, and when I dipped my wounded shoulder into the stream, he held it steady while the hunks of avocado fell off. Even the seed had stuck to me, and when the water finally forced it away, I felt like Jules must have felt in surgery. I imagined I could feel the kindness of Dr Zir as he removed my bullet, and I thought, This world is made up of many people, not all of them working for Mr Smith, not all of them headed in evil's way.

"That's enough," I said. "Thanks a lot."

When the guard turned the hose off I picked up the avocado seed, holding it so that I could see it in the light of the moon. This is my husband's heart, I told myself, small for not having within it the courage to include me, to open up and welcome me, no matter what kind of trouble he was in. And this is my own heart too, small for its selfishness, for its unexpandable quality, for its inability to focus on more than one thing.

This was also, of course, an avocado seed, driven into my shoulder by an attacking monkey, and when I walked over to the edge of the garden, to the edge of the slope that led to the valley where the monkeys had gone, I hefted the seed in my hand, wound up like a javelin thrower, and threw the seed up in an arch as if aiming at the moon. I could see it for an instant, but then all I could do was listen, the security guard beside me, both of us hoping to hear a monkey scream.

Is this what everything is really about, I wondered, revenge, getting even, keeping an even score? Judging from his letter, that's what Jules seemed to feel, but would I, if I could, turn my avocado seed into a rifle bullet and aim it at the fleeing back of Kamau or Mr Smith? I was hurt by that monkey, I somehow understood, in quite the same way I had been hurt by my husband and by my father too. It was painful, in part at least, because of its surprise. But I would survive, I knew that now. All I had to do was hose myself off and go on.

When I went into the house everything was quiet. My father's bedroom door was closed, and in the living room the embers of the fire he had built were nearly gone. Out the back door I could see Beatrice sitting in front of her room reading her Bible by the light of a paraffin lamp. She had undoubtedly heard the ruckus of the avocado attack but had decided to stay in her chair with her God. Such constancy was what I needed now, and as I watched her I vowed that in the morning I would find it, somehow.

In the meantime, however, I went into my room to sleep. I cleaned myself up and climbed into bed, having left my door ajar so that the moonlight could play on the wallpaper in the hall and I could see in it the myriad images of childhood, which for me, strange to tell, had not been frightening at all.

12

Mortification Sets In

I should have known better than to suppose my father had gone to bed early that night. His penchant for staying up late was legendary. In the old days, when he went to bed at midnight my mother used to say that he was ill. It must have been the business with the avocados and the fact that he had slept a lot since his return from London that made me believe a closed bedroom door meant a sleeping father within, but at breakfast my father told me he had spent the night at Dr Zir's. He had eaten there and he had stayed up late playing chess, finally falling asleep on Dr Zir's front-room couch. He had asked Beatrice to build the fire, he said, so that it would be roaring, waiting to welcome me when I came home.

"We've also done some organizing," he said. "Zir and I

have set aside next Saturday afternoon for Julius's wake. We'll hold it here at home in the afternoon."

"Julius is already buried at the farm," I said. "He isn't having a wake."

My father had never lived in Ireland, but his Hennessey heritage came out to find him once in a while, especially after somebody died. I remember that at the time of my mother's death he left the house open to visitors for two days, crying in front of them and bringing me out from my bedroom every hour or so to cry by his side. I had done it on cue, I had done it easily, simply because I knew that he wanted me to.

"Of course he is," said my father. "Zir is sending out the notice this A.M. There'll be an announcement in the paper the day after tomorrow."

"Julius isn't having a wake," I said again, but then I said, "I am sure you've forgotten to tell anyone out by the farm. The few friends that Julius had didn't live in Nairobi, you know."

"I am aware of that, my dearest girl," my father said. "Notices will be going to whomever you dictate as well."

After he spoke my father pulled a notebook out from somewhere and before I knew it I was trying to remember the names of old friends, to conjure spellings and let old faces float up. Because little else weighed upon my father's mind, it had not occurred to me that something like a wake would be weighing on it, but in a moment I got into the idea too, imagining our house aflower and full of friends. I even startled myself with the thought that had my father mentioned the wake earlier, we could have kept Jules in Nairobi. Had my father mentioned it earlier, I grimly noted, I might not have done that horrible thing with his arm.

When he left again, walking down into the valley of the

monkeys to take the shortcut back to Dr Zir's, I was alone in the kitchen with the same feeling I'd had yesterday, namely, no idea of what to do to pass the time. It was Tuesday and though Dr Zir would no doubt work fast, the wake wouldn't be held until Saturday, so what could I do with the intervening days? Could I go to bed again, sleeping until Tuesday morning became Saturday afternoon? Could I wake up to a house full of guests and be pulled from my room by my father to come out and cry? I didn't know what I could do, but just then the telephone rang. Beatrice answered it and called me right away.

"Please," she said, "it is Ralph Bunche Road."

I was both pleased and somehow not surprised to be hearing from Ralph. I would tell him to come on Saturday, tell him to expect his invitation in the mail. When I said hello, however, it was Miro's voice that answered back.

"It's the real Ralph Bunche Road," she said. "The place, not the person. What are you doing for lunch?"

She sounded like one of my old Oxford girlfriends. There was a briskness about her, a sophisticated tone that made me think of her as on stage.

"Nothing," I said.

"I've got rehearsals at ten, but after that can we meet for a while? What do you like? Anywhere's fine with me, only not the Norfolk again—if I stay too close to the theatre, no pun intended, I get butterflies."

"How about Trattoria?" I asked, and Miro said, "Okay by me. Does two o'clock sound all right? Rehearsal will be over by then and I'll be starved."

It occurred to me that *Madama Butterfly* might open on the night of the wake, and I tried to ask about that, but Miro cut me off. "I'm late as it is," she said. "I can see that the other singers have already gone inside."

Miro hung up and I put our own phone back down on the piano. That was an odd conversation. She hadn't been calling from her father's house on Ralph Bunche Road, but from the theatre or perhaps from a phone box in the Norfolk bar. Otherwise she wouldn't be able to tell me what the other singers were about to do. I remembered the scene from last night. Was Detective Mubia still sitting at our table with Mr Smith? Did they have their heads together, conspiring against me while they watched her call?

I stayed next to the piano quietly for a moment, but pretty soon I picked up the telephone again and found the number I wanted on a piece of paper taped to its side. The Norfolk Hotel not only had a bar, it had a hairdresser's too, where Jules and I both used to go for haircuts. When the matron answered the phone I made an appointment for eleven A.M.

By the time I got off the phone it was ten, and when I went back into the kitchen to look for the Land Rover keys I could see my father again, trudging up from the valley with Dr Zir. The two of them were leaning into each other as they walked along.

I found the keys and put them in my pocket, hanging them up on that ubiquitous tusk. I then took two mugs down from the shelf and poured them full of coffee. There was fresh milk in a jug in the fridge, so I put a cup of it on the stove to warm. By the time the men came through the kitchen door the mugs of hot coffee were ready.

"Nora, sweetheart," said Dr Zir.

I cut them each a piece of Beatrice's apple tart, and while

they had their coffee I told them that I had made an appointment to have my hair done. And it pleased both men when I
added, "If this wake is really going to happen, I don't want to
look like I'm bereft."

"In that case go to the Norfolk Saturday morning, not
now," said my father, but I jangled the keys at him and went
out of the door. The drive was still strewn with rotting avocado flesh, but the night guard had cleaned the Land Rover, so
I stepped over the carnage and got into the car. Somehow,
where only yesterday I'd still been overwhelmed, dodging that
cloud that had been stalking me since the afternoon of Jules's
death and not having the slightest idea what to do, this morning my heart was primarily at ease. All the way into town my
lightness of spirit held, but when I entered Harry Thuku Road
I did wish that I had another car to drive. If I parked the Land
Rover in the National Theatre car park again, I felt, it would be
like announcing myself, so I continued down quite a long way,
turned onto Kijabe Street, and found a parking spot right
away.

The Norfolk is a beautiful hotel, my favourite, even though
when Jules and I came to town we mostly stayed at others. We
could, of course, have stayed at my father's house, but Jules
liked hotels. He had a kind of obsession about making love in
strange rooms, the opposite of his lack of desire when sleeping
under the stars, so we had stayed once in the Six Eighty, once
at the Milimani and the Boulevard and the Fairmont, and even
one time at the Hilton.

The hairdresser's was tucked away in the back, and when I
went inside the matron greeted me warmly, as if I'd been there
the week before. There were no other customers in the place
just then, so she and her assistants called me immediately into

the back room to wash my hair. When Jules and I came in from the farm this was usually my first stop. I loved the smell of the place and I liked looking through the hairdo books, at the strangely beautiful women. Their photos reminded me of the animals that we'd see at our pond. There was a catlike litheness to them, the lines of their jaws were predatory, their hair set like that of the ardent queen in my father's chess set, pulled back in leonine tightness, or with strands of it swooping about their eyes. My father had been right in telling me that I ought to wait until Saturday to have my hair done, and it occurred to me that I might come back again, not only on Saturday, but on Wednesday and Thursday and Friday too. I would turn my hair perfect in daily installments as I stepped away from shock and grief, as I prepared to take up normal life again.

These were calming thoughts and I clung to them, but when the ladies tipped me back over the shampooing tub my idyll was interrupted by the matron's chatty voice. "Did you hear about the trouble last night? I don't know about Nairobi anymore. Even the Norfolk's not immune."

"What trouble?" I asked. Since I was looking up at the woman from the odd angle of the shampoo sink, what I saw was the soft underside of her chin and the weird movement of her lips, like an upside-down sting ray washed up on the shore.

My hair was heavy and I could feel the assistant's fingers dancing over my scalp.

"It was ever so late," said the matron. "Almost all of the customers were gone, but a man got killed in our bar last night, stabbed through the heart with a bread knife. He was a crazy man, a street beggar who had somehow got inside."

When my shampooing was done and they sat me up again

I felt light, as if the dirt washed from my hair had pulled the blinders from my eyes.

"Who killed him?" I asked. "What was the dead man's name?"

They led me from one chair to another without speaking. When I was sitting down again, the matron shrugged, "Who knows the names of wild men off the street?"

Since I wasn't having a perm I let the setting and combing go on with as little conversation as possible. I had to try to think clearly now. I had been in the Norfolk last night. Upon leaving I had seen Mr Smith sitting in my chair, and if this killing had anything to do with him, as I knew it must, then I also knew I had to get help, I couldn't go on alone anymore. I hadn't allowed myself to believe it before, but Mr Smith might harm me, he could easily do it, and he might also harm my father.

The shop door had opened a few times and the matron was greeting newcomers. "Did you hear about the trouble last night?" I heard her say.

When they were finished with me I paid them quickly, glad I didn't know any of the other women in the waiting room. I'd been in there for an hour, but two hours remained before I had to meet Miro. I went out through the hotel foyer, past the magazine stand, and when I passed the bar I could see that lunch was in full swing, with most of the tables taken and all the waiters hurriedly walking by. I tried to see if last night's table was occupied, but I tried too hard and the maître d' came over and asked me if I wanted to sit down.

"I'm looking for someone," I said, and then I asked, "Did something bad happen here last night?"

The maître d' nodded solemnly. "Alas," he said, "even we are not immune."

"Who let the man in?" I asked. "And where did they take him when they took him away?"

The maître d' looked at me a little keenly but answered my question. "He came in by himself, off the street and out of control. He attacked one of our customers and made the others run. When they took him away he was dead, so he went to the Nairobi Hospital mortuary, I suppose."

I had more questions, but the maître d' looked over my shoulder. "Do you need a table, sir?" he asked, and when I turned around I found Ralph standing there. Ralph wasn't wearing his business suit this time but his Wildebeest Road safari uniform, tan khaki pants with a short-sleeved jacket. The Wildebeest Road logo was on his breast pocket. He looked smart.

"Are you working today?" I asked. "Are you heading out of town?"

"As a matter of fact I am," said Ralph. "Cottar's Camp and the Mara."

"When are you coming back?" I guess I still had Jules's wake on my mind. I hoped that Ralph would be in town by the weekend, that I could mention the wake to him and he'd say he would come.

"Thursday night or Friday morning," he said. "The first and last nights we're camping, so I'm not sure how long they will want to stay out."

Because we were both standing in the maître d's queue, Ralph offered to buy me lunch, and I found myself making a counter-offer. "Come with me for a little while instead," I said. "I need help, Ralph. I will buy you lunch at Trattoria later."

"I am hungry now," Ralph said, but it was clear that he was coming along. I told him I had my car, but his Wildebeest Road van was parked right out in front, and when we got in, Ralph asked where I wanted to go.

"Nairobi Hospital," I said.

Ralph shook his head, but, maybe out of respect for the recently widowed, he didn't ask questions. He just put the van in gear, telling me he had to pick up his tourists at the Hilton Hotel at four.

/   /   /

Nairobi Hospital had several large car parks, with signs pointing to outpatient and emergency rooms. I hadn't told Ralph my reason for wanting to go to the hospital, but since there were no signs for the mortuary, I had Ralph stop at admissions and park his van under the shade of an old and sloping flame tree, next to the helicopter pad and directly below the ward where Jules had been. As I looked up, I could see the wide ledge, the easy footing that someone walking on it might have. Of three windows, I knew one had to have been Jules's. All three were open now, with white curtains flicking out into the warm Nairobi air.

"Julius died there," I said, pointing up, but Ralph looked down. "Are we visiting a memory, then," he asked, "or are we simply passing time?"

We were in the hospital's outer hallway before I told Ralph why I'd needed to come, that these days I feared I was connected to everything, even, perhaps, to the previous night's death at the Norfolk. "Maybe it's pointless," I said, "but someone told me recently to leave no stone unturned. Just a quick look, down where they keep the bodies, and then we'll go have our lunch, I promise."

I thought Ralph might be reluctant to search out the mortuary, but he was nothing of the kind. Rather, he went over and asked the admissions nurse how to get there.

Maybe mortuaries are always in basements, but this one was a long way down, and once we were on the stairs it was I who had trouble going on. I thought of Jules's body passing this way. Though, of course, there was a lift, I imagined rigormortised corpses taking these sharp turns, exhausted orderlies at each end. At the bottom I was as much out of breath as I might have been had I been going up, and when Ralph opened a heavy door I nearly decided to retreat, to catch my breath while climbing the stairs.

We were in the hospital's lowest basement. There were labs and changing rooms and hospital workers milling about. And there were living patients too, lined up in the hallway in front of the laboratory doors, coloured tags on the backs of their wheelchairs or pinned to the sleeves of their gowns.

Ralph asked an attendant to point out the mortuary, and as we went that way we found that the crowd quickly thinned, that activity was pretty much limited to the area by the stairway door. The wall paint, at no spot in the hospital anything but drab, was all but missing down here, and though the hall was properly lit, it was poorly cared for. This was an area of defeat, I realised; if the business of hospitals was saving lives, here the business had failed.

The mortuary had double doors with heavy glass windows, both scratched and dirty, impossible to see through. One could easily imagine a stretcher knocking the doors quickly open, though the patient on the stretcher wouldn't care about speed.

We were surprised to find that the mortuary was empty. That is, I had expected a worker or two, but there was no one standing up to meet us, no one asking what we wanted in such a cold and quiet place.

The chamber we were in appeared to be an anteroom. There was a desk in it, and on top of the desk a clipboard with a list of names, perhaps twenty in all. Each name was followed by a notation—dates and scribbles, often with a doctor's signature at the end. There were several sheets of paper below the top one, and on impulse I flipped back a few and soon found Dr Zir's name next to an unreadable version of "Julius Grant." As I looked closely, in fact, I could see that they'd called him James, and that made me mad.

Ralph took the clipboard from my hand. "Let's clear up the matter of last night's murder, if that's what we came for, and get out of here," he said. He turned back to the first page and found the man in question immediately, third entry from the bottom, under the heading "Unknown male."

He was listed as D-2 on the clipboard's location index, but when we turned to face the mortuary, even Ralph became hesitant. To venture farther seemed an intrusion, a formal violation of the rules. Still, there were doors leading out of the anteroom and since they were marked A through F, I walked over to door D and opened it up. And even though a cold dead breath came out to meet us, Ralph and I both walked inside.

"There has got to be a light switch," said Ralph.

We knew we were in a refrigerator, but until Ralph found the switch and we let the door swing closed, the thought stayed with me that what we might find lying about in this room would be tusks, that we were still in Mr Smith's domain.

There was only one bare bulb, but it was so powerful that both of us at first put our hands up to our eyes. There weren't drawers in this room, as I'd imagined there'd be, but free-wheeling stretchers, just like the ones they used in the upstairs wards. There were five of them, with large numerical placards pinned to the sheets covering the corpse on each one.

"It's D-2," I whispered, and Ralph nodded, walked over to the D-2 stretcher, and pulled the sheet back right away. What we saw there was the face and upper body of a very young woman, her mouth a grimace, her breasts round and hard.

"They must have marked them wrong," said Ralph. He was looking at the breasts and he touched, for an instant, this young girl's upper arm. "She is not a crazy man," he said.

Although the stretchers had been marked wrong, the good condition of this young girl gave me courage rather than taking my courage away. And since there were only five stretchers, I felt sure we'd be able to find the man by looking under each sheet in turn. He would have a wild look, the muscles of his face frozen at the moment he screamed through the Norfolk Hotel, scaring all the patrons in the bar.

Ralph and I went to the next table and he pulled the sheet back on number five, an old man of about my father's age. This man didn't look human. His face seemed made of burlap as thick as one of our coffee bags, and his chest was so caved in that its encompassing skin appeared to rest on his spine. Seeing the young woman had been easier, and after covering this old man up again we paused. There were three more bodies. "Let's try number four," I said.

"This one really might be him," Ralph said, and by that I understood that it was my turn to take the sheet away. The sheet was cold and as soon as I touched it the D-4 placard fell to the floor. Ralph was behind me when I pulled the sheet away, so I couldn't see his reaction, but I immediately knew that this was the man we sought. His hair wasn't long and he didn't have the slightest vestige of a mad look on his face, none of the disconnected wildness that life on the city streets always seemed to give, but this was our man just the same. His mouth was wide and his eyes were open. In his upper chest we could see three bloodless wounds, deep slits that looked like places for coins and did not bring bread knives to mind. Seeing him made me feel so bad. I could remember the stacks of letters in his room, the picture of his family, and the way I had taken his *panga* away.

"It's him," I told Ralph. "His name was Kamau."

Room D had been quiet, but as I spoke a compressor came on and a cold breath touched the backs of our necks, an icy wind from a grate above. I covered Kamau again, and picked up his placard from the floor, and pinned it carefully to the sheet over his chest. I couldn't remember whether I had told Ralph that I was sure Kamau was the one who had finally taken Jules's life away, sneaking back into his hospital room, and I don't even know whether I have written that the last time I saw Kamau, the time he stood in my living room with my husband's rifle over his shoulder and Mr Smith by his side, he had a strange hopeless look in his eyes, but that is what I remember now. While all those words had come from Mr Smith's mouth, Kamau's face had contained only sorrow and resignation, as if he were about to drown.

When we left room D there was still no one in the ante-room, but as we made our way through the mortuary doors and up the hall, passing all those labs again, we found Detective Mubia sitting on a bench. Like rags on a statue, his red suit conformed to his thinker's pose.

"It was who I thought it would be," I told him. "Kamau, our foreman. The man you never met at the farm."

"I saw you entering the stairway," Detective Mubia said. "I came along only this far."

The detective stood and followed us into an adjacent lift, which opened conveniently to take us up. There were several doctors in the lift, men of Dr Zir's era, older and stooped and bald. Next to the starched whiteness of their jackets and the bright black polish of their shoes, Detective Mubia looked even worse than he had on the bench below. He had the look Kamau was supposed to have had the night before.

By the time we got to Ralph's van it was a quarter past one. Because Ralph had parked under a tree, the van's cab wasn't hot, but he opened the doors anyway, then sat inside while the detective tried to tell me what had happened at the Norfolk after I'd gone. He said he had remained at our table to finish his tea, had just, in fact, received more hot water for a second cup, when Mr Smith appeared. Mr Smith demanded to know what I'd said, who the woman with me had been, and how much money we'd offered the detective to come into this thing on our side.

"How much did Mr Smith offer you in turn?" I interrupted to ask. It was a crass kind of question and maybe it was unfair, but my decision by then was to assume the worst in everyone.

Detective Mubia's body had been slumped on that bench

in the basement, and he had followed us into the lift in an abject and defeated way, but when he heard my words he filled up again, remembering his natural dignity and expanding into his suit, which made it look better.

"If I am connected to any mortal man outside of my policeman's call," he said, "it is to N'chele, from whose good seed the evil man has come. The father helped me when I fell on difficult times, but he never asked more than that I monitor the activities of his son, that I tell him of those activities in order that he might correct them before I needed to tell my superiors in the law. So that is what I have done."

"Yes, and I'll wager you never told your superiors in the law," I said.

I had liked Detective Mubia from the beginning, but he was the kind of African man for whom I usually had no affinity. His demeanour was too serious, his beliefs too literal, his view of the world too dull. And now, after my second harsh comment, his eyes flashed, even while the anger within them turned the volume of his voice down low.

"Everything in this world is not clear," he said evenly. "I have been a detective of police for eleven years. My salary is small and it does not grow to meet the increased prices of our goods. I house my family in two rooms at the edge of town. I have six children and must pay their school fees every term and buy their school uniforms and the other necessities of our daily life. When another Kikuyu man says he will see that those school fees are paid if only I allow him the chance to exorcise the devil from his own son, do you think it is God's will that I tell that other Kikuyu man no? Who will make judgements such as those? Maybe he is God's vehicle, God's messenger sent to keep my children strong."

Detective Mubia had controlled his anger as he spoke—by the end it showed only in the muscles of his jaw. But if what he said was true, if he was not on Smith's payroll but was instead on Mr N'chele's, helping him keep his son in line, then Detective Mubia knew everything. He knew of Jules's long involvement with Mr Smith and he knew of my father's, and he knew what it was that Jules had stolen and hidden away. If what he said was true, in fact, then his value to me was far greater than I imagined before. I softened my own voice and put my hand on his arm.

"How did Kamau present himself last night? And where did the bread knife come from? How did he get killed?"

Detective Mubia spoke as if what he said were memorised. "They bring bread knives right to the tables in that hotel. They bring an entire loaf of bread and let the customers carve it up themselves!" He seemed furious with the hotel's policy, but he continued. "Kamau had come there to speak with Mr Smith, to petition him for money so that he could leave Nairobi, go to his village or somewhere. When Mr Smith dismissed Kamau, he found the bread knife on the table next to us and used it to try to cut some of Mr Smith's evil away."

"But if Kamau had the bread knife, then why is Smith uninjured and Kamau dead? The reverse would be a better outcome, if you ask me."

"It is because I did not have my police revolver to calm him down," the detective said. "My police revolver is under repair, so I stood and splashed my tea in Kamau's face, just as my training told me I should do. I then turned his arm inward and pushed it back from whence it came. I am skilled at disarming, but he puffed his chest out to meet the bread knife and the bread knife went inside. Your foreman killed himself, I think, but the devil gave him the use of my hands. And now I am disgraced. When my superior came, Smith told the story differently, and from this morning I am suspended, without the return of my revolver or the benefit of my pay."

I looked at Ralph to see what he was thinking, but his face was hollow, his hands on the steering wheel, his eyes staring down.

"We are going into town now," I told the detective. "Thank you for taking the trouble to find me here. I appreciate knowing the details, the truth of my foreman's death."

"Now I am suspended without my pay," the detective repeated. "My revolver is repaired but I cannot retrieve it from the shop."

"But surely Mr N'chele . . . He has been your benefactor before."

I might have gone stupidly on, but a new look on Detective Mubia's face stopped me. Three times now my words had told him how little I understood, how slightly I perceived his dilemma or his mind. Indeed, he spent such a long time staring at me that I thought he would leave without speaking again, but finally he said softly, "Like the school fees of my children, my debt to Mr N'chele has been paid in full. Now it is only Mr Smith whom I must find. Your foreman killed himself using my hands, and I must do battle with the devil for the salvation of my soul."

He pointed at the faded side of his red Toyota, which was parked nearby. "As you engage yourself in defeating him," he said, "I will be around."

Detective Mubia walked away when I got into Ralph's van, and as soon as he could, Ralph put the van in gear and quickly drove down the hospital hill. As usual, I wanted to speak about what we'd just heard, I wanted to go over everything one more time out loud, but Ralph's face was closed, nearly as troubled as Detective Mubia's had been. He drove well enough, but everything about him demanded quiet, and with quiet all around, I finally began to think a little bit more clearly. Detective Mubia was a rigid Christian man. He wasn't a social believer, his sect was not of the charismatic, Sunday drumming, kind. I remembered his comment when I had asked him if he was a believer before—"It is better to believe and know you are mistaken, than to disbelieve and know you are correct," he had said, but such an answer, with its syntactical appeal and tricky intellectual charm, was not the product of his heart, I knew that now. Detective Mubia was not casual, he had no cynicism, he had no nonchalance. And now he was in a state of pure mortification, as surely as if he were wrapped with barbed wire underneath his shirt; he was not only denied his pistol and his pay, but he was out of favour with his God. I could see it now. At Mr Smith's table and under Mr Smith's evil sky, Detective Mubia had lent my foreman his hands and guided that bread knife not only into Kamau's wayward heart, but also into his own.

13

The Page-
Six Man

Because traffic was light, we got to the restaurant quickly, about fifteen minutes before we were to meet Miro. Ralph parked his van behind another one just like it, but with a different logo on the side. Ralph had been perfectly happy rummaging around inside the mortuary, but now he was morose. The detective had upset him, and I thought that was strange.

Inside the restaurant there were empty tables everywhere, but when a waiter greeted us, Ralph told him that we wanted to sit upstairs, in a section that was normally closed during the day.

"Mama is up there alone," the waiter said, but Ralph insisted, and we climbed a winding metal staircase and chose a table across the room from the large Italian woman who owned the place. We had to take the chairs down off the table-tops to sit up there. When the woman heard us she welcomed Ralph, waving a big arm and calling out his name. Ralph said hello, but he still had a bad look on his face and when we ordered coffees he finally spoke his mind. "Sometimes we do stupid things for reasons we cannot fathom," he said, "neither at the time we do them nor afterward, when we try to reflect."

I thought he was talking about me, that he'd been thinking about my behaviour with Detective Mubia all this time, but Ralph took a piece of folded paper from the inside pocket of his safari jacket and put it on the table between us.

"I think I intended to bring this back to you all along," he said. "I know I did. I imagined myself showing up with it some night at your home."

"What is it?" I brightly asked. "What have you got there?"

With Kamau dead and Detective Mubia suspended from his job, I didn't want a melancholy Ralph on my hands, so I used my most cheerful voice. As I touched the edge of the paper, however, my hand and my voice turned cold.

"It is page number six," Ralph said. "The important missing part of your husband's letter. After we left the circle of singers I found it hung up on a thorn."

I took the paper from the table and opened it, but I couldn't concentrate on the words. If Ralph had found the missing page of Jules's letter, why hadn't he given it back to me at the time? I remembered his being helpful, searching everywhere, running around. The motivations of men were peculiar, to be sure, but this didn't make sense at all.

Ralph shook his head. "It was a horrible impulse and most

unexpected," he said. "All I know is that it had something to do with our school days, with the way you were then, and with your not recognising me when we happened to meet. Seeing you reminded me of how much I disliked those years, and it occurred to me how little you'd changed. I was invisible to you then, so I guess I thought I'd make your letter disappear now."

"Did you read this page?" I asked. "Did you learn anything from what it said?" Since there was nobody but the owner in the upper part of the restaurant, I let myself go, this time allowing anger to push my voice up high. Men were bastards, every one. He had kept a page of the letter because it occurred to him how little I'd changed? I was furious with him, but Ralph answered normally, as if I'd asked my questions in a civil way.

"I did read it," he said. "It was after reading it, and after listening to the detective back there, that I knew I had to give it back now."

The white border of page six seemed to swell a little when Ralph spoke, so I picked it up and read what it said, while trying to calm down.

. . . terrible dupes we had been. I don't know where he got the know-how or how he made everything seem so authentic that night, but I discovered only recently that the tusks we'd been smuggling all these months were real. Think of it, Nora, your father and I have been doing what we detested in others, laughing about it and making money. Your father sold the things all over Europe, Nora, at least he did before he had his stroke, and I shipped them out so confidently and so well! And all the time this man was buying tusks off poachers or poaching himself, amazed at what fools, what easy marks we had been.

I feel terrible about everything, Nora, and too ashamed to express it except in this poor way. When I confronted the man, asking him why he needed to involve us in such a scheme, he laughed in my face, said it was a mere by-product of his real work, and that he'd done it to get even with your dad. He beat us, Nora, took us both so easily in, but I did do something about it, and aside from confessing my stupidity and guilt, I'm writing you now to let you know what I've done. He sometimes kept his tusk supply in an un-likely building, right here in town. I've had easy access to that building for months now, and one recent day I stole the centerpiece to everything he was about, the eye of his storm, and I buried the bounty out on our farm. Now here's the key, told, Nora dear, so that only you will understand. It might seem silly to do it like this, but I really can't come up with a safer way.

> *Under our bed*
> *yes, under hot covers,*
> *where the sweet smell of sex*
> *draws the sharp claws of others.*

Do you get it, Nora? I hope you do.

That was all, and since I didn't have the rest of the letter with me in order to place it properly in context, I folded it again and tucked it away. And when I looked at Ralph I not only under-stood why he'd felt he had to return the page, but a little about why he'd taken it. Something to do with our school days, Ralph had said. Though Julius Grant was gone, two kinds of men had come a little bit into focus for me that day. Ralph and Detective Mubia, two kinds of men that I'd never understood before.

"My God, Ralph," I said, "this is all so bloody crazy. What am I supposed to do now?"

"First of all, do you get it?" he asked. "Do you understand what your husband's riddle means?"

I did, without the slightest doubt, and I was about to say so, but right then we heard someone rattling up the metal stairs and in a second Miro came in, grimacing and twisting her mouth and asking why in the world we weren't eating down below.

"This is Ralph N'deru," I told her. "You know, Ralph Bunche Road. It was his idea, he likes it up here."

She and Ralph shook hands and Miro sat down. It turned out they had met before too, and while they were remembering when and where, I took a moment to try to think clearly for a second time that day.

My husband and father had been dealing in real tusks, not acrylic ones, and when Jules discovered how easily and thoroughly he'd been tricked, he took something from Mr Smith and hid it on our farm. Mr Smith hired Kamau, a man who'd worked for us for years, to get that something back, and Kamau proceeded to shoot Jules and then go into his hospital room and smother him with a pillow. When Mr Smith punished him for the mistakes he had made, Kamau followed Mr Smith to the Norfolk Hotel and was himself then killed, stabbed through the heart with a bread knife, wielded by his own hands and those of Detective Mubia, whose skill in self-defence had cost him his peace of mind and his job. And now here was Ralph, the fellow for whom Miro had said I should look out, giving me back a page of my husband's letter that he had kept for deep-seated reasons of his own. And on top of all that, though I did understand the poem that was on page six, though I did know where Mr Smith's stolen property was, I still didn't know *what* it was. I only knew that I had to go and get it, and that I had to give it back to the unspeakable man if I ever wanted this ordeal to end. I also knew that I couldn't give it back if I wanted to honour my husband's dying words.

Miro and Ralph were ordering their lunch by the time I looked up. Miro, who set up this luncheon with her own odd phone call, didn't seem miffed that Ralph was there, nor did she appear to be in any hurry to say whatever it was that had made her call. Ralph, on the other hand, was relieved and had come completely back to himself. And since they both seemed content with small talk, I went along. If it weren't for small talk, after all, how would I ever find time to pause?

The woman who owned the restaurant delivered our food herself, kissing Ralph when she put it down. Her English was cooked in a thick Italian sauce, but she told us that Ralph was the only man in town for whom her second floor was never closed. A few years back Ralph had taken this woman's mother, visiting from Italy, on a wonderful safari, and since that time she'd been forced to think of him as family. And family always ate upstairs.

I had no memory of ordering anything, but the food that came was good, and by the time we finished eating, Ralph had told Miro about the murder and about everything that had happened at the hospital, leaving out only the part about my husband's letter's sixth page. His tone was serious and quiet, full of respect for the complicated situation and a desire to continue to help. When the owner came back with more coffee and our bill, Ralph excused himself for a moment, insisting that the lunch was on him, and when he was gone Miro was all business again. "I thought you'd be alone," she said. "It doesn't seem so ominous now, but look at this, look at what that waiter gave me last night."

It seemed to me that the pain of Jules's death and the difficulty of my present life was unveiling itself in a series of letters and notes and coincidental meetings. This time, however, not only was the little square of paper unimpressive, compared with the solid sheet of Jules's good bond, but its message was paltry too. It was clumsy and snide, calculated only to upset Miro. "The woman you are with is a dangerous woman," the note said. "She has violated one of Kenya's sacred laws."

I laughed and handed the note back, saying only, "Awkward phrasing."

"But listen," said Miro, "I know your heart is broken, but you better try to remember whatever it is you know about African men. Don't be frivolous, don't be flip, and above all don't assume that in the end you'll win. Awkward phrasing or not I almost took this thing seriously. I nearly believed it, I worried about it all night long."

"Well, if you almost took it seriously, then he almost achieved his goal," I said. "He wants me to remain alone in this. If I build up a circle of friends, he worries that I'll find the strength to go on." I then somehow told her about Ralph's returning page six. I also said that the three holes in Kamau's body looked like slots for coins.

Miro touched my arm and said, "My dear, Nora, you're not listening to me. Be careful of this man. You have lived here all your life, I know, but you're a white girl who has floated around on the cream, and he is fighting you in purely African ways. You think you have a foot in both worlds, but maybe you do not. Remember this, there is no nuance in the things he says, no double entendre, no sarcasm, and no underneath side. He has taken away your husband and killed your foreman and ruined your detective's career, and though Ralph seems very nice, what is he doing but playing like a schoolboy? Go back, my dear, to your childhood, remember what you know of this place and this man. Otherwise you will not beat him at his game."

Ralph came back just then and said, "I have to go. I pick up my tourists at four."

When we stood to leave I told them both about the wake, but I was looking only at Miro. "You have to come," I said. "I need you there. Otherwise I really will be alone."

Opening night at the opera was Friday, but Miro said her Saturday performance wasn't until eight o'clock. She promised she would come to the wake and after that, when Ralph went over to say good-bye to the owner, Miro and I wound our way down the stairs. "Let me catch a taxi," she said, and just as Ralph appeared her cab pulled away from the curb.

When we got into his van I already knew what I would ask Ralph, and I wondered whether or not he would be surprised.

"I want to go with you today," I said. "I want you to drop me at my farm."

"I've got three British tourists," he said.

If he had only three tourists, there would be plenty of room in the van, so I wasn't sure whether he was agreeing to take me or not.

"Surely your tourists would like to see a farm," I said. "Or, if you must, just drop me off in Narok and I'll catch a ride the rest of the way up the hill. When I'm finished doing what I have to do I will bring our lorry back to town."

It was clear that Ralph didn't want me along. Since he'd taken part of Jules's letter, however, it was impossible for him to say no. So what he said instead was "I leave at four. What are you going to do with your car?"

The Trattoria was only a few minutes from the Norfolk, and since Ralph's safari office was in Westlands, I asked him to drop me at the car and told him I'd be at his office, ready to go, before his customers arrived.

"I'm picking them up at the Hilton," said Ralph.

I had got out of the van and was looking back inside. "I won't cause you any trouble, Ralph," I said.

When he left I didn't waste time watching his van depart. I jumped into the Land Rover and drove away fast, before it was properly warm. Down Kijabe Street I went and into the round-about that led me up by the museum and onto the sports-club road.

And though it must have been there all along, I didn't see Detective Mubia's faded red station wagon in my rear-view mirror until I was out of Westlands, almost home.

14

Michael, the Lion-Hearted

I had told Ralph I would meet him at his office, but in the end I asked my father to drop me at the Hilton Hotel instead. I told him only that I wouldn't be home for a while. "No, Dad, not for dinner," I said, "but in a day or two, in plenty of time for Julius's wake." I said I was going on a short safari, that what I really needed now was some time alone.

I bought some safari clothes in one of the shops off the hotel lobby and changed in the lavatory. I bought the clothes so that I'd look as touristy as possible, so that I wouldn't look like myself sitting beside Ralph in his Wildebeest Road van. I had the .380 with me, but since the safari clothes weren't bulky enough to hide it, I bought a loosely woven sisal bag too, wrapped the pistol in my old clothing, and stuffed it all in that.

The Hilton was a hotel I knew well, so I went to a room on the mezzanine to wait for four o'clock to arrive. This room served as a lounge for hotel guests, as well as for Nairobi residents who had special memberships, but even though I didn't belong, I managed to talk my way past the room's attendant and sit down in one of the wide and smooth-armed chairs. There was a writing desk next to my chair and a fanned-out selection of cheap plastic pens. I knew about this room because Jules used to come here sometimes—he actually did have a membership—and as I sat there it came to me that it might have been here that he wrote his seven-page letter of revelations. He used to come here to drink brandy and sit and think things out. Such behaviour was in Jules's nature, but it isn't in mine. I'm not the kind of person who would take out a membership in a private lounge, yet Jules, who loved the farm more than I did, liked this kind of thing inordinately well. He was a loner but a joiner too. He was a believer in the fraternity of man, yet he didn't enter into easy confidences with others. He was a man of action, a man of movement and hard work. He was knowable in an instant, as I'd found out in London, yet on the other hand he was not knowable at all. He had loved me deeply, I still absolutely believe it to be true, but his feeling was in some ways quite a shallow one.

I moved to the little wicker-backed chair in front of the writing desk and rifled around looking for the kind of good stationery Jules had used. In the drawer there were hotel postcards and pamphlets advertising various safari companies. I searched among them for mention of Wildebeest Road, but there was none. Ralph's was a word-of-mouth safari company and I hoped the word was spreading around.

I took out a piece of cheap stationery with the hotel's emblem at its top and wrote my name with one of the plastic pens. I wrote it this way: **Nora Hennessey Grant**, going over it several times so that it would be bold. Under my name I put the number one and to the right of the number one I wrote "My Farm." After that I squeezed in the words "Last Will and Testament," in tiny letters, just below my name, and then I scratched out the "and Testament" part.

I had no idea I was going to write such a thing—I was just doodling, passing the time—and I had no desire to list other numbers past the number one. Our farm was now "my farm," and it was the only thing I could think of as actually being part and parcel of me. I had some small amount of money, Kenyan shillings in a bank nearby and a few pound notes up in London, but what did those things have to do with me, how were they connected with my will as I had displayed it during my time alive? And was my will, my own true will, really represented by the words "My Farm" on the paper in front of me? It had been Jules's farm more than it had been mine, it had been his idea to grow coffee and live there, and now that it was mine alone, I didn't know what to do with it. Could I run it by myself? Did I even want to? And to whom could I bequeath such a thing? Who on earth would care, now that Jules was gone, to have a bit of what I, too, had worked so hard to make, to remember me by?

/ / /

I left the paper where it was and went back downstairs quickly, with the sudden fear that Ralph had already arrived. The narrow street in front of the Hilton was always packed with safari vans, and when I went out to look for Ralph's I fit right in, in the new clothing that I wore. The German and Japanese tourists were dressed as I was, and the British and Americans were too, though in less flamboyant ways. Because it was already late in the day, most of the vans were returning. Everywhere I could hear expressions of joy over Kenya's beauty, the names of various animals peppering the air. No matter where I looked, however, I couldn't find Ralph, and I was beginning to think he'd left without me when I saw three people emerge from the hotel's front door. Where everyone else was wearing khaki or green, these three wore white. I heard one of them mention Ralph's company's name and I walked right up to them.

"Wildebeest Road," I said. "Nora Hennessey, at your service. Ralph N'deru will be right along."

"Who?" said the older man, but the woman smiled. "We're the Cooleys," she told me. "I am Dorothea and he is John. That one is my brother, Michael."

It was John Cooley who'd spoken first, but Michael who came forward and shook my hand. I liked Michael right away, and I liked his sister, too. She had self-possession in her posture and her voice, the thing I had lost, somehow. She was pretty, in a big sort of way, and meeting her brought my spirits up. It was only John Cooley toward whom I felt a little cool. He had a small mustache that made him look stern.

Ralph's van didn't show up until four-fifteen. I was surprised at his tardiness—I'd have guessed he would be a strict keeper of time—but when he jumped out of the van, full of apologies, I realised that he was late because he'd waited at his Westlands office for me, while I had inexplicably come to the hotel. Since the Cooleys were travelling light, we were on the road in about two minutes, and as we headed out of town I tried to make things up to Ralph by telling odd bits of local history and trying to act as if tour guiding were as much a part of my makeup as the outlandish garb. It was only when I happened to say our first stop would be my farm, however, that the three of them perked up.

"You've got a farm?" Michael said. "How nice. I've got a farm, too."

"We were both raised on it," said Dorothea, "but John and I live in London now."

Ralph had said earlier that they were camping near Cottar's, and that he didn't have reservations for them until tomorrow night, so I decided that offering to let them stay at the farm would be a good idea. It might help make up for the trouble I'd caused Ralph, and it would solve my problem of having to spend my first night back there alone.

"Would you like to see my place?" I asked. "Would you like to stop over? It's right on the way and there's no extra charge."

Michael and Dorothea both said they thought that would be great, and though I should have asked him first, Ralph seemed to think it was okay too, so by the time we got to the escarpment, to that little Italian prisoner-of-war church where I'd stopped with my dad, only John retained any of the dour mood that had been set by the late start. Ralph pointed down at the Great Rift Valley and talked about the origins of man, about the recent discoveries that had been made. He was clever and interesting, very much on stage. When a group of baboons leapt up on the escarpment wall and Ralph pointed out details of their hierarchy, we could immediately see it in the way the baboons stood around. When he spoke of anthropological matters Ralph sounded like an absolute professional,

and by the time he began to talk about the behaviour of the
other animals they would see, even John thawed out. I had no
idea Ralph would be that good. Before we knew it we were at
the outskirts of Narok and I was telling him where to look for
the road to our farm.

For an hour I'd been happy, listening to Ralph, but when
we started to climb out of Narok again I began to see a certain
rashness in inviting these people to spend the night. I'd made
Ralph bring me so that I could follow the directions in my husband's poem, just as I'd told him at the restaurant. I wanted to
work, to dig the contraband from its hiding place, not fill the
farm with tourists, possibly endangering their lives. It was unlike me not to have thought of such a thing before, and it made
me worry about my own impulsiveness. Still, since it was
nearly dark I knew I wouldn't do any digging tonight. In the
morning Ralph and his customers would leave and after that, I
told myself, I'd go outside with my shovel and my nonspecific
plan.

We drove through the latent coffee, barren plants still
thick enough to hide whatever damage the elephants had
done, and into our yard. I knew the place had been guarded
well enough by the Maasai, but I'd forgotten to worry about
the condition of the quickly reassembled inside of my house,
and when I remembered it I turned in my seat to apologise.
The Cooleys, however, had just then turned in their seats
too, all three of them looking at our pond.

"My goodness," said Dorothea. A couple of wildebeests
were drinking. They looked like the ones in the logo on the
side of Ralph's van.

"Is this where you live?" Michael asked. He leaned forward
and let his hand touch my arm.

Ralph parked the van next to the dormitory, and when we got out and slammed the doors, the two wildebeests trotted away.

"I've got lights for that pond," I told them. "One bright light. We'll turn it on when it gets dark and see what comes to drink."

Since Michael had touched me in the van and was standing too near me now, I wanted to find a way to mention Julius pretty soon, and when I turned to him Michael himself provided it.

"Surely you don't live here alone?" he asked. "I'd think it would be too much work."

"I do now," I told him. "My husband just passed away."

Michael closed his mouth and John said, "That's certainly bad news," but Dorothea came over and threaded her arm through mine. She didn't speak, but it was a kind and helpful thing for her to do. I had begun to discover, since Jules's death, that I missed the presence of other women in my life. I felt it with Dorothea and, of course, I felt it very strongly with Miro. But if I missed other women now, why hadn't I missed them when Jules was alive? Why hadn't I particularly noticed that in ever so many subtle ways I was going through my daily and my weekly and my yearly routine alone?

Inside the house things were just as I had left them. No one had come in to ransack the place again, but the front room was arranged haphazardly, as if only bachelors used it now. The Maasai I'd hired as guards were nowhere around, so I asked Ralph to make tea while I went back outside to find them. Previously we had only hired Maasai guards when Kamau was gone and there were otherwise only temporary workers on the farm, but the petrol station man had never let us down, and sure enough, I found a Maasai sitting under a tree behind the workers' quarters, a few feet from our generator. As I got closer I realised that this was one of the men who tried to help Jules on the night of his wounding, the same one I saw at the petrol station when coming back with my father from town. I thought Maasai boys would be guarding the place, not a warrior, and when the man looked up I said, "Oh mister, thank you for coming back."

I thought I remembered that this man spoke Swahili pretty well, and I was right. "I have killed the lion," he quietly told me, "the big female. She ran but I followed her well, killing her only this morning with the sun."

He spoke so softly that I got confused and very nearly asked what he was talking about. But since he had a bundle on the ground beside him, I held my tongue while he opened it up. The bundle was wrapped in a red Maasai cloth which covered another wrapper of thick and sticky leaves, like pieces of parchment. Inside the leaves, warm as toast, was the big female lion's heart.

"I have waited for you," said the Maasai.

"I don't know your name. My husband knew your name," I told him, "but not me."

"I am Sosio," he said, and for some reason he said that part in English.

When Sosio stood away from the lion's heart, I finally noticed the two Maasai boys whom the petrol station man had hired to watch the farm. They'd been seated on the other side of the tree and came around it now.

"We will go," Sosio said. "We only waited for your return."

They left so quickly then that I had to run to catch up, taking the nearest boy by the arm and pushing some bills into his hand.

Because I had no idea what to do with it or how I could explain to Ralph's three guests how I'd gone to see if my guards were around and come back with a lion's heavy heart in my hands, I nearly left it by the generator for the scavengers who would come. But in the end I picked it up by the edges of its leaf wrapper. And when I came past the near side of the dormitory with it, there was Michael, standing in his starched white shorts and looking around.

"What have you got there?" he asked. "What did you find?"

His face was composed and pleasant, his eyes deep and earnest and bright. He was a kind and good man, I thought, someone who'd been looking forward to his Kenyan holiday for a long time.

"You don't want to know," I said.

I could see the others seated on the porch, teacups in their hands.

"Oh, but I do," said Michael. "That's why I asked, you know, because I want to know." He had his hands behind his back and was lightly rocking, very British, on the balls of his feet.

"It's the heart of a lion," I told him. "Of a lioness, to be exact."

Michael laughed but then stopped laughing and stepped near. "Are you quite serious?" he asked. "Wherever did you get it? Wherever did you find such a thing?"

"From the Maasai warrior who killed the lion. He gave it to me out back just now."

Michael's eyes were open wide. I gave him a steady look,

finally deciding to make his holiday as memorable as possible. "It's in retribution," I said. "She was the lioness who caused my husband's death, who started it, at least. The warrior who brought her heart to me was here at the time but he couldn't intervene. Come on, help me get rid of it. My husband is buried up here, just overlooking the plains."

It was only as I spoke that I had any idea what to do with the heart, but Michael, eyes like saucers now, readily followed me across the soft ground. Jules's grave was unmarked, I hadn't even ordered its headstone yet, but a dozen feet away from it stood our ever-ready campfire, fresh logs crisscrossed on top of burnt ones, and everything surrounded by stones. "Julius and I used to sleep out here sometimes," I said, "and I'm going to have a small ceremony now, if only to honour the effort of the man who brought this thing back to me."

"Quite right," said Michael. "Quite proper that you should."

Michael was keeping up a calm front, but it was all beyond me by then. Before I spoke I had no sense of wanting to perform any ceremony. I think I said it in order to give Michael his money's worth, but my tongue was getting to be unreliable. I was still living each day under the whim of random impulses, and in order to keep them away I put the heart down and asked Michael about his own farm at home.

"It's sheep, mostly," he said. "It's in England."

"I did gather that it was in England," I told him, "but where? Is it anywhere near Oxford? I lived in Oxford for a while."

"It isn't, actually," he said. "It's up north, in the lake country, you know? It's nothing like your place here, mostly rocky terrain."

Michael was friendly but I wasn't really interested in his farm. My thoughts were still controlled by the lion's heart and by my husband, buried twelve feet away. And since I couldn't think of another thing to ask or to say, I picked the heart up again and began pacing around the perimeter of Jules's grave. My God, I thought, it has been only a week since Jules died, three days since I buried him here, under this heavy blanket of ground, so what am I doing inviting all these strangers to our farm? What am I going to do with this lion's heart, and after that, what am I ever going to do with my own?

As I walked I thought about saying a proper prayer, something memorised when I was a girl, and then flinging the heart off the embankment, down the way the snake had gone. I considered digging it a grave of its own, and it even crossed my mind to take the heart back inside and boil it, slice it thin, and eat it on crackers to give me strength to continue with this charade. But in the end I could come to no decision and I surprised myself by saying so.

"I haven't got a clue what to do with this thing," I let Michael know.

"Well," he said, "was your husband brave?"

"Boy, I'll say. He was a fool in more ways than I can count but he was almost always brave."

Michael smiled. "Did he have a good heart?"

"Yes," I said. "He was brave and he had a good heart, bigger than this one most of the time."

"Well, then, the heart of this lion was good, and of course by definition it was brave," he said, "so maybe you could just draw that parallel and otherwise leave it alone. Let nature take its course, so to speak."

I held the heart up but instead of drawing parallels I found myself saying, "He wasn't very honest, my husband, sometimes. And he had his shallow side."

"Ah, well," said Michael. "His shallow side, yes."

"And he had no idea at all about intimacy. I mean of either the verbal or the emotional kind."

"So far as I can tell, that's pretty much the definition of a man," said Michael. "What was his nationality? What passport did he hold?"

"He was Canadian," I said, "from the English-speaking part."

"Ah, yes," said Michael, "Canadian."

"He had a great knack for physical intimacy," I suddenly added. "I wouldn't want you to think that I was complaining about that."

"No," Michael said. "Verbal intimacy was where he was weak, not the other kind."

"And my God he loved hard work. He loved this farm so much."

This time Michael only nodded. As I looked at him I knew that whatever ceremony I would ever be able to perform was over, and that an Englishman, an absolute stranger, had been its medium, in solitary partnership with my heavy lion's heart.

At the edge of the orchard, a few feet past our campfire site, there was the stump of what had once been a large jacaranda tree. Leaving the lion's heart on the stump was exactly the right thing to do. I knew it because my own heart settled when I put it down.

It was already very nearly dark and I said, "This will be gone before the moon comes up."

"Ah, yes, the animals," he said. "I can't wait to see them come to the pond."

When Michael and I got back to the house, John and Dorothea were still on the porch and Ralph was inside, mixing drinks. I went in to help, but Ralph was finished, and was cleaning up the kitchen before bringing the tray outside.

"Listen," he said. "Maybe we can work something out. I mean make your place a regular stop. These people are ecstatic, Nora. They love it here."

I smiled, then said I was going to stay inside and think about dinner. There was nobody like Beatrice up here, never had been. When the dormitory was full and the harvest was taking everyone's time, we sometimes hired a cook for the workers, but Jules and I cooked for ourselves, and we did our own housework, too. Jules was adamant about it. That was something I could have mentioned at the ceremony. Jules was unusual in that way, always an equal partner where work was concerned.

There wasn't much food in the refrigerator, but we had a pantry full of staples, so I was able to find rice and spices and enough stored vegetables to make a proper curry. The one I knew how to make best originally came from Dr Zir. There was wine in the pantry too, and a little bit of clean linen in the bottom drawer of an old English bureau that I had.

It was just about then, just about the time I was getting the linen out of the drawer, that I noticed it was too dark to work anymore with only the camp lanterns on, so I went back outside and stood behind the others for a while, listening to the quiet comments they made, while they strained to see as far as the pond.

"There are usually giraffes," I said. "Every night recently, right about now."

I stepped off the porch and headed for the dormitory. It had been Kamau's job to start the generator, and in the beginning, during our first half year or so, Jules and I would run to the front window when we heard it burp into life, in order to watch the pond. It had amazed us that the animals, whatever might be drinking there, would never so much as raise their heads when the noise and the lights went on.

As I pulled the generator cord this time, however, I knew that though the animals at the pond might not move, four heads would look up from the four wicker chairs on my porch, and I thought about the nature of composure, the simple act of responding, of living one's life through.

When I started back around the dormitory again everything was as I knew it would be. A dik-dik and a tommy were drinking, noses down, and the four people on the porch were watching me come. A giraffe had walked out of the bush on the far side of the pond and was looking everywhere at once, its high eyes taking in the other animals and the five of us as well.

"It's a glorious place," Dorothea said.

Her husband and brother both agreed with that, and before I went inside to see if the curry was done, we all saw a warthog and a small baboon. It would be a stellar night. And in later days, when I thought back on it, I would be glad that they had had at least that much. For in the morning things changed, and the change, don't you know, was just as Miro had predicted it would be. It was not for the better, not to my advantage at all.

15

The Fire of Our Loins

The dinner was good, and afterward we all stayed outside until midnight, talking some, but mostly watching the animals in silence. Since this time there wasn't enough sleeping space inside the house, Ralph and I got clean sheets from the supply cupboard and made up three of the empty dormitory rooms. These were rooms that hadn't been used by workers for a season or two. They weren't spotlessly clean, perhaps, but I thought that with new linen they might appear that way, at least in the dark, at least for the single night that my guests would use them.

When we finished, Ralph went back to the house to call the others and I stepped into Kamau's room to look at it in light of what I knew had been his fate. I expected, I guess, that the room would give me something more than it had when I went in there before, but it did not. The table was still cluttered with his letters, and the photograph of Kamau's family, though it had moved me in the first place, was merely a photograph now, camera-ready faces, a white backdrop to make their features clear. Kamau had been a careless man, that's what his room said. He hadn't known what he was doing, he didn't know what he had done. I felt worse for Detective Mubia than I did for our foreman—that was my eulogy to Kamau.

When Dorothea and John came into the dormitory I showed them the larger of the rooms we'd prepared. Dorothea seemed exhausted but leaned against her husband in contentment. "What a day," said John.

John's abbreviated mustache appeared softer to me now. He was a veterinarian, of all things, but even as I watched him watching the game coming and going from the pond I found it difficult to imagine him with his sleeves rolled up. He had the physical bearing of a businessman, a stockbroker or a banker, perhaps.

Ralph and Michael were to sleep in two smaller rooms nearer to the front of the dormitory, across the hall from Kamau's. Michael wasn't in his room, but Ralph was in his, and when I knocked he said, "Everything went perfectly. Thanks for the invitation, for the idea of having them stay."

I touched Ralph's sleeve but was too tired to talk anymore, and though I really considered Michael a wonderful man for coaching me so well with the lion's heart, I didn't want to speak with him, either, or find him still sitting in a wicker chair on my porch.

Back in the house I turned the pond light off and moved the dinner dishes from the table back into the kitchen. Michael hadn't been on the porch, nor was he in the house, but before I could find the energy to muster up anything like alarm, I saw him through the window, coming down the path from the orchard in the dark.

I went back outside and said, "It's dangerous to walk around here. This isn't England, you know."

"I had to see whether or not it was gone."

"It was, wasn't it? No trace left on that stump, I'll bet."

"It was there when I arrived," said Michael. "I watched it get taken away."

Michael came closer, not up onto the porch, but to the spot where the weak porch light played on his face a bit more.

"What animal was it?" I asked. "Who took the lion's heart?" I could see now that Michael wasn't composed. His white shorts were dirtied and so was his face.

"You won't believe it but it was a leopard," he said. "I'm sure that's what it was. I was just standing there, looking down into the valley to see what I could see, when it appeared out of the darkness. When I first noticed it, it was already sitting down, staring past the stump and directly into my eyes. It had a white front and a long stiff tail. It sat there watching me for the longest time."

"I know that leopard," I told him. "He killed a Maasai cow last year and some warriors tried to hunt him. It's a lot easier killing a lion."

"This will sound odd," said Michael, "but after a minute or two I lost my fear. I could tell that he wouldn't harm me."

I didn't like such talk. It reminded me of mistakes that Jules and I had made, mistakes that could easily lead to my having a dead tourist on my hands, but I only said, "Imagine having him around when you're trying to run a farm."

Michael went off toward the dormitory then, after saying that in the end the leopard simply lifted the lion's heart off the stump and disappeared back into the night, and when I went inside my house I turned off most of the lights. It was expensive and wasteful to leave the generator on all night long, but because I hadn't provided paraffin lamps for the dormitory rooms, that's what I decided to do.

In my kitchen I couldn't face the mess again, so I made it disappear by turning that light off too. And in Jules's office I shut the drawers and somehow lined up the pens and squared the blotter with the edges of the desk and closed the curtains.

In my bedroom I thought, "Tuesday's over, Tuesday's done," and since these days really did seem like months, I looked at the wall as if I might find a calendar there, something to mark up with Xs, in commemoration of slowly passing time. I was thawing out, I was sure of it. On the only other night since Jules's death that I'd slept in this room I had stayed in the shocked posture of dumb disbelief, like Michael when the leopard came. Now, however, one week after Jules had died, it was me in the bed with all my faculties, and when I pushed my leg over to where it usually found Jules, it was me that let a little cry come out, a little tremor to represent all the misery that was still inside.

What I'm trying to say is that after only a week, the pain was less. May God forgive me and may Julius Grant forgive me too, but the pain, without any question, was less. I could tell, don't you know, because it was beginning to come out

now, and because it hurt so very much more than it ever had
before.

/   /   /

When I awoke in the morning the first thing I noticed was
that the generator was shut down. It was nearly eight, so I
thought that Ralph must have done it, but I knew right away
we'd have to turn it on again if we wanted to get breakfast made. I'd slept well enough and was looking for something fresh to wear. I was sick of those stupid safari clothes
and had just kicked them under the bed when I heard the
sound of our farm lorry starting up. It was an unlikely sound,
since the key was stuck in one of the office drawers, but our
lorry's voice was unmistakable. I dressed quickly and went out
of the room.

"Hello?" I said. "What's going on?"

I was smiling hard, lest any of Ralph's clients think I was irritated that they'd started the lorry without asking, but the
front room was empty and the front door was open wide. And
when I turned to go into the kitchen, there in the doorway,
leaning against the jamb, with my own .380 automatic pistol
loosely held in his hand, was Mr Smith.

"Everything is now out of control," he said. "Everything has
gone too far."

"What have you done with the tourists?" I asked. "You
haven't killed them too, I hope."

It was a stupid thing to say, at the very least rash. If I was
ever going to beat this man I would have to stop acting like
that. Luckily, however, Mr Smith didn't seem to care what I
said. He didn't consider me a formidable opponent, and, so far

as I could tell, he had no idea I knew about Kamau. That much, at least, was still on my side.

"Of course I haven't hurt them," he said. "Our economic future depends on tourists like those." As he spoke he shook his head at my lack of understanding; the lines on his forehead were pronounced.

Mr Smith was dressed in a suit again, like a cool businessman. I remembered feeling some sense before that maybe he was a man I could reason with, but I knew now that that impression was made almost entirely by his English and his clothes.

"I do not want to hurt you or that fool policeman or the wildebeest man either," Mr Smith said. "Under different circumstances you and I might even have become friends."

When he said that, I tried to speak with less hostility in my voice. Miro had been right in telling me to take care, and since all of the physical strength was on his side, all the power, I could take care only by using as my weapons the trickery of language and insinuation and tone. And by trying to play upon his already iron-clad image of a woman's role.

"It has taken me ever so long to piece all this together," I said. "I know you don't believe me, but I knew nothing before. I hadn't the slightest inkling that we were involved in anything but coffee growing."

Even as I spoke I was irritated that though I was now trying to trick him with innocence and guile, what I said was basically the truth. If I hadn't followed Jules that night I wouldn't have known a thing. Maybe Jules was a lot like this man here, maybe all men were. Isn't that what Michael had said the night before?

"Then you had a very old-fashioned marriage," Mr Smith said. "My father told me as much, but I doubted him until now."

The end of my pistol was loose in his hands, tick-tocking around. I thought it represented Mr Smith's disrespect for me as an adversary and his indecision as to what to do next. It turned out, however, that he was only waiting for a signal, and the appearance of our farm lorry just off the porch made him move.

"Let's go outside with the others," he said. "Let's end it all this morning, right now."

I could see when he stepped away from the kitchen door that Mr Smith's other hand held my sisal bag. He'd taken the pistol out of it and he had taken Jules's letter, all of its pages intact. But though he ordered me to, I didn't move toward the front door. Instead I let him get close to me and then I grabbed my bag back fast, snatching it out of his hand.

It was a bold thing to do, but it wasn't stupid, for I needed to see how he would react. The bag came loose from his fingers easily, and for a second I thought he would strike me with the pistol. However, in the end all he did was sigh and point with it, aiming at the door. "Don't do that again," he said. "Do not act that way."

I wouldn't, but I was enlightened by the exchange. If he didn't want to hurt me, if, for example, his father had begun to intervene, warning him not to go too far, then the weapon of words might be mine.

This is what I was thinking as I walked in front of the man, but when we got outside I forgot about it. Ralph and his three guests were standing in the bed of our lorry, and to my great surprise, Detective Mubia was there too. All of them had their hands tied behind their backs, and positioned around the lorry were half a dozen horrible-looking men. These men were poachers in oily black rags, with rifles slung over their arms. Their hair was matted and their eyes were wild and terrifying.

"You don't want to do this," I said, but now my words were so weak, so powerless against what I saw, that I was glad when Mr Smith let them go unanswered. He spoke in Kikuyu, which I don't understand, and the man driving the lorry forced it into gear. We walked behind it over the trampled ground.

"Your husband's letter is excellent," said Mr Smith. "I love the mystery of it, the way it gives you knowledge and makes it necessary for me to have to worry things out."

We were going so directly toward the orchard that I was beginning to fear Mr Smith had already worried it out. He was too expansive, and he clearly smelled victory in the air. We finally stopped, however, in a clearing about halfway between the house and Jules's grave. I had seen immediately that the people on the lorry bed were tied together, Ralph with Dorothea, Michael with John. Only Detective Mubia was tied alone, and he was also the only one who appeared to have been injured thus far. He had a bruise on his left cheekbone and a bit of dried blood under his nose. When Mr Smith saw me looking at him he said, "We found that fool sitting over on the Narok-Nakuru road. Is he your security guard, is that his new job? If so, you should know that he's a poor one. We found him sleeping in his worthless car."

There wasn't any question that Detective Mubia was their fellow captive, but the three tourists and Ralph were staying pretty far away from him. Like healthy wildebeests, they sensed they should distance themselves from wounded prey.

Though he still had his red suit on, the detective's shirt was torn and his tie had somehow been pulled around and thrown over his shoulder so that it hung down his back like a noose that could be pulled tight at any time. He was subdued but he was frightening to look at. His eyes kept darting between his captors and then rolling away.

"Now," said Mr Smith. "I have already spoken with your friends. They have agreed to keep quiet. I told them that if things go well I will soon be letting them go, leaving your land altogether, never to return."

I looked up at the people on the lorry's bed, but there wasn't any contradiction in the faces I saw. John and Dorothea were watching each other, and Michael and Ralph were both looking down. Two of Mr Smith's henchmen had climbed onto the lorry and lit cigarettes. The others were standing very close, making a circle around Mr Smith and me. With the possible exception of Detective Mubia, everyone was dreadfully calm.

"What do you want me to do?" I asked.

"Ah," said Mr Smith. "It embarrasses me to say it, but I want you to read your husband's poem and explain its meaning. After that we will be gone."

"It is a private poem," I said. "It shouldn't be read for others to hear."

Mr Smith nodded as if willing to concede that point, and I suddenly got a small idea, "You read it to me," I said. "You say the words and I will answer questions about them."

There is an oddly prudish strain in Kenyans sometimes, and I guess I spoke because I hoped I might detect it in him. Still, I had no idea what such a strategy would get me, even if he was reluctant to read the poem. My only idea was to take up time, to remain standing there, to have the issue of his property unresolved until a better idea came along.

Mr Smith thumbed through the pages of Jules's letter until he found the poem. After that he spoke Kikuyu again, and immediately one of the men in the lorry cut the ropes that bound Michael with John. Both men began rubbing at the sore spots on their wrists. And just then the poacher who'd cut them loose took a long puff on his cigarette. He shook the ash away and pushed the bright red end of it into Michael's arm.

"Ouch! Christ!" said Michael, and John shouted with him, jumping aside.

Mr Smith tried to pretend that he hadn't ordered the burning; he yelled at the poacher and the poacher threw the cigarette away, and in a second Michael's arms were tied again and the poacher made John jump down. Mr Smith held page six of Jules's letter up in front of John's face. "Read this," he said. "Read it so the lady can refresh her memory and tell me what it means."

John rubbed his wrists some more. He shifted his weight from foot to foot and cleared his throat. We all understood he didn't want to, but in the end there was nothing for him to do but to read the pitiful poem.

> *Under our bed*
> *yes, under hot covers,*
> *where the sweet smell of sex*
> *draws the sharp claws of others.*

"Is he talking about your bedroom?" Mr Smith quietly asked. "Is he talking about passion here? Must I tear your house apart to find what I want?"

If I said yes it would buy us a world of time, but it would also destroy my house, and when he found nothing he would be furious. And since the two poachers on the lorry, at least, wanted to cause us pain, keeping Mr smith engaged was the only hope we had.

"I haven't given it much thought," I told him, "but no, Julius would never hide anything in the house. He was an outside man."

"Where, then?" asked Mr Smith.

I told John to read the poem again while I put on a thinker's pose, as if I were finally paying close enough attention to worry things out. I stood there, chin fisted, my other arm laid across my middle, and said, "Maybe he means the New Stanley Hotel. We used to stay there once in a while. When we were feeling romantic and wanted to get away from the farm. My husband loved the New Stanley Hotel—maybe he means he has left your property there."

But this time I went too far and Mr Smith barked, "I don't care about your mischief, I want my property back! Tell me where it is and stop the rest! I'm not one you should trifle with, Mrs Nora Grant, this is not the good old days. My patience is as thin as that fool detective's ridiculous coat."

John was so frightened by Mr Smith's raised voice that he actually began to read the poem again.

"No need for that," I said. "I know it by heart."

"Do you understand it or do you not?" said Mr Smith. "I am asking for the final time."

"I do not," I said. "I realise that my husband thought he was making it easy for me and difficult for everyone else, but I'm notoriously thick where puzzles are concerned. You can ask anyone."

If we were playing poker I wouldn't last a minute with a strategy of this kind, but I didn't know what other strategy to use. I was lost, and Mr Smith smiled down at me, calling my bluff immediately.

"Very well," he said. He looked at his poachers and this time he spoke in Swahili. "Burn the house," he told them. "We will find my property in the rubble."

"Wait," I said. "There's nothing you want inside."

Mr Smith held up a hand, stopping the poachers, who'd already started to walk away. "If you know that's so, then you know it from your husband's poem. And if you know where my property is not, then you must know where it is, too. That is deductive reasoning. Didn't we both learn that in school?"

"It's outside," I said. "As I have told you, I know it because my husband was an outside man, but I know it also because of the poem's last line, the one about the sharp claws of others. Once when we were sleeping out here we drew the interest of some lions and had a bit of a close call. He must have buried your property, as you call it, at the spot where that event occurred."

"Good," said Mr Smith. "Show me the place. Find it for me and I'll be on my way."

"But you see, my husband was the romantic in the family, not me. It was in his nature to remember such things but it isn't in mine. That's the truth. I do know that it was around here somewhere, but I don't know the exact spot. We slept outside often, but so far as I can recall, we never settled down twice in the same place."

Three of those still remaining in the lorry, Ralph and Dorothea and Michael, seemed to be trying to affect disinterested looks, as if other business was occupying their minds, but Detective Mubia, over the past few minutes, had been taking up a progressively more aggressive pose, getting our attention by staring down at Mr Smith and growling, making a gurgling sound deep in his throat. When Mr Smith noticed it he spoke in Kikuyu again, and in a split second all four of them were pushed out of the lorry, left to land on their feet or not, but without the use of their hands.

"If what you say is true, you will give us the general area and we will look everywhere," said Mr Smith, ignoring the falling bodies and turning back to me. "We will all take shovels and search for places where the ground is no longer hard."

Michael and Detective Mubia came down off the lorry pretty well, feet-first, and rolled away, but because Ralph and Dorothea were still tied together they had no way of turning in the air and therefore landed hard. It wasn't a great distance from the lorry bed to the ground, but Dorothea's right side took the brunt of the fall. She shouted and then turned pale. Ralph was wiggling around to try to get his weight off her.

John and I both ran over to them. "Give me a knife," I yelled. "Quickly! Can't you see she is injured?"

I couldn't see Dorothea's face, but she was so quiet now that I thought she might have passed out.

Mr Smith only stared at us, but when I stood again, he finally did take a knife from his pocket, flipping it my way. "I don't need this," he said. "Cut them all loose."

The ropes were easiest to reach by Ralph's arm, and since the knife was sharp I got the job done in a second or two, but Dorothea didn't move, even when we turned her onto her back.

"Get some water," said John. "Dorothea's pain threshold is low."

"I'm going into the house," I told Mr Smith. "We need to bring this lady around right now."

When Mr Smith nodded I left quickly, got to the house without a guard, and rummaged around in my kitchen. I put cold water in a bottle and took ice from the freezer compartment of my fridge. I got a washcloth from the bathroom, and a bottle of aspirin from above the sink. Before I went back outside I tried to think what weapon I might find, but in the end I only grabbed our first-aid kit and ran. Dorothea was sitting up when I got there. Michael was beside her and John was at her back.

"Her bones are brittle," he told us. "That arm's been broken before."

Maybe that was true, but when I knelt by Dorothea and looked at her arm, it seemed to form a straight-enough line, and there wasn't much swelling. I gave her water and made her take four or five aspirin tablets, and then I found an elastic bandage in the first-aid kit and wrapped the arm, tying it off at her elbow.

"Can you think straight, Dorothea?" I asked. "Do you understand what's going on?"

Mr Smith had surprised me by letting me go into the house alone, surprised me more by waiting patiently since my return, but now he seemed to have had enough. When he spoke to his men in Kikuyu again, three of them pulled Detective Mubia and Ralph and Michael away from Dorothea and John and me, pushing them up toward the orchard.

"Enough of this playing, Mrs Grant," Mr. Smith said. "I

want you to help me right now." Dorothea was standing by then, so John and I supported her as we followed the others.

Until that moment everything I'd thought and everything I'd said, however muddled, had been with the intention of doing what Jules had asked me to do in his letter, namely, to seek a modicum of revenge, to avoid giving the property back. But by the time we reached the edge of the orchard I had pretty much decided to resign the fight. Someone else would surely be injured if I didn't; someone might even be killed. I would simply have to honour my husband's memory later, and in some other way. Michael, however, turned and spoke before I could, surprising us all.

"This is a graveyard," he told Mr Smith. "It's a cemetery. If you dig here you'll find nothing but human bones."

He spoke in a strong, loud, English voice, evoking what he assumed to be a universal respect for the dead, and Mr Smith blinked.

"There are no markers here," he hissed. "British graveyards have markers. They have headstones and fences surrounding the graves."

Michael resolutely pointed at the stump where the lion's heart had sat the night before. There wasn't a trace of it now, no hint of the leaves on which it had rested, not even a blood-stain on the dried-out wood, but Michael forged ahead, keeping his finger pointed out and his voice strong.

"What do you call that?" he asked. It was such a wild and wayward question, such a hopeless ploy, that it caused Mr Smith to pause again. In a minute, though, he stopped looking to any of us for guidance and ordered Michael's hands retied.

"Dig where the ground is soft," he quietly told his men.

Since our farm was big, my first mistake had been letting Mr Smith come in this direction at all. I could have taken him out into the coffee or past the pond in the direction of the Mara plains or down toward the main Narok-Nakuru road. As it was, however, I had told a near truth, and now his horrid men were strewn across the orchard, poking the ground. If they got near Jules's grave, if they started digging him up again, I'd have to stop them, wouldn't I? Isn't that what Jules would have me do, stop the interruption of his eternal sleep at the price of his revenge?

"There is soft dirt over here," said Michael. He had walked away from Jules's grave and was standing near the site of our campfire, pushing at the earth with his heel, hands behind his back.

Michael's gesture was brave, and he had inadvertently moved close to the spot that Jules had mentioned in his poem. All I had to do was nod, all I had to tell them was to dig right there and it would all be over. But just then Detective Mubia took over Michael's job. He twisted free from the poachers who held him, and tried to run away. Mr Smith's men caught him in a minute, and when they brought him back Mr Smith got mad. It seemed to me that Michael had done far more to anger him, but when Detective Mubia defied him, Mr Smith ordered one of his men to light Jules's always-ready fire.

"I've had enough of you," he hissed. "You followed me everywhere, you are my father's spy. Let me hear you say something truthful, let me hear you speak like a man. I'm going to stop asking this woman and find out if you know where my property lies."

Mr Smith had his men push the rest of us down on the

ground and told two of them to walk Detective Mubia closer to the growing fire. "Don't you sometimes use this place for roasting pigs and goats?" he asked me. "Don't you sometimes cook your meals outside?"

Things were getting more serious and the detective made them worse by nearly freeing himself one more time. "Babylon is fallen!" he shouted. "Let its ruler be gone!" Mr Smith's men had been pushing him back, but his words made them loosen their grips. The detective was quick on his feet and for the moment, though one of the poachers had hold of his jacket, he wasn't getting very much closer to the fire.

"Why don't you get a stake?" shouted Michael. "Why don't you get a big boiling pot like in all the old African cartoons?"

Detective Mubia was still struggling, but Michael's question was wild enough to make Mr Smith look up, giving me one last chance to intervene.

"Mr Smith, this is a question between Kenyans," I said. "We shouldn't air our grievances in public, in front of strangers from abroad. Can't we settle this alone?"

That stopped him. His men had just caught Detective Mubia firmly again, but he immediately ordered them to stop marching him toward the fire.

"You think of yourself as Kenyan?" he asked, his voice quiet and containing true surprise. "Are you telling me that we are Kenyans, you and I, and should settle this matter alone?"

Because I had spoken unambiguously I nearly made another flippant remark, but Mr Smith was so incredulous that I stopped myself. Miro had told me there was no sarcasm in the man, that the things he said had no underside. But as I sat there, only nodding, Mr Smith seemed to grow demented before my eyes. He puffed hot breath into the morning and cursed and ran his fingers through his short and dusty hair.

"How dare you tell me that? You are a hybrid, a mongrel combination that has nothing to do with Kenya!" He was shouting now. "You are the daughter of a disgusting English bully, of a mother like these tourists I have scattered around. You are not Kenyan! Never say that again! You are a grotesquerie, not Kenyan at all!"

Mr Smith had pretty calmly put up with all the nonsense of the past half hour, but now he was wild, his mouth trembling and his hands slicing the air. He came over and stood above me, his right fist clenched and his voice breaking in a way that suddenly made me remember playing with him all those years ago. I could see us in front of his father's house, a white child and a black one, eyeing each other and not playing well.

Though he had told them not to, Mr Smith's men held Detective Mubia directly in front of the raging fire. The hot air was licking us all, so I had to be extremely careful now.

"Please let him go," I said quietly. "What you are doing is barbaric."

But once again my words were a bad miscalculation. Mr Smith was still so aghast at my claiming to be Kenyan that his face had taken on an ugly purple hue, and when I spoke this time, he shrieked at me, all restraint gone.

"Barbaric! You are calling me barbaric? I am not barbaric, you are barbaric! Barbaric is your very family name!"

His screaming was blood in the water, exciting his shark-like men. One of them pulled a *panga* from his belt and another picked up a stone. I believed they would kill us, and all of my efforts, everything I'd chosen to do or say, seemed to bring them closer to it. Miro had been right again. I thought I had a foot in both worlds, but I didn't have a foot anywhere.

"If you let us go, we will all look for soft ground. No more talk," I said. "We'll find what you want and then you can take it away. I promise I won't interfere. I resign from my position as your opponent. I declare that I have lost."

Mr Smith came up to me, arms above his head. I thought he would slap me out of my reasonable pose, but just then thick smoke sprang up from the backs of Detective Mubia's legs. The two men holding him had acted on Mr Smith's anger, not his words, and pushed the detective right up next to the fire.

I knew I couldn't speak again, that whatever happened next would be Mr Smith's call. My eyes were on the detective and behind him I saw Ralph and the others, frozen in this moment too, and I could also see, as clearly as if he were there, my own young father's arms raised. His image had replaced Mr Smith's above me and he was about to strike me down.

Detective Mubia didn't scream, even when his smoking trouser legs burst into flame. He would have died without speaking, I was sure, but Mr Smith told his men to let him go. As soon as his hands were free the detective leapt away, un-buckled his belt, and let his burning trousers fall to the ground. Ralph ran over to swat the flames. Smoke was everywhere, and the detective's thin legs were covered with white blisters.

In the first-aid kit there was burn cream, but when I made a move for it, Mr Smith stopped me. "No," he said. His calm voice was back, but when he took hold of my wrist and told me to stand, that image of my father returned, arms still raised high. I was a little girl and watching now, no longer the victim of his blows. This was what I had almost seen, almost allowed myself to remember, a few days earlier, when leaving Mr Smith's father, when going down the stairs of that nightclub.

"We were in a hallway," I said. "We were not at your father's place at all."

For a second Mr Smith didn't know what I was talking about but then he did, and as he let go of my wrists, the image of my father went out of my mind.

"Yes," he said, "that's right."

Mr Smith was staring at me intently, and I believed I could see a less hostile expression in his eyes, a human element slowly appearing. Dear God, I remembered it now, how could I ever have forgotten? There had been a terrible argument, my father and Mr Smith's father yelling and standing near the top of a flight of stairs. I could see the bannister along the landing, with its thickly painted yellow rungs, and I could see the triangular shadows formed by a partially opened door at the bottom of the stairs.

"We were in that building on Market Street, outside of my father's office," I said. "Isn't that right?"

"It was 1956," whispered Mr Smith. "I was just a child."

I could see it all. Mr N'chele had come to complain about my father's recently published book, *Elephants of Tsavo and Other Lands*, about my father's contention that all of the poachers in Kenya were Kikuyu. Mr N'chele called the book offensive and stupid and wrong—I could hear the words colliding in my head—and my father went berserk. He stopped shouting and raised his hand like an angry god and slapped Mr N'chele hard across the face, knocking him halfway down the stairs. I remember trying to believe only that Mr N'chele was doing cartwheels, but in my sudden flash of memory I saw the son now too, skirting around my father and flying down the stairs. He took my father's book and tried to tear it, screaming at us as he did so.

As I looked at him I understood that Mr Smith was seeing everything I was, but from a vastly different point of view. I had suppressed the incident, I'm ashamed to say, while he had relived it countless times, screaming at us, and plotting, through all these many years.

The others seemed frozen in various poses, a catatonic and surreal array. Ralph had somehow got the burn salve from the first-aid kit; he had it in his hands, and was crouched with everyone else, down around the detective, all of them looking at Mr Smith and me. Mr Smith's main henchman still had his *panga* out and was standing over them all, lips wet, arms waiting for the order to slice Detective Mubia's life away. I think it would have happened if I hadn't remembered that scene so well, but now Mr Smith's anger was deflated, and when he told them to, his men left the detective alone. They took up their shovels and began poking haphazardly, walking about again, looking for soft ground.

How long would I act the emissary, the fulfiller of my husband's last wish, the settler of scores, in the face of what I'd just remembered but should not have allowed myself to forget since the day it occurred? Could I not end it now, as I'd said I would before, by giving this hopeless man whatever he was trying to find? He hadn't intended to kill my husband but to exact revenge upon my dad. My husband's involvement had come through an invitation from his father-in-law, that was all, his death from the accidental configurations of a vile and fateful day. In modern parlance, in the West, at least, Mr Smith was a victim too, scorched by a childhood gone wrong.

The ground was softest where Jules was buried, and when the men got near that spot, a dozen feet to the east of the fire, I had to interrupt my newfound notions, keep the conciliatory thoughts I was having at bay. They had started digging in the hole I'd dug for Jules's arm, but they were quickly moving toward Jules himself, and that spot was off-limits. No matter what the past had done to Mr Smith or me, the rules of our engagement would have to allow that this one small rectangle be out of bounds.

"My husband's buried there. His bones aren't ivory," I warned, "and the expression on his face will frighten everyone."

I was sure those words would stop him, and if they had, I would have given everything up, I swear it, and kept my promise by finally telling him what he wanted to know. But in the short few seconds that my thoughts had run his way, Mr Smith's face had grown stony once more, that human element I had seen reburied under his own soft ground. He looked at me and laughed and told his men to dig where I had just said they should not.

My father did a horrible thing, I knew it now. Not only had he slapped a man down a flight of stairs in front of his child, but he had lived and worked dishonourably during his whole career. Though he'd been a good father in many ways, he had been a bad public man, neither ministering to the country's wildlife well nor calming the awful wild life within him. I knew it was true, but I also knew, from his wicked face and his laugh just now, that Mr Smith was a worse man than my dad. Detective Mubia had been right in calling him evil, for where my father was weak and arrogant, a racialist bully no doubt, Mr Smith was a man who had allowed the gift of perfect outrage to turn him perfectly wrong.

But whatever I thought, whatever knowledge I had gained, I knew also that if I didn't stop it, this horrible cycle would never end. Jules had wanted to get even with Mr Smith because Mr Smith had tricked him, and Mr Smith had tricked him in order to get even with my father. Jules was dead, and my dad was unreachable, though he was alive. It was in my power to end it, and I wanted to do it now, but Mr Smith wasn't letting me. In fact he was making me want to seek my own revenge, by daring to dig up my husband's grave, by never letting up, by going way too far.

"Very well," I finally said. "I didn't think I'd be seeing him again so soon." I stepped back over by the others, over by the bluff that led down to the valley below. Detective Mubia lay muttering, mad as Macbeth, on the troubled ground.

Since Mr Smith wasn't listening, I guess I hoped my words would stop his men, but these poachers, these grave robbers or whatever they should be called by now, didn't seem to have any idea that what they'd find at the end of their digging was a wooden box with my husband inside. They dug him up quickly, and before long we could hear the first taps on the top of the coffin.

"That's Julius Grant," I said. "I hope he doesn't tap back."

Maybe Mr Smith truly thought that the box contained some of his missing contraband. When his men pulled it out of its hole, however, he didn't suggest that they take the lid off.

"We can't dig everywhere," he said. "You have a big farm. And what I have here is your husband, you say?"

"It's his body, anyway," I whispered. "Shall I open it for

you? Shall I show you the face of the man who has suffered most?"

Mr Smith looked at me for a long time but finally said, "No, we have just agreed that your farm is large. I will keep this box and let you find my property alone."

After that he spoke Kikuyu, but I knew he was telling his men to carry Jules's coffin away.

"We have our own transport down the road," he said. "You will find your lorry parked there. I suggest you use it to bring my goods back to town."

Dorothea tried to protest, but the rest of us just stood there speechless as we watched Jules's coffin moving on the shoulders of the rotten pallbearers.

"By the week's end," Mr Smith said.

Five of the poachers got onto the back of the lorry with the coffin and the sixth man got into the cab. Mr Smith was about to join him, my automatic pistol still tucked in his belt, when he paused for a second, staring over at us. He told two of the men to pick up Detective Mubia, to put the poor detective in the back of the lorry as well.

"You will have enough to do," he said. "Let me take care of your garbage. I will dump it in town."

When the engine started and the lorry began to move away, John took a couple of steps, but Dorothea got hold of his shirt, keeping him back with her one good arm.

"Let's go inside," I said. "It's over now. We can wash up. We can tend to Dorothea's arm and take a look at Michael's, too."

Michael had forgotten the cigarette burn but my comment made him look at it and say, "That poor charred man."

When we got inside the house Ralph went straight to the radio in Jules's office. He wanted to call the police station in Narok, but I told him not to. Dorothea was sitting on my living-room couch and Michael was next to her with the first-aid kit in his hand. John was pacing the porch, looking off toward the pond. When Ralph came out of the office, he called John back inside. "You will get a full refund," he told them all. "And my services for as long as you are here. Am I correct in assuming that you want to go back to Nairobi tonight?"

Dorothea's arm was sore, but it wasn't seriously injured after all, and Michael said he hadn't come to Africa merely to turn around and go home. John said what he really wanted to do was get a gun and follow the lorry down the road. I tried to give a speech then, to tell them how terrible I felt about everything, about Michael's burn and Dorothea's arm, about ruining their holiday and almost getting them killed. As I stood there watching them reinvest themselves, however, regaining a part of their original spirit, I regained some of my own original spirit as well. I, too, wanted to get a gun. I, too, would follow my lorry down the road. "God damn you, Mr Smith," I said. "God damn you to hell." And it was only when I glanced at the others that I realised that for once at least I hadn't spoken out loud.

/   /   /

Ralph's van had an opening in the roof for the easy viewing of animals, and Dorothea and John were already standing in it later that day, when I went outside to say good-bye.

"Honk if you see my lorry," I told Ralph.

They left quickly—John and Dorothea sat down almost

immediately and the top closed. I listened to the departing van and waited for the sound of its horn. Dust had risen up around the pond and then settled, and when the noise of their motor disappeared, the farm was quiet and I was alone.

I was exhausted and filthy and worried about what Detective Mubia's fate might be, so it surprised me greatly to notice that it felt good to be by myself again. It was the end of labour. It felt something like it did when the harvest was done and the workers were paid, something like it did when Julius Grant had found some excuse and gone, one more time, taking the lorry to town.

16

Myself, Alone

I was inside my house for what seemed a long time before I heard Ralph's horn telling me that there was some kind of honour among thieves, that Mr Smith had really left my farm lorry where he said he would. I cleared the table and washed and put away the cups and plates, and then I started the generator and hoovered everywhere throughout the house, pulling a lost pair of Jules's socks from behind the sofa in our office and finding a favourite old jumper of his stuffed between the mattress and box springs of the bed in our room. I started out slowly, since I intended to do only a light cleaning, but soon I altered my intentions, going several times to the storage shed for mops and buckets and a stiff-bristled brush. I moved the furniture from the living room to the verandah and when the floor was washed and shining I moved everything back inside again.

When our bedroom was as clean as the room in the front I took two suitcases from the cupboard in the spare room and packed Jules's clothing into them, leaving only his recently found jumper on the top of the bed. I locked the suitcases, carried them out to the dormitory, and threw them into one of the empty rooms. After that I took the occasional chairs from my verandah and scrubbed the whitewashed boards. I refilled my bucket and washed all of the windows of my house, both inside and out, noticing as I did so that the sun was going, that most of the day was gone.

After everything but my body was as clean as I could make it, I got into our shower and washed myself too, and before I dried and dressed again I washed the bathroom walls and polished the fixtures until their dullness disappeared. There is such peace in mindlessness, in the unthoughtful passage of time. I had worked for half a dozen hours before the sun went down.

I was in my living room and wearing a clean pair of trousers, with Jules's old jumper on over them and that little tusk of mine in my hand. I sat down on the freshly aired sofa and put the tusk on the table and looked at it from the distance of three feet or so. Here was the crux of the matter, the symbol of all that was at hand.

"Should I dig up your brothers and sisters?" I said aloud.

The sound of my voice in the room was startling. When last I'd spoken, it was in farewell to that stunned quartet, and ever since then, all during my marathon cleaning, the intrusion of words would not have been welcome. The moment after I spoke I felt as if something had moved in the house.

"Who's there?" I asked, but, of course, there was no one. I was alone on my farm, just as I was alone in the world at large, with others passing through my life to visit, but with no one staying long. This, I understood, was practise for the years to come.

I stood and carried the tusk along with me as I locked the windows I'd cleaned, but when I got to the front door, though my intention was to lock it too, I somehow opened it and stepped outside, reaching back in to turn the generator off. Now I was in a natural darkness as complete as any human being had ever known. The stars were out and there was a moon, which looked at me through a squinting eye, but there was no artificial light, nothing from Narok and nothing from the house, and there was no lit fire anymore, by which I could sit to stir the memories of what this day had brought me or of what my earlier life had been.

I walked out to the mid-point between the house and the pond, thinking of the false nature not of man-made light anymore but of humans in the natural world. Suddenly I took Jules's jumper off, and then the rest of my clothes. I was the same colour as the moonlight, milky on the dark path, and since I was still holding the tusk in my hand, I raised it up and turned it until its shape conformed to that of the moon. It seemed a perfect fit, as if this man-made tusk could fill the hole in the sky, and I thought that if only I were tall enough and could place it there, then artifice would triumph and every-thing would turn truly dark and I would die.

When I put my arm back down and came to my normal senses once again, I looked toward the pond and was aston-ished to see a female elephant there. She was on the pond's far side and must have been there all along, since I hadn't heard her come. I must have been an odd vision, unclothed and glowing in my moonlit skin, for when the elephant saw my eyes her pinned-back ears came forward again, like kites dancing out, and then her hind legs bent and she turned on them, lunging into the bush behind her, crashing through the underbrush like a runaway lorry off a road. She'd run as soon as I'd noticed her—wasn't that strange? Was this the fear of a grieving mother at the sight of a grieving wife?

The surprise of seeing the elephant made me drop the little tusk, so I fell to my knees as soon as she was gone, oddly worried that I mightn't be able to find it again. And once I felt the coolness of the ground I stayed there for a while. I had a vision of the elephant before me, her living tusks dancing in the distance like two white Maasai gourds or like the moon unblocked of its ivory plug. I found the tusk beside me and held it tight, and then I let all my muscles go, stretching out, staring up, and feeling the earth beneath me, heavy and solid and wide. I will stay the whole night through, I thought, with only this unsharp tusk to protect me should trouble come my way. I thought of my father for a minute but chased him from my mind. I thought of Jules in his coffin on the back of that lorry with Detective Mubia's burned body by his side. I listened for the leaving elephant, but her sound was long gone, and when I looked at the sky, a dark cloud had covered the little moon, as if to protect it from any more meddling by me.

I was alone on the surface of the planet, the masthead of my ship, pushing into unchartered space. Suddenly I seemed to know that this was how Jules had felt too. Superimposed on my body I could feel his own, complete with its shredded arm and its wide-open, bullet-torn wound. I could see the land around me and the pond and the house and the dormitory, and I felt my body move and I knew that this was the agonised way in which Jules had moved only ten short nights before. I was at the exact spot where Jules had fallen, I knew it now, and the moon was as dark now as it was then, and I was as free of pain as Jules had been and as ambivalent about whether or not to go on. I could see it all, whether in my mind's eye or from the elevated height at which my husband still hovered, I do not know, but I was Jules on the ground with the little elephant's tusk suddenly stuck between my legs to prove it, not burrowing in this time but standing up tall like the carved phallus on a primitive doll. I could see that my breasts were flattened and that the light from a re-emerging moon made the muscles of my arms and legs look wrong, moving me manward and back again like an optical illusion, a creature designed through cataracts on the eyes of God.

The moment was strong and I gave in to it, unafraid and sure that from all this misery I was finally learning a universal truth of some kind, when abruptly I was just as sure that Jules had fled and the devil had come. Where before the breeze had cleansed me, now it was thick with the choking smell of feces and urine and burning flesh. It was as if I'd been captured by the evil in the night because I had not been watching for it, as if a blanket of hot and rancid air had been thrown over me to keep me warm.

I grabbed the tusk from its resting place and leapt to my feet and shouted "No!" And when I thrust the tusk at the devil's horrid head I so startled him that he jumped away, fell on his haunches, and twisted around, as the elephant had, to run. This devil had thought I was dead and was there to retrieve my soul. This devil was a big hyena, alert and hungry, come to sniff me out.

I snatched up the clothes I had worn and hurried back to the house, since the hyena's retreat might only be momentary. I closed the door and locked it and put my back to it and then I turned and pulled the shade down too. From the front room window, where I crouched and peeked, I could see the hyena again, standing where I had been, smelling the ground and laughing like Mr Smith, and looking at the house.

While the hyena was out there I didn't want to move, and the hyena was out there for a good long time. My eyes were near the bottom of the window, peering over the top of the sill, and then they were down a little, surfacing occasionally periscope style, and then they were watching the ceiling, for I was lying down, safe this time, across my spotless wooden floor. When the hyena left, probably because he'd forgotten why he'd come, I didn't know it, and it wasn't until I heard a knocking on the shaded front door that I knew anything at all. It was morning and when I looked out, naked but rested in my immaculate home, I found Ralph standing there.

Whatever had happened the night before, whether I had encountered my husband or only hallucinated my way into a nearly deadly meeting with a hungry animal, it was all gone now. Only ordinary worries were reflected in Ralph's glassy face and harried eyes.

"I've been cleaning here," I said. "Give us a moment and I'll let you in."

Ralph didn't move away from the window, so I did, slipping quickly into the same clothing I had worn the night before. And when I opened the door I told him to take off his shoes.

There was no dirt on Ralph's feet but he did as I asked and while he was doing it I stepped briefly onto the verandah again, to make sure that the hyena wasn't still hiding nearby. He wasn't, but my knickers were there, folded neatly on the top of a chair. Ralph saw me see them and shrugged.

"I was worried about you," he told me. "I walked over from the main Narok-Nakuru road. Those things came tumbling up to meet me when I entered your yard."

Ralph said the Cooleys had urged him to come back, so he'd asked a friend, a Cottar's Camp man, to drive his van for him, taking them on the rest of their safari and then bringing them back to Nairobi when it was done. He also said he saw Detective Mubia's station wagon, still on the Narok-Nakuru road, but a hollowed-out shell, burned far worse than his legs had been.

Ralph wanted me to be glad he was there, he wanted me to see ordinary human concern in his presence, and in the insistence of Dorothea and Michael and John that he come. I saw it, but it couldn't make me glad, and strangely, instead of turning me friendly, Ralph's presence turned me inward again. It made me remember Mr Smith and it re-engaged me in the puzzle of defeating him, of evening the score one last time. There were murderers and grave robbers in my world, yet civilised human beings wanted me to tell them I was fine. I was not fine. And, in a word, Ralph's kindness and the kindness of strangers on whom I would never lay eyes again continued to make me mad.

17

Baby Ahmed

I asked Ralph to go into the dormitory room where Jules's clothing was stored, and when he came back out he was dressed for work. I tried to tell him that there was a solitary aspect to what I was about to do, that I needed him and was glad he was there, but that I wanted, one final time, to do the actual digging alone. Don't ask me why I felt that way, but it seemed imperative, the only thing to do. Like Detective Mubia before him, Ralph said that he would assist me. He would pull the charred logs of the fire away and keep my workplace clear.

In Jules's office there was one more rifle standing behind the door. It was single-shot, not much good, but I feared that Mr Smith might have left men behind to watch me, to spirit his goods away once I dug them up, and as ghoulish as Mr Smith himself could be, I didn't relish facing any of those men without him there to temper their moods.

"If anyone comes, shoot him," I told Ralph, and Ralph nodded, taking the rifle and filling his pockets with shells. He then walked to the end of the lane, drove my farm lorry back into the yard, and followed me in it, across the increasingly busy ground.

Parts of the fire were still warm, so Ralph set the rifle down against the lone peach tree that gave our orchard its name, and used a shovel to spread the fire out. As I watched him I thought of Detective Mubia's legs, his own charred logs. Would he be able to walk on them when Mr Smith let him go? Would Mr Smith let him go at all?

When the logs were gone I dug under the fire, moving big shovelfuls of soil and sand away. Compared with the work of digging Jules's grave, this was easy. In ten minutes I was a foot down, and in ten more the tip of my shovel hit something wooden, making the same dull sound that the poachers' shovels had made. I'd intended to do a disrespectful, careless job, smashing the box open and yanking the contraband out, but as soon as I hit its top I knew I couldn't do that, because the wood felt thick and the shovel's blade was small. And though Jules had been satisfied with burying the contraband in a shallow grave, the box was far longer than the one he was in, so once I got to it I had to expand my digging, to perform a careful excavation for another long time.

I didn't have my watch on, but as the sun reached its apex Ralph found a tarpaulin and belts in the storage shed, and by attaching the belts to the lorry's hydraulic hoisting arm we were finally able to pull this second coffin out from under the blanket of ground. It was a monstrous kind of stillbirth—a box four feet wide and ten feet long, and of superior material and better craftsmanship than the one my husband occupied. It surfaced like a whale, clean and grey, leaving the dirt behind as if it were water. Seeing it made me pause, wretched in my soiled clothes. I told Ralph I wanted to get washed before opening the box, and when I went in the house again he stayed where he was, rifle loaded, and looked around.

Nothing was changed inside my house, no dust had settled on the surfaces of my tables and chairs. Even in our bedroom, where I went to take Jules's now-filthy jumper off, everything was so clean that there was nowhere I thought I could put dirty clothing. I was a Kenyan farming woman, so what was this new penchant, this desire I recently had for keeping everything so spotlessly clean? I didn't know, but as I took my dirty clothes into the bathroom with me, put them on the floor of the shower stall, and kneaded them with my feet, watching the water turn brown, I found myself thinking of next scrubbing the Land Rover.

Once I was dressed again, this time in a flowered skirt and white jersey, favourites of Jules's, I took the sodden clothing from the shower floor and ran out of the house with it, and around the side to the line. And when I went back to the orchard I at first got worried, because Ralph was gone. He wasn't at his post at the edge of the hill, and he wasn't leaning against the peach tree. But just before I began to shout I heard Ralph's voice, calling to me from the other side of the bluff, from over the edge of the hill.

"Nora," he said. "Come down here, please. My God."

Ralph's voice was strained, but it didn't have the urgency that his words seemed to call for, so though I went to the edge of the bluff, I went slowly, with no sense of purpose in my stride.

"What is it, Ralph?" I called.

"Nora, come down here," he said again.

Had he been standing, I would have been able to read his face, but Ralph was crouched behind a stubby bush, examining something on the ground.

"I've brought a better tool," I shouted, holding up the crowbar I had taken from the shed. "I am ready to go on."

Maybe I sounded a little short, but I didn't care. I had my own schedule to follow, a big enough job to do without getting involved in whatever Ralph was up to. Ralph, however, stood up just then, letting me see him over the squat tree. "You need to come down here now," he told me. He was only about twenty feet away, so I could see that his face was gaunt, its patience and calmness gone.

"What is it?" I asked. "Was there a kill last night?" Ralph was more experienced than I in such things. I expected a dead animal—considering his gravity, perhaps a cat, our resident leopard, choked on a lion's heart. What he had found, however, was nothing of the kind. Rather it was something long and thin and barren and alone. It was Julius Grant's left hand and arm, devoid of its flesh but still together, and with its wedding ring on.

"What an evil man he is!" Ralph hissed. "He has opened the coffin and left this here for you to find. Something barbaric to remember him by."

Ralph believed that this crime could only have been

committed by Mr Smith, so I didn't correct him. I don't think I
ever thought that the snake had eaten Jules's arm, since I knew
that pythons liked living things, but as I stared at it, at my husband's humerus and the two twisting bones of his forearm, at
the intricate carpals of his wrist and the no-longer-fat fingers
of his hand, I began to realise how saturated my mind had been
with images of that arm departing, of that wriggling Christian
symbol, of the horrible thing I'd done. It had been my own
greatest sin, casting that arm away, and now our farm was giving it back to me, clean as the coffin full of contraband. I'd seen
dozens of kills and hundreds of kill sites, but I don't remember
ever seeing one where the bones were left attached. Yet here
was the missing part of my husband, with not even a finger
gone. Despite all else that had happened, so far as I was concerned this was singular evidence of order and wonder in the
world. I bent down and touched the arm, and then I picked it
up. And though the wedding ring now had a hugely unnecessary circumference, it got hung up on a knuckle bone and
stayed on.

"An animal must have eaten what was left of his flesh, " I
said, "something small and solitary, without others to feed."

"What will you do with it?" Ralph asked. "Where are you
taking it now?"

I was moving carefully and didn't want to speak. The arm
had been returned to me whole, but I wasn't at all confident it
would stay that way, so I only whispered, "Please, Ralph, go
into the house. Find something to put it in. Hurry."

Ralph left right away, visibly glad to have a practical job to
do, and when I got to the excavated box I sat down on it, laying Jules's arm across the folds of my skirt. His humerus was up
against my right hip bone, the back of his hand resting on my

left knee, his fingers curled toward the sky. I could hear Ralph looking through the house and I wanted to call out where the empty boxes were, but I feared if I did so, all of Jules's bones would fall from my lap, detaching themselves and landing with such randomness that I'd never be able to put them back together again. Finding Jules's arm had been shocking, but I hadn't been fearful when picking it up. Now, however, it was impossibly difficult to touch that wedding ring, to unhook it from the knuckle where it still was wedged.

"I am your wife, Julius," I said out loud. "Should I leave that ring with you or take it as my own?"

The nearby birds seemed to stop singing when I spoke, and when next I looked down at the arm in my lap I saw that my right hand was reaching over and taking the wedding ring away, with no fanfare and no decisive thought. I put the ring on my own ring finger, where it surrounded my own wedding ring and settled down.

Ralph took a long time, but when he finally came back he had a wooden box with him, a well-made affair that had once held four bottles of good French wine and still had the coat of arms of the winery embossed on its side. The wine had been a gift from Jules on our first wedding anniversary, but because we'd been immersed in the work of the farm at the time we had put the wine away and hadn't remembered it until our first orchard fire, when first we worried the animals with our outlandish ways. The box was perfect. It contained the original straw that had padded the wine, and it was wide enough and long enough to contain my husband's arm.

Ralph saw the arm across my lap. He saw the transferred ring and said, "I am sorry I took so long."

The box was nailed shut, but its lid came off easily under

the even pressure of Ralph's hands. And when he held it out to
me I lifted Jules's fingers from my knee, moving the whole
thing to the waiting straw. It was a grand feeling, like lifting a
scar from my soul, but all I could think to say was "Now at
least I'll have something to display at his wake on Saturday.
When our friends and neighbours come, now they can pay
tribute to his arm."

After the box was closed I apologised to Ralph for my self-
absorption. "Will you continue helping me?" I asked. "Will you
take the crowbar and force the lid off this larger box as well?"

Ralph said he was glad to have work to do, so I got up and
put the small box, the only true coffin left in my domain, over
on a bit of clean ground. I think I expected a long moment of
exertion, as the lid to the contraband box tried to keep itself
down, but in fact this lid behaved much like the one on the
wine box. Its nails screeched a moment; then they gave way
with so little work that I imagined Ralph could have opened it,
also, with his hands. As soon as the lid was loose Ralph let it
fall to the other side, down into the hole from which it came.

What I expected was dozens of tusks, a cornucopia, an obscene array, but what I got was harder to deal with than Jules's
arm had been. There were just two tusks in the box, longer
than the bed of my lorry, old and scarred and impossibly
grand, with the circumference, at their thickest spot, of a
young elephant's leg. These were the largest and most glorious
tusks I had ever seen. They were unmatchable, the tusks of a
lifetime, and my first thought, once I could think at all, was
that there was nothing in the box to pad them, no straw, as in
the wine box, and no proper velvet cushions to signify their
beauty and their worth.

I leaned against the box but for the longest time I couldn't make myself understand. I tried to remember Jules's letter, which Mr Smith had taken away. In the letter Jules said that what he wanted to do was hurt the man who had most hurt him, and if these tusks belonged to Mr Smith, then he had certainly done that, though in Mr Smith's father's kitchen I had seen fourscore smaller tusks with my own sharp eyes.

I put my hand inside the box and touched the tusk nearest me, and finally I saw that these giant wonders had not been buried alone. Sitting between the tusks, in the oval enclosure made by their natural bend, was the skeletal construction of a small and perfect elephant, a model eight inches high. It was like something one might use in an anatomy class or an expensive gift that a wealthy parent might buy for her child, and it had a single tusk coming out of the right side of its small skull. The tiny elephant's tusk was the same colour as the two mammoth ones that surrounded it, with identical markings that made it look old, and as I looked at it I felt my heart go upside-down. In the left pocket of my skirt my hand touched the missing piece that would make the puzzle whole, my talisman all these days, the crutch I'd leaned upon in such a wide variety of ways.

"These are Ahmed's tusks," I said.

I walked around to the far side of the box and took my own tusk from its warm and lonely bed. There was a cavity in the left side of the tiny elephant's skull, and when I pushed my own tusk into it, the fit was fine, with no resistance and no room to spare. It was like putting a key into a lock, I suppose, for as I placed it there, another door opened inside me and understanding finally flooded in. Mr Smith had stolen Ahmed's tusks and replaced them with acrylic models he had made, that had been his intention all along. It was the theft of a lifetime, a grand and dazzling plan, but Detective Mubia had found out about it and immediately told his dad—that was the detective's second job, after all. And just when Mr N'chele's outrage was at its height, just when he'd demanded that his son return the tusks or he himself would go to the law, Jules had stolen them. It was an unproven deduction, perhaps, but I knew in my bones that I was right.

I don't know how long I stood there, but even when I heard the lorry engine cough and realised that Ralph was bringing it a few feet closer, I couldn't take my eyes away. My own tusk seemed happy now, absurd as that may sound, and I noticed that the chipped side of its tip, that flattened part that had worked for me so well, was mirrored perfectly by the huge tusk that rested at my side.

Ralph got out of the lorry and fixed the hoisting arm in place and dropped the lorry's rear gate. And when he got to the box, when he looked in and once again saw the off-white expanse and the decades' worth of scars, his face grew soft.

"How beautiful they are," he said. "How great he must have been when he was alive."

"Do they look real to you, Ralph?" I asked. "Do they look manufactured at all?"

"Oh, they are real," he said. "Can you imagine the strength it must have taken to carry them around? These are teeth, Nora, do you understand that? Incisors on the rampage, that's what they are. Ahmed was Africa's glory, Africa's past retold."

"Let's load them as they are," I said, "box and all. Let's put them on the lorry and take them back to town."

It was nearly two o'clock when I said that and by the time the work was done it was four. Ralph and I didn't speak again as I locked up the house and fixed things around the farm. We didn't speak until after we had passed through Narok, until after we had stopped at the petrol station to hire some more guards, until we were on the road again and noticed that there was trouble ahead, that there was a police vehicle waving at everyone and telling them to pull over to the side. This wasn't a tactic of Mr Smith's, as I feared at first, but a bad accident. It was a surprise, therefore, and a small pleasure to realise that when the policemen saw us they waved us through. They removed their hats and were quiet, taking a moment to ignore those dying around them, in order to salute in honour of someone who had died before.

18

Tusker Premium

The National Museum, where Miro's father worked as an assistant curator, had been closed for the past two months, but there were always long queues at the ticket windows. Ahmed the Elephant had recently died and the people interested in buying tickets to see his tusks and skeletal remains were legion. Schoolchildren would be coming by the busload, office workers in Nairobi would be given time off, and village leaders from as far away as Lake Victoria wrote, asking whether entrance fees could be waived for the children of the poor. All this was in anticipation of the exhibition's opening, which was still a few days away.

Without question the most remarkable public event of the year was the death of Ahmed, who'd been under twenty-four-hour guard during the entire first half of the decade. The guards had been posted by presidential decree as a protection against poachers, a situation that allowed Ahmed to die of natural causes—at a game reserve in Marsabit, way up north—but that greatly restricted his freedom and his movement. If Ahmed's tusks were Africa's glory, as Ralph had said, then there was irony in the last four years of Ahmed's life. He had been a prisoner of his own grandeur and his age, just like the continent. And a second irony was that although his life had been protected, people weren't prepared for his death. Ahmed's carcass was left in the sun too long, and when he was finally brought to a taxidermist in Nairobi he was peppered with scavenger bites, and the initial stages of rot had set in. His hide was beyond saving but the taxidermist prepared him for exhibit anyway, building a skeletal elephant ten feet high, with his stunning tusks swooping toward the ground. It was an exhibit that Jules and I had looked forward to. We read about it in the papers and told each other that once the crowds died down we'd go.

And now, as Ralph and I worked our way into Nairobi after dark, I understood that we had seen a part of the exhibition without paying our fees. Mr Smith must have broken into the taxidermist's and switched the tusks, and that, of course, meant that what Ahmed himself now wore, what the schoolchildren and lunchtime visitors and village elders would soon line up to see, were Mr Smith's acrylic replicas, the coup of his entire criminal life, his extraordinary and mammoth duplicity.

To steal Ahmed's tusks was everything to Mr Smith, I saw that now. He didn't care about making smaller tusks or fooling the tusk-buying world—that had been a product of the chance he'd seen to punish my dad. Those were prototypes, the tusks Jules and my father had been shown, and my little tusk, the one I'd been transferring from pocket to belt, my little phallic partner during this endless week and a half, was the smallest one. It was an almost perfect plan. The value of Ahmed's authentic tusks, to an Arab king or among rich North Americans or Japanese, was incalculable, for they were the purest representation of the capitalist collector's rallying call: one of a kind. They were the largest and most famous elephant tusks in the world, and they had taken sixty-five years to grow.

How furious Jules must have been when he discovered the truth, how he must have raged! Now that I understood the enormity and sophistication of Mr Smith's plan, now that I could believe completely in Jules's surprise, I could also finally believe what he said in his letter, that he hadn't told me because he'd been embarrassed beyond speech of any kind, able to focus only on the idea of turning things around. And the real truth must have come to him very late, at just about the time I saw him in Mr N'chele's kitchen that night.

I guess I felt some relief at knowing everything, but what should I do now? What could I do with Ahmed's actual tusks, and how was I to deal Mr Smith a final blow?

/   /   /

I offered to drop Ralph at his office, but he said he'd see me safely home. And on impulse, when I got to Dr Zir's gate, I turned in there. Who knew, Mr Smith might be in my father's drive right now, waiting to hijack my leverage away.

Dr Zir's lights were on but he didn't open the door when I sounded my horn, so I knew that my father was there with him, that chess had prevented Dr Zir's hospitable nature from bringing him outside. Dr Zir's dogs greeted us, barking and jumping up as we got out of the lorry, but Ralph had the wine

box in his hands, and when the two dogs sniffed it they immediately settled down.

"My father's house is up there," I told Ralph. "It's a brief
walk through the valley, a short drive up the road."

When we got to Dr Zir's door I said, "Open it." I was
speaking under my breath, to a vision of the slow-moving doctor inside, but Ralph thought I was talking to him and reached
for the latch, stepping back again as the door swung wide. Dr
Zir's house was larger than my dad's, but we could see the two
men right away, in the middle of the living room, seated at the
chess-board and staring down.

"Daddy," I said, "Dr Zir."

Since it was his move, my father didn't respond, but Dr Zir
was so startled that he almost knocked his chair over as he
tried to stand.

"Nora, darling," he said. "Come in, dear, and how do you
do? And, oh, you shouldn't have."

Ralph stepped forward to shake his hand, but did not,
thank God, extend the greeting by giving him the wine box
that the doctor clearly thought was a gift. Instead he put the
box on a table by the door. And when my father finally moved
his chess piece, he stood up too.

"Did it help to get away, Nora?" he solemnly asked. "Did it
do you any good to be alone for a while?"

"We've parked the farm lorry in front," I told Dr Zir. "I
didn't want to chance taking it home."

Both men went over to the window, pulled back the curtains, and looked at the lorry. The box on its back made it look
strange. "When did you get that one?" my father asked. "I
thought your lorry was a flatbed."

I told my entire story then, so far as I knew it. When I

mentioned Ahmed, my father at first seemed to think I was talking about a man, and when I said I believed that the tusks in the lorry were real and that the ones at the museum were the crowning example of Mr Smith's craft, the point of everything he had done so far, my father sat back down. I hadn't yet mentioned Mr Smith's own father's humiliation, or the son's decision to make revenge a by-product of his endeavour, but my father's face was so pale that I feared going on.

"I've been reading about the museum's opening," said Dr Zir. "I've even got tickets—one of my colleagues at the hospital gave them to me today."

"When is the opening?" I asked. "I don't even know that for sure."

"It's Monday," said Ralph. Since my father had his face in his hands, and since Dr Zir was searching for the tickets in the pockets of his worn-out vest, Ralph had gone over to the couch and picked up a newspaper.

"Monday morning, ten o'clock," he said. "President Kenyatta will be there, as will the vice president and everyone else. It says here that the folk dancers and singers are rehearsing tomorrow. It also says that the taxidermist and the contractors will be working through the weekend to get everything done."

"I was the Minister of Wildlife for five good years," said my father. He was looking up with tears in his eyes and his voice had such resonance yet expressed such shame that I thought he was about to let everything out. When he got up and came over to me, however, all he said was "They should have invited me."

I looked at my father standing there. He seemed much older than the number of his years, he was fragile and wayward of mind, he was contemptible for what he had done, and

he was all the family I had. I thought of him slapping Mr
N'chele and shoving him down the stairs. My father was a big
man, and that had been in 1956, when he was undoubtedly fit
and strong. I could see the expression on his face as he turned
from the top of the stairs and took my hand, walking with me
back down the hall to his office door. It was nothing like the
expression he had now. Then there had been arrogance in his
eye and he had walked slowly, looking satisfied and proud.

I asked Dr Zir if I could leave the lorry where it was—I
would take my father up the path and home. Their chess game
wasn't over but the doctor said I could do what I liked, and
when my father nodded I took his arm. Ralph took the box
again, and we made our way back out the front door.

I got the little model of Ahmed from the lorry; then Ralph
and I followed my father into the valley and onto the path.
The valley was dark, but my father knew the way so well that
he left us behind. We could hear him, and we could see him,
sometimes, in the odd patterns of darkness, but twice I had to
call, asking him to slow down. When we got to the edge of our
own yard, however, my father was waiting there. "I don't want
to go inside," he said. I stepped past him, looking around to
make sure everything was calm, but it wasn't fear of a dangerous house that kept my father standing outside.

"In the morning, Dad," I said. "It will all start to unfold
tomorrow."

"Our family has always been small," my father said. He
shook loose from me when I tried to take his arm again. He
was speaking not to me but to Ralph on his other side. "Only
Nora and me and her mother years ago. When Julius came
along I didn't like him at first. He had a strange way of speaking and I didn't want him around."

"It's natural for fathers to resent the men who take their daughters away," said Ralph.

"But when we were working together Julius was quick and thorough. He did a fine job. He knew more than I did and he was faster at knowing it, and his shipments were always on time. Do those things count for something when a man looks back, after his life has turned wrong?"

I tried to move my father across the grass again, but he was a heavy man, and as he refused to go I imagined him turning and slapping me, pushing me down into the valley and watching me fall.

"I'll bet his farm was run well too," he told Ralph. "I've found that when a man is thorough, his thoroughness is uniform."

"It was well run," I said. "Now let's go inside."

My father finally took a step toward the house but Ralph stopped him by suddenly speaking passionately. "I've never seen such a farm," he said. "Even after all this ruin I can tell that it was very well managed, very well run. The current mess is superficial, it doesn't take the eye of the farmer to see that."

I was surprised at Ralph. I hadn't thought, on any serious level, that he'd taken stock of the farm. He'd been so quiet out there, in fact, that I assumed he was only trying to get through a horrible day. My father, however, was moved by Ralph's words. "Oh, thank you," he said, and then he walked straight into the house, forcing Ralph and me to follow along. Beatrice had left a snack for him on top of the piano, a thin sandwich and a glass of milk.

"You play, don't you?" my father asked Ralph. "You will, won't you, while I eat my snack?"

When I went into the kitchen to make sandwiches for

Ralph and me I could hear my father going on. He was friendly and talkative again, not eating his sandwich until I came back with ours.

"However this thing unfolds, it will begin tomorrow," I said again, "so let's eat up and get you to bed."

My father nodded and it was just then, as I stood there with an unwanted bite of sandwich in my mouth, that the idea of having Ralph sleep over entered my head. I'd intended to lend Ralph my father's Land Rover, to thank him and send him on his way, but when my father took his plate into the kitchen and walked down the hallway to his room, I found myself saying something altogether different. "Do you want a beer, Ralph?" I asked. "Do you want to sit out on the verandah for a while, or would you rather go?"

My God, had I brought Ralph home to help me with the tusks, or in order to regain my equilibrium with Jules by exacting a final revenge of my own? Could I take Ralph to my childhood bedroom ten days after my husband had died? Was I still so angry with Jules that I could do something like that?

"A beer," said Ralph, "the verandah."

The smallest bottles of beer in our refrigerator were the Tusker Premiums with the foil around the top. I took two and opened them and followed Ralph outside.

"Why have you never married, Ralph?" I asked as soon as we were sitting down. "In all these years why haven't you ever taken a wife?" It was difficult to see Ralph in the odd patterns of light, but when he spoke he contradicted what he'd told me in the market that day.

"I was married," he said matter-of-factly. "As it is with your husband, my wife died."

Could that be true? Could he have left such a thing unsaid for so long, could I have simply not heard about it in the expanding smallness of our town?

"She was killed in a road accident," said Ralph. "She was driving one of our safari vans and swerved to avoid a pothole. A *matatu* hit her head-on."

Ralph's words seemed rote, as if he'd said them that way many times before, and I wondered how often he changed the order in slight little ways. Was he still experimenting or had he long ago left it alone? I considered how I would tell about Jules's death, whether I would easily find a way. I looked at Ralph but held my next question back, sensing that he would answer it anyway.

"That was in 1966," he said, "eight years ago now. Her death was horrible, but beneath it all was the unavoidable fact that we had married too young. And I have to say that the worst thing for me was that I felt relieved when she died. Is it bad to say so if it's true?"

It had been another long and impossibly difficult day. Nothing was impossible anymore, but I was struck dumb by Ralph's words. Could he be telling the truth, could such a thing be universal, or had Ralph read my mind? And would I speak of Jules this way after only eight years had gone by? Would I say, "He was killed on our farm. A lion mauled him and then he was shot"? Would I say, "Beneath it all was the unavoidable fact that I felt relieved when he died"? Would I say it the same way every time?

I suddenly felt like falling to the ground and weeping, in grief not only for poor dead Jules, but for our inability to grieve properly. All I did, however, was tell Ralph that what he said sounded too cold.

"Did you not love her then?" I asked him calmly. "When she died did you not mourn?"

Did Ralph understand my questions, with their rigid diction and negative syntax? Did he know I loved Julius Grant too much when he died, and that I was furious with myself now?

"She was leaving," said Ralph. "She had told me as much on the morning of the day she died. She was an educated girl."

From the verandah we could see into the kitchen. On the counter was the wine box containing Jules's arm, and on top of the wine box, with its two tiny tusks touching the window pane as if about to tap, stood the model of Ahmed the Elephant, eight inches tall. From where I sat I could see the model well enough, but had I not known what it was I could never have made it out. It seemed a jumble of circular lines and angles, and its bones somehow seemed black, as if someone had pasted a peculiar ebony rose on the glass. I tried to make it be an elephant again, but it was stubborn, insisting on the abstract, the way a fortune teller's bones do when they're cast on the ground.

"A couple of nights ago I was attacked by monkeys," I told Ralph. "They came up from the valley. They hid in the avocado tree, attacking me when I came home."

Ralph glanced into the valley, then turned to look at the tree. We had put our beer bottles on the table between the two lounge chairs where we sat. In the moonlight Ralph's pants and shirt looked clean, though I knew them to be streaked with dirt from the work he'd done. He sat near me but his face was impossible to see.

"One of my wife's complaints was that I was not ambitious," he said. "She told me I didn't have a master plan."

"If Jules had been unfaithful to me with women I would

consider getting even in kind," I answered. "That would have been easy, but he was unfaithful in the oddest possible way."

When Ralph stood up, preparing to go, I felt relieved. It had only been a few minutes since I had the idea that I could ask Ralph to stay, but now I knew that that was wrong.

"We should sleep," I said. "Will you help me again tomorrow?"

Ralph said he would help me not only tomorrow but every day, and I picked up the beer bottles and turned to take them inside. Ralph's bottle was still one-third full but the beer in my bottle was gone. "Do you want to finish this?" I asked.

"If you will allow me I will take it with me in the car," said Ralph.

That was all. We didn't speak once we were back in the house, and when I gave him the keys and showed him to the door again he didn't turn around.

Alone in the kitchen I leaned against the counter and peered out the window at the spot where we'd just been. I could see everything plainly, the pattern of the lounge chair ribs on the moonlit ground, the tops of the trees in the valley, and the movement that their leaves made in the wind. I could even see two wet circles on the table made by the beer bottle bottoms.

If I could see everything so clearly from here, then why, when I was out there, did I have such trouble seeing things inside? Now the little elephant model was before me, still looking out. I touched it and lifted it off the wine box and turned it in the air and set it down again. Whatever happened, I would keep this little elephant as my own. Without thinking about it I reached up and took Ahmed's left tusk out of his skull again. I hadn't touched the right one, but it looked locked in place, and this left tusk was worn better anyway, its end less pointed. Though I worried that the solitary habits of my widowhood were starting far too soon, I would have turned and taken the tusk with me to my bedroom, I think, if I hadn't suddenly been sure that Ralph was back, that he'd come in quietly and was standing at the kitchen door.

"Our time has passed, don't you think?" I said, but when I turned, my entire body stern, there was no one there to scold. Ralph stood only in my mind, and when I turned again I put the little tusk back in Ahmed's skull, pushing it in until, this time, I heard it lock in place.

I went to my bedroom alone after that, no Ralph, and my hands empty at my sides. There was a connected bath, and as I let the water roar and watched the room fill up with steam, I remembered poor Detective Mubia again. I went back into my bedroom and picked up my bedside phone: 222-222. His number had been my mantra for so long. As I listened to the phone ring and heard the water in my bathroom splash, I knew, of course, that Detective Mubia would not be there. I saw the charred logs of my husband's ever-ready campfire spread out before me on the ground, and as I watched them I had a clearer vision of what the next few days would bring. Tomorrow I would begin my engagement with Mr Smith, finally taking the baton my husband had handed me with his note, finally knowing what to do. And with that baton I would run the rest of the race with speed and determination. And I would not pause, this time, until the race was done.

I dialled again: 222-222. Why wasn't anyone answering at the police department? Were Detective Mubia's colleagues sleeping or were they gone?

19

A New
Mercedes-Benz

When my father came out for breakfast, he had his old Minister of Wildlife uniform on. I'd been up for an hour and had made pancakes, but my father insisted on standing while eating because Beatrice had just ironed his trousers and he didn't want them spoiled.

"But how will you get to town?" I wanted to know. "And whom will you impress, wearing such a thing?"

"Uniforms impress," said my father, "never mind whom."

All during his time as Minister of Wildlife my father had worn a business suit, never this quasi-military thing. The uniform had been given to him at the time of his promotion to the job, but I could remember his wearing it only twice, at President Kenyatta's inauguration, and once on Kenyan Independence Day. The uniform was in good condition, dark blue and well made, but it had gold braids at its right shoulder and reminded me now of something worn in a military band. The fit, however, was fine, and since I could tell my father was not going to change, I turned my attention to the food.

Through the kitchen window and across the valley I could see the top of Dr Zir's house. I could see his bedroom window and the red awning that covered his porch, but I couldn't see the driveway where our lorry was parked.

Now that the day was at hand, what was I going to do about Mr Smith, how would I resolve things and begin to take up my ordinary life again? I was sure I'd had at least the beginning of a plan last night, but now, standing in the morning light, I couldn't remember what that beginning had been. I had intended to negotiate with him from a position of strength, I think, since what I had was of value and what he had was not, but beyond that, I no longer had the slightest idea what my first move ought to be.

I went into the living room and looked at the telephone. I would call him and dictate how and when we could effect an exchange. I would tell him I wanted my husband back but that I wanted money too. There was an obscene aspect to asking for money, but what else could I do, in what other way could I be sure of causing the man pain? Ah, but it was a horrible plan. I didn't know how much to ask for, and at the same time I knew that no amount would even things out. In pounds and pennies how much was my husband's life worth, how much should I demand?

When the phone rang it seemed a telepathic response, since I'd been staring at it all this time. And when I didn't make a move, on the third ring my father came out of the kitchen and picked it up.

"Hello," said my dad, and Beatrice, her hands in dishwater, said, "There is another someone at the door."

I wanted to listen to my father, but Dr Zir's big nose was pressed up against the glass, so I had to go let him in.

"Ah, lovely, Nora!" said Dr. Zir. "It's a beautiful day!"

"No one bothered the lorry last night?" I asked.

"Safe and sound, Nora. I had my security guard sleep on top of it just to be sure."

Dr. Zir's exuberance was something I had never tired of before. Now, however, I wanted to concentrate on the telephone conversation. "There are pancakes in the kitchen," I said, but Dr Zir put both hands on his belly and said no.

"I understand," said my father, "but I think that's a very difficult place to meet."

"Who is it?" I asked. "Give me the telephone."

"Yes, yes," said my dad. "I know all that. Who do you think I am, young man?"

"Give it here," I said. "Let me talk."

My father had the receiver clamped to his ear, but when I got my hand around it he suddenly let go, throwing me off balance and sending the telephone crashing from the piano to the floor. Its grey plastic cover cracked around the dial and its back fell off.

"Hello! Hello!" I said. "Can you hear me? Who is this? Are you still there?"

"Your house is not in order," said Mr Smith's voice. "That is why things have gone so wrong."

"Tell me what you told my father," I said. "And tell me

what you did with the detective yesterday, where you let him go."

"Your father has just said that you finally brought my property back to town. Is this true?"

"I have it," I said. "What about the detective? What else did you say?"

"This morning I saw the announcement of your husband's wake in the newspaper. My own father showed it to me and made me feel sorrier than before. We were playmates, you and I, and we should remember better times. Also, my father's memory is shorter than my own. He has forgiven the issue at hand and does not want me to bring it up again. He does not want to think of it. My father is an old-fashioned man. He has stopped me in my dealings with your father and has saved this detective of yours. As I promised, all I did was give him a ride back to town. I dropped him at Nairobi Hospital, where so much of this latest round seems to want to unfold."

Could I believe that much? Could I believe that Detective Mubia wasn't lying dead somewhere, as charred and immobile as his car? I wanted to find out more about the condition he was in, and at the same time I wanted to hurt Mr Smith with words, but I didn't do it. I had learned that lesson twice before. Now I had to find the discipline to restrict myself to the business we were about. "What else were you telling my father?" I asked. "Where do you want to make the exchange?"

"We will meet at the opera tonight," said Mr. Smith. "Drive your lorry to the National Theatre car park and when the performance is over walk around the foyer with your keys in your hand. The room will be crowded and well suited to a quick exchange."

"What kind of exchange is that?" I asked. "What about my husband? Are you going to bring a crew to switch the boxes, to put my husband where your goods have been, all while the opera-lovers are filing out to their cars?"

"Please," said Mr. Smith. "I am not finished. Listen carefully to what else I have to say and be careful, do not call things by their names. Your husband's death was accidental. If you take time to think about it, you will agree that no one could have planned a death like that. If you want to ask my father, he will tell you as much. A lion works for no man, do you understand that to be true?"

"Kamau was not a lion," I said.

"Ah, yes, he was not, but listen again. That fool was actually trying to shoot the lion when he fired. That is the second truth of your husband's horrible final day. Since your husband was the only one who knew the location of my property, though I was angry with him for stealing it, I would have a vested interest in keeping him alive, would I not? What happened at the hospital was Kamau's mistake, that is all, the mistake of an amateur and a reckless man, something done out of fear and completely on his own. And I have seen to it that he paid for his mistake. He was working for me, that much is accurate to say, but what he did on your farm and at the hospital was the product of his bad aim and bad judgement, nothing more."

Detective Mubia's name was on my tongue again and I very much wanted to speak it into the phone, to tell Mr Smith that I knew Kamau was dead and who had killed him, and by doing so somehow twist in a blade of my own. I wanted to express everything in outraged terms, but I said only, "It was all an accident. Everything that's happened so far."

"My original idea was simply to trick your father into acting on my behalf, into thinking that my tusks were not real," Mr Smith said. "I have wanted to disgrace him, to avenge my own father's humiliation, as you now understand, my whole life long. In the end we must all strive to defend our fathers, however trying they are, no one knows that better than you and me. But things have gone too far now. I actually liked your husband. I never had violence in mind."

Mr Smith's voice was close to conspiratorial, as if, through our moment of shared remembering, we had now become accomplices. But did he think I was as big a fool as Kamau, that I would make the same mistakes my husband and father had made before? He knew I had his box, but did he think I hadn't looked inside?

"So you believe that our exchange tonight will make us even?" I asked. "That after we trade boxes things will be fine?"

"No," he said. "My father has told me that something more must be done. So listen one time more. Your husband's remains are loaded on the back of a new Mercedes-Benz flatbed lorry. I bought it only today. When I come into the National Theatre foyer we will exchange keys, not words, I hope. After that we will simply walk away. I will keep your farm lorry and you will keep my new Mercedes-Benz. The particulars will be in the glove box. It may seem a cold solution, but it is my gift to you for the mistakes that have been made. Anything more would be untoward."

"Untoward," I said. "Untoward" was a word I had always enjoyed. Its meaning wasn't clear in its make-up, but it had the ability to fit in nicely, to add oddness to an ordinary phrase. "All right, so I get a new lorry, a Mercedes-Benz."

I tried to make my tone pleasant and I must have

succeeded at least this one time, for Mr Smith heard acquies-
cence in it and suddenly sighed.

"Oh, good," he said. "I was worried you might not see it
that way. Until tonight then, when *Madama Butterfly* is done."

I was about to hang up, to turn to the others in the room
and begin to think about what in the world I would really do,
when Mr Smith spoke one more time. "May I add that I am
sorry for your loss?" he asked. "I am a married man. I don't
know if you knew that, but I know the pain I would feel should
I somehow lose my wife."

"Pain," I said. "Yes, I'm sure that's true."

"Everything was an accident," he said, "that is all. Most of
what has happened was a big mistake."

Mr Smith risked a laugh then, and his laugh was uncon-
trolled, and telling in its way. It had a rising intonation that
said he had been under pressure too, and that he could not
quite believe that now it all might end.

"There is someone at the door," I told him. "I've got to
hang up now."

After that I let the receiver move from my ear to its cradle
without saying good-bye. Was that a mistake? I had been con-
vincing, I think, but had my deception needed cementing by a
solid farewell, an uplifting note like the one in his laugh, a
vocal modulation of my own? When I turned to the others
they were all staring at me, sober-faced and strange.

"What?" I said.

"You have given comfort to the enemy," said my dad.

Dr Zir seemed to concur, but I felt quiet inside. I knew by
then that the day was mine to win. Mr Smith was like my
father; in a way he was like Ralph and Dr Zir as well. By that I
mean that Mr Smith was a man, and among men, when every-

thing is finished, there is always the matter of verbal sincerity
and form. A man may cheat and he may lie, he may even commit crimes such as those that had been committed against poor
Jules, but when one man speaks forthrightly to another, when
he comes out and actually says he was wrong, form dictates a
reply in kind. That is why Mr Smith believed whatever it was
that I had said, and that is why not speaking at the end, not
bidding him a clear and cheerful good-bye, might have been
my only mistake, the only flaw in my telephone behaviour that
day.

"Tell me," I asked, "how much do you suppose a new lorry
costs? A Mercedes-Benz."

This was such an unexpected question that both men lost
their critical attitude. Dr Zir was the first to thaw.

"A new Benz? Oh my dear, it's a bundle."

"In England you might pay twenty thousand pounds," said
my dad.

"Pshaw! Not anymore," said the doctor. "Twenty thousand
last year, maybe, but more now, twenty-three or even twenty-
five. Prices are going up everywhere."

When they started to argue the point, I left the room.
Since I had dressed improperly for what I now had in mind, I
went into my bedroom to change. Twenty thousand pounds,
last year and in England to boot. That meant that in Kenya my
new lorry would be prohibitive beyond belief and that therefore Mr Smith thought his offer to be grand.

When I came out again I was dressed in my smartest
clothes, clothes I hadn't worn since my university job. My
father was wearing his uniform and Dr Zir always wore a suit,
so we were ready to go.

"We have to hurry," I said. "The day's half gone."

"What do you want of me, Nora?" asked Dr Zir. "Do you want me to go home?"

I took his arm then and said simply that he and my father should both go to his house, and when they got there they should warm up the lorry. "It's old," I said, "and needs to idle for a good long while."

After they were gone and I was alone in the living room I picked the telephone up off the floor, my fingers moving slowly in its broken dial. Miro answered on the first ring, and when I told her what I wanted from her, I could tell that she smiled.

"Where I am concerned he'll do anything," she said. "But give us an hour, I have to go by the theatre for a final fitting of my kimono."

When I rang off I went out of the house and into the valley alone. The sky was clear and the monkeys were gone. At Dr Zir's both men were in the drive, standing around the lorry.

"I want you to take my dad and go in your car and find Ralph at his office," I told Dr Zir. "Ask him to meet us at the National Museum at two and ask him to dress up, not to wear his safari clothes."

I was giving orders without much latitude in them, but both men hesitated only long enough to see if there was anything else I might say. Like Mr Smith, they could sense a real denouement, and so far as my father was concerned, all he wanted was to make amends, for me to tell him that he had done nothing wrong.

"I'll meet you there," I said. Then I looked at my father carefully and said the words "Maybe after this we will be able to go on."

That was what he'd been waiting for, and it was only as I watched them leave that I thought of Jules again. Mr Smith not only had his body, but he had his pistol and his letter too, and I would insist that he give back all three. In the letter Jules had asked me to finish for him what he had so clumsily begun, and I suddenly wondered whether or not Mr Smith had read the letter carefully. It worried me, for if he had, then he might understand that though I'd been weak at the gravesite and sounded weak on the telephone, the word "revenge" was not an anagram. By that I mean that it could not be found in the letters that made up his offering. It couldn't be found in "Mercedes-Benz."

20

J14767

I was stopped at the museum gate by a security guard, but ahead of me I could see various lorries not unlike my own, and when I told the guard that I was with the taxidermist, he let me through. On the museum grounds there was a lot of confusion and as many people as one might find at any large construction site. Less than three days remained until Ahmed's unveiling, and security, I happily understood, was the last thing on anyone's mind. Getting in had been easy. Now all I had to do was look as though I knew why I was there.

I parked the farm lorry with the others at a spot near the back and walked past a crew working on the new building's flower beds to the museum's front door. I nodded at a man who was sitting there, then turned and headed directly toward him.

"I've brought the last of what they need, but I've been working in the shop all this time," I said. "Where's the set-up? I haven't been here in so long I've forgotten where the mammals are."

I spoke Kiswahili, in a very polite and friendly way, and the man said, "Everything is over on the near side. They are making a whole new room for this guy. I don't know about now, but earlier this morning they were driving their lorries all the way into the building, through a big hole in the far wall."

I thanked him and said, "I wonder if they're ready for me yet. Let me go this way first, find my boss, and ask him. If I drive in before they need me all he'll do is get mad."

The guard gave me a look that said he knew how bosses were, and let me pass. It was true, I hadn't been in the museum for years, and it had changed—grown larger and better appointed—since I was a girl. When I stepped through the door it was just after half past one. There was noise coming from somewhere, but I was alone in the entryway, facing an impressive collection of guns.

To my immediate left was the museum shop, and when I saw that it was unoccupied too, I began to feel a little more at ease. I went down a long hall carefully, and once past the shop I made a sharp right turn and immediately found myself outside again, in an enclosed garden between the old section of the museum and Ahmed's new room. This was an ordinary garden except for one thing; standing at its center was the largest elephant I had ever seen, twelve feet tall, not ten, with medium-brown skin that waved across his frame as if the wind had pushed it up, and tusks that stopped only an inch above the ground. He was impressive in his way, but anyone could tell that this elephant had never been alive. He was a fibreglass dummy, a fake-looking replica, from the tips of his tusks to the end of his tail. Judging from the sign that stood in front of him, he was supposed to be the guardian of the gate, here to approximate what the real Ahmed had looked like with his flesh and skin intact. He was Ahmed's likeness and more than Ahmed's size, but he wasn't Ahmed, he couldn't fool a child, and seeing him made me appreciate anew the quality and precision of Mr Smith's work. The tusks he'd made were in some inexplicable way as much a wonder as the real ones were. Could I concede such artistry to a man who was evil in so many other ways?

This plastic Ahmed watched the new mammal room, but when I walked past him and found myself inside again, there were so many workers that it was easy not to be seen by anyone. The room was large with a high ceiling and, as the guard had said there'd be, a huge opening at its unfinished end. I expected to see Ahmed again, skeletal and standing in front of me, a slightly smaller version of the one outside, but what I saw instead was more amazing than that. The whole floor of the room was laid with bones, large and small, and men were standing around looking at them as if they had no idea what to do. It seemed to me that it would be more than easy to kick a bone away, or break or misplace one. Everything was so haphazard, in fact, that it made me mad. My God, I thought, didn't they realise that the work they had to do was special, that the grand opening was only a weekend away? I fumed where I stood, but in a moment I began to notice that there was a calmness in the air which seemed shared by everyone but me. This was Ahmed, all right, but Ahmed with his leg bones and his pelvis and his ribs splayed out, Ahmed with his tail and his spine and the enormous bones of his shoulders and skull all lined up on the floor. The more I looked, the more I realised that there was a method to the particular madness here. No one was kicking anything and, as a matter of fact, they all appeared to be waiting, ready, each man with a job to do. Ahmed's tusks, those wondrous replicas that Mr Smith had made, were on the floor in front of Ahmed's skull, and everything except the tusks was connected by what seemed to be lines of thick brown string. As I watched I began to hear a voice, though I was sure the voice had been there before. Almost incredibly I had wandered in at the exact moment of Ahmed's rising, at the second the flattened elephant would stand. The voice told me that what I'd supposed to be string was cable, and that they were just about to draw the cable tight, bringing the elephant bones up into the air like a ship in a bottle, making Ahmed whole. There were ladders precisely placed for the workers to climb upon, bolters and welders standing behind them like a formal rear guard.

"Everybody should know exactly what to do," said the voice of the man in charge. "Just like yesterday we have one easy chance. If we fail, the cables will tangle again and it will be late tonight or tomorrow before we can try once more. Let's get it right this time. Is there any man who doesn't know his task?"

He spoke in English, a chancy thing to do. I could see him walking around in the widest possible circle, peering at the bones and into the eyes of his men. When he got back to his original place he said, "Very well, no mistakes now. Winchmen, start your engines."

It was all quite military and captivating, and obviously

orderly. As soon as he spoke, two small engines burped into
life at the corners of the room, starting up easily, but so loud
they made further comment from the man nearly impossible to
hear. They were high-pitched, screeching things, like lorry-
size dental drills.

"Phase one!" he screamed. I could hear him because he was
comparatively nearby, but nothing happened and he had to
scream again.

"Phase one!" This time one of the engines bogged down
into first gear, and as if pained into movement by a gigantic
alarm clock, Ahmed's head and his shoulder blades and the
previously connected components of his spine woke up, turning a little on the floor and causing a number of men to grasp
them before they actually lifted off. "Phase two!" yelled the
man.

Now the first engine changed voices and the other one fell
in below it making all of Ahmed come to life. His head and
shoulders were waist-high to the workers and the rest of him
started to rumble, in a swinging, shimmying skeleton dance,
the hip bone connected to the leg bone and so on. It was as if
he were alive and shaking off a long dream of death, as if he
were actually yawning and stretching on the new-made floor.

This entire spectacle was far beyond strange. It was
miraculous and seemed to me to promise—to prove—that
change was possible, that anyone could undo the things he
had done. I found myself concentrating on Ahmed's left
humerus, if that's what it's called on an animal his size. I fixed
on it and conjured his bicep torn and flapping away, and imagined myself repairing it, fitting it back in there, making it work
again.

Once Ahmed was in place the cables were anchored to the walls, the engines stopped, and silence returned once more. The cables, taut and thin, led from the bones to the ceiling, like the strings of an absent puppeteer. The men holding most of Ahmed's larger parts had climbed their ladders by then, and the men controlling his legs and feet, his rib bones and his tail, were stretching their arms outward or upward or down, and every man, though they all tried to hold their pieces still, shook the bones in a slight but constant way, making me lose my just-found feeling of hope and optimism. Once again it seemed that Ahmed was doing a dance, but not back into life anymore. Now he did a sad and slow shuffle to wherever it is that dead elephants go. Only Ahmed's tusks were unmoving before me; lying solidly on the floor at his front, they seemed to be the gods that Ahmed's dance was dedicated to, as if he hoped in his ascendancy to convince them to rise up and join him so that their wonderful weight would settle him down.

It was incredible and absurdly moving. I was crying on the stairs I'd found to sit on, and my heart hurt in ways I can't begin to explain or describe, hope and despair doing their own stiletto dance within it. Out in the room, though it seemed long past time for the next stage to begin, the men appeared to be captured by the event too, all of them aware of the pageantry.

"Good," the leader said quietly. "Look at him standing there. Everything's fine."

After that it seemed to me that another long moment passed, but I'm not sure, for when I began to notice things again, the welders and bolters and seam hiders were all over the elephant, making him settle down even without his tusks.

When I looked at my watch I was amazed to find that it was not yet two. I had been there less than half an hour, though it seemed as though what I'd witnessed should have taken all day. It would be a fine exhibit, with a wonderful Ahmed for every Kenyan to see. Then I noticed that the man in charge was coming my way, so I backed up into the darkness at the top of the stairs, finally going all the way up to the second floor. I watched the man passing below, and I could hear the workers going out the opening at the far end of the room.

The second floor of the new building was poorly lit, but it contained an exhibition too, already prepared. Up here there was a gallery. On the walls, under lights that would no doubt shine brightly come opening day, were dozens of photographs from Kenya's past. Directly beside me was a placard that read, "Freedom Fighters of the Early Days," and in the very first photograph I saw President Kenyatta standing with a group of men. The caption beneath the photograph identified these men as Mau Mau leaders, key members of the early independence fight. The photo was taken on the occasion of Kenyatta's presentation of a "Collector's Letter" to each of these men, giving them the right to retrieve and sell the tusks of elephants who had died of natural causes; this was a gift from their country for having fought so well. I knew of such letters but I hadn't known there were so many men who had them. In the photograph most of the men wore business suits. They didn't look like revolutionaries, they looked like government officials, unsmiling and stern. One of them was familiar but I didn't understand why until I studied the list of names below: this was Mr N'chele, Mr Smith's father.

It was an accident that I should have come upstairs at all, and a bigger accident that I should see Mr N'chele's photograph and discover that he had an authentic Collector's Letter filed away. What it meant was that Mr N'chele had the right to export tusks by presidential decree, that there was no real need to smuggle. And if Mr N'chele had a Collector's Letter, Mr Smith knew about it and could more or less legally claim it as his own. *No real need to smuggle!* Such was the degree, then, of his willful involvement of my husband and my dad.

I wanted to stay in the room a little while, to see if I could find photographs of Mr N'chele in his earlier days, say around 1956, but a commotion drew me down the stairs again. There was noise coming from the front of the museum, as if the queues had already formed. Since Ahmed's room was now empty, however, I took a moment to bend down and touch the tusks that lay before him on the floor. The left tusk was the one I knew intimately, so I ran my hand across the bevel of its tip, over the spot that Ahmed had used most during the sixty years or so of his life. That these tusks were artificial seemed impossible now. They were worn and oddly coloured and covered with intricate layers of deep and shallow scars. They even bore his registration numbers from the Ministry of Wildlife files, J14767, just like his real ones.

I heard steps behind me and turned, sure I'd be facing trouble, but Miro was there, with a man beside her who could only be her father.

"I thought we might find you in here," she said. "They've only just completed the set-up outside, they've just now finished the stage."

When she introduced me to her father I wanted to address

him using his surname, but I didn't know what it was. I had
asked Miro on the phone that morning to talk her father into
showing us around today, into letting us stand in the back during the rehearsals, while the opening-day performers were
practising their acts. I had asked especially that my father be
allowed to come, in the hope that his old Ministry of Wildlife
suit might turn him into a dignitary, the rehearsal into a more
formal affair. Now, however, it seemed a hopeless ploy and I
had no idea what to do next, other than go outside. I'd been
taking heart only in omens, like seeing Ahmed dance and finding Mr N'chele's photograph upstairs.

"You have a wonderful daughter," I told Miro's dad. "She is
my closest friend."

It was an odd thing for me to say, especially since she'd no
doubt told him we'd met just the other day, but Miro's father
smiled. "And no less do you have a wonderful dad," he told me.
"We were just speaking with him outside."

We'd been hearing the activity from out there for several
minutes by then, but it was only as Miro's father spoke that I
realised what we heard most recently was music.

"What's happening now?" I asked. "How long will this go
on?"

Miro's father was about a decade younger than mine. He
was a gentle-looking man with white hair and a soft and ready
face. He'd been an assistant curator for a dozen years but his
primary work was in the main part of the museum. He had little to do with the new exhibition.

"I'm not sure—I am in charge of weapons," he said. "But I
think the show will continue for quite a while."

We had walked back past the plastic Ahmed in his garden

and into the main building once again. "From elephant rifles to pistols to poison arrows," Miro's father said, "if Kenya's past had weapons in it, then I have collected them, catalogued them, and put them on display. Would you care to have a look?"

I said I would, but we were back on the museum steps by then and the sun was so warm and time was so much of the essence that I also said it would have to be another day. A group of Samburu dancers were in front of us, jumping and chanting on a wooden stage that hadn't been there when I'd entered the building forty-five minutes before. Below the Samburus were a bunch of Maasai, and beside the Maasai was a secondary-school choir that had come all the way from Marsabit, about fifty boys and girls in dark suits and dresses, each wearing a huge round badge embossed with a profile of Ahmed and a caption that said: *Marsabit—Ahmed the Elephant's Own Home Town.*

The choirmaster was watching the Samburu dancers impatiently. He seemed to be complaining to one of the museum officials, saying the Samburus were taking too long. It was then that I saw my father. He approached the choirmaster and the museum man, Dr Zir behind him, nodding as if he were a military aide.

"Oh, oh, your father's been asking to hear the singers now," Miro's father said. "I think that's my cue."

When he walked past the Samburus, Miro and I followed, and though I was worried that my father might ruin whatever chance we had by saying something idiotic, his posture was impeccable and his old Ministry uniform really did let him look official and grand. There was something about the direct sunlight, I think, that made the cut of it stand out, the band braids on his shoulder all aglow. Everyone was watching him. Some of the Maasai had come closer to listen as the Samburu dancers were filing off the stage. When Miro and I got near I heard my father say, "Scheduling problems, don't you know." He was an old colonial dignitary, come unexpectedly, maybe, but full of the old colonial expectations. Only I knew that this was no act at all.

My father was insisting that the Marsabit school choir perform between the Samburu dancers and the Maasai, and when the performance coordinator finally agreed, Miro's father had to go over and explain everything to the Maasai. Real Maasai, people like Sosio and the others who lived out around my farm or up in the Loita Hills, didn't worry very much about time, but these dancers weren't from the Mara. They were members of a newly formed dance troupe housed just outside of town, on Langata Road. Their leader listened while Miro's father spoke, and then he looked directly at my dad.

"Wouldn't he rather see us dance?" he asked. "White people can hear a choir anytime."

The choirmaster heard him and started to complain. "This is a Rendille choir," he said. "What white person can hear that? We sing not only the familiar fare but traditional Rendille songs. No one knows them in Nairobi, black or white, no one here has ever heard them before!"

The Maasai dance troupe leader had deep red ochre stains on his skin and wore a huge lion headdress over long braided hair, but he spoke English pretty well, and he seemed to hold his ground. Finally, however, the Rendille choir director pointed at the fifty boys and girls. "These young people will be disappointed," he said. "They each knew Ahmed personally, you know. And they have never been to Nairobi before today."

The Maasai sighed and nodded his head. "You go next then," he said. "After that maybe he will want to stay and watch us dance."

My initial idea was a far-fetched notion that had come to me upon seeing my father in his uniform that morning, but it was beginning to seem that what was happening now actually might allow me to drive my lorry into the museum's new exhibition hall unopposed. Everyone was engaged by my father, and my father was in rare form, every inch of him the Minister of Wildlife again.

Even after the Marsabit choir took the stage, I lingered, like a ghost watching an old world. Miro's father was tending to my father and Dr Zir again, all three of them now sitting with the higher museum officials, in chairs that had been brought from inside. And when the choir started singing, Miro had to pinch me before I could make myself walk away. The first Rendille selection was chilling and innocent: a dead-slow rendition of "God Save the Queen."

When we got to my lorry the box was still on the back but there was a man inside the cab.

"That took forever," said Ralph. Ralph had changed out of his safari outfit and into a suit that nearly matched the one Miro's father wore. I explained in a minute why I had asked him to come. "Give me the keys," he said. "You two walk in first. Make sure no one's there."

Walking into the museum from this direction made the mammal room seem less large. I could quickly see that it was still empty, that even those who might have been told to stay were standing somewhere near the front door, listening to the choir. No one was expecting trouble, after all.

Ahmed was alone, the artificial tusks in front of him on the floor. Miro and I walked all the way up to them before Ralph brought the lorry, turned in a tight circle, and backed up very close to Ahmed, perhaps four feet away from his huge left side.

Ralph jumped out of the cab, leapt up onto the bed of the lorry, and pried open the box. "Let's do this fast and get out of here," he said. He didn't even look at the elephant.

Each of Ahmed's tusks weighed at least one hundred and fifty pounds, but Ralph reached into the box, grabbed one, and hoisted it onto his shoulder as if it were light. Miro and I reached up and took the hollow end of the tusk, then guided it to the floor and held it there while Ralph jumped down. The tip of the tusk was five feet above us in the air.

Ralph moved in front of us, picked up Ahmed's artificial left tusk, and had us steady it while he placed the real one in precisely the same spot on the floor. Then he got back onto the lorry and we felt the fake tusk lift out of our hands. "God Save the Queen" was over. It had been a long rendition, funereal in tone, and by the time the choir started its Rendille song we had replaced the second tusk and Ralph had lightly tapped the box lid shut again. He gave me the keys to my father's Land Rover. "Go back outside and listen," he said. "Meet me at your house when you get away."

Ralph jumped into the cab and drove immediately out of the mammal room and across the museum grounds. We could see him there, waving at the security guard, waiting for a break in the traffic. After that he was gone.

That was all there was to it. It had been profoundly easy to do what we had done, to exchange the real for the artificial, the naturally grown for the manufactured. When Miro and I stepped back in among the crowd, the Rendille boys and girls had finished only their second song, and though my father and Dr Zir and the cadre of museum officials were flawlessly attentive in their chairs, the leader of the Maasai dancers was now impatient over at the side.

The Marsabit choir's third song was "Greensleeves." I got the feeling that they had added it late, that they sang it because they felt it captured my father's world in some way, but they nevertheless did an excellent job, an absolute longing for England in their tone. Now that I could take time to notice, I saw that the boys in the choir were younger than the girls, by so many years, in fact, that their voices intermingled as if there were no gender difference at all. The choir sang as one, really enthusiastic now, and the choirmaster, using the exaggerated body movements that were popular at the time, seemed completely connected with the majesty and power of the song. When I looked at my father I could see that he was connected too, won over not only by the singing, but also by young faces that seemed to contain only sweetness, by children who had nothing but music in mind.

When "Greensleeves" was done the members of the choir looked up, and their Ahmed badges flashed in the sun. We applauded and the Maasai applauded too, an odd sight. Since I'd seen a lifetime's worth of Maasai dancers, I squeezed Miro's arm, waved at my father, and quickly turned away. I would take the Land Rover and go home, just as Ralph told me to do. And in a few hours, when I bumped into Mr Smith in the post-opera crowd, I would give him back his artificial tusks and take Jules's bones away. Surely that would be enough, surely I could end things there. Mr Smith might never discover the switch I'd made, he might sell those perfect replicas to a sheik or a businessman who in turn might live his whole life through believing that the tusks he had purchased were real. The only questions that remained for me, then, were these: Did the rules of revenge demand that one's enemy feel its full weight? Did Mr Smith have to know he'd been beaten before I could finally slow down?

In twenty-four hours my husband's wake would begin, in less than eight I would meet Mr Smith, but when I got into the Land Rover what I wanted most to do was read Jules's letter again, on the chance that there was something in it that would help me answer complicated questions like those.

21

Un Bel Dì

In Nairobi expensive art such as theatre has always been primarily supported by subscription. That's why I didn't have to worry about tickets for the opera that night. Jules and I had season tickets for opening nights at all National Theatre productions, and so did Dr Zir. For Jules and me it had been an unused patronage much of the time, but even so, when we arrived at the theatre all I had to do was go to the season ticket holders' window and pick the tickets up. With Dr Zir's we had four tickets for the three of us, so when I saw Ralph earlier in the day, I asked him to come along, to meet us in the foyer at a quarter to eight.

Dr Zir and my father and I pulled into the car park at seven-fifteen, forty-five minutes before curtain time, all dressed up and in the farm lorry with the giant coffin on the back. Even though we were early, however, there was such a large crowd that it became immediately clear that parking would be impossible. There were already cars all over the lot, and well-dressed people walking toward the theatre lobby stared at us as if we'd made an absurdly wrong turn.

Because I was driving and because there wasn't space enough to turn the lorry around, I let my father and Dr Zir off at the door, then drove off toward the bushes at the back, where there were some more parking spaces by my old dance studio, the room where I had first discovered Miro.

I hadn't seen Mr Smith's lorry when we entered the main car park. Back here there was an attendant who would park the larger cars of the officials and otherwise important people who had come. There were big cars with embassy flags on them—I saw the British High Commissioner's Rolls—and there were several Kenyan government vehicles, long and dark. Drivers stood against the bushes smoking, and beyond the drivers, over by the farthest hedge but facing out, was a shiny new Mercedes-Benz flatbed lorry with Jules's coffin on its back. It was a pitiful box compared with the one that held Ahmed's tusks—it was filthy and dirty, just as it was when it came out of the ground.

When the attendant came up to my window I was prepared to pay him to let me stay, but he said, "Good evening, madam, I have awaited you."

He opened my door, and after he helped me down, he got into the cab of my lorry and drove it in an impossibly tight circle, narrowly missing everything, and then backed it past all the fancy limos and into a space just in front of the Mercedes-

Benz. The manoeuvre reminded me of the way Ralph had
driven it in the museum earlier in the day. When the attendant
came back I gave him five shillings and asked for my keys.

"Oh, I must keep the keys with me," said the man. "I must
be able to alter my configurations should someone unexpectedly decide to leave."

He had my keys in his hand, and a peg board full of keys
was nailed to my old dance studio's door.

"I need them," I said. "I have to give them to someone inside." I was ready to take the lorry back out onto the road
again, to park it in front of the Norfolk Hotel or all the way
down on Kijabe Street if he wouldn't give me my keys, but
first I asked, "What about that other big lorry back there, the
Mercedes-Benz?"

The attendant smiled. "In my car park even Mr Smith must
comply," he said. He walked over to the peg board and, lifting
some others away, hung my keys under my enemy's. "The two
lorries together," he said. "Mr Smith expressed the same concern but I put his mind at ease."

Walking into the theatre alone made me feel as if I should
have Jules by my side. Quite suddenly I remembered that we
had parked the farm lorry at the theatre once before. We
sometimes used to try to coordinate opening nights with trips
to town to buy supplies, and I remembered Jules's speaking to a
parking attendant, telling him to guard our purchases well.
Could the same man have been working then, so many opening nights ago? Jules had loved the way our farm lorry insulted
the vehicles that surrounded it, the way our farm clothes drew
stares as we walked through the audience to our row.

Jules's opinion of his own hard work had been too high,

and he'd been arrogant in other ways too, about such things as
not dressing up, about somehow putting down the crowd.
Now, however, as I entered the foyer, I wore formal mourning
clothes, black on black, and severely combed hair. It was
strange that I should be going out on the evening before my
husband's wake, and when I remembered Mr N'chele admon-
ishing me for it before, I realised that one small part of Mr
Smith's plan was to add a final insult to his list of other crimes,
to see me embarrassed in front of the gathered patrons, the
power brokers and politicians of the town.

"Good," said my father. "They wouldn't give me your tickets without you or Julius to sign."

"His wake is tomorrow," I whispered. "I think now that I
shouldn't have come."

I might have made the decision to stay in the foyer, or perhaps even to go home again, but just then Ralph arrived. He
took my arm and walked me back out to the ticket window,
clean fingers strongly gripping my arm. "I was backstage just
now," he said. "Miro has had our seats changed. We are to be
in the first row."

I don't know why such a comment, such a trivial change of
plans, should have made a difference to the sense of impropriety that I felt, but it did. If Mr Smith wanted me embarrassed,
then somehow sitting in the front row would serve to turn that
embarrassment around. It made me think of Jules in his farm
clothing once again, unnecessarily visible and proud.

The four of us went into the theatre together, but since Dr
Zir's two seats were in the back somewhere, Ralph and I ven-
tured down the aisle alone. Though I wanted to, I didn't look
around for Mr Smith or for others in the crowd I would know,

schoolmates and university colleagues and old family friends,
people who'd known for decades that my father was capable of
slapping another man. It seemed an extraordinary moment, as
if I were permanently being defined, widowhood locked forever on my brow, a father's daughter, beaten by the genes he'd
passed on. I was sure that everyone was watching me, that the
hush that had just then come over the hall was in observance
of my entrance and not of the fact that the house lights had simultaneously gone down.

"We're almost there," Ralph said, but all I could see was the
orchestra pit, and around Ralph's calmness all I could hear was
cacophonous sound.

Our two seats were in the centre of the front row, next to
Miro's father, who stood and embraced me when we arrived.

"My dear," he said. "It is good of you to have come, to honour my daughter on her big night."

When we sat down Miro's father kept hold of my hand,
and it was just then that applause greeted the conductor and
the orchestra stopped its coughing and sweetly found its voice.
It was good of me to have come out for his daughter's big
night. I turned around and stared at the full house behind me,
black faces and Asian faces and white, like the intermingling of
independent planets, together right now but with no common
orbits on ordinary nights. I looked at Miro's father again, and
had the music not kept me from it, I would have told him that
it wasn't good of me at all, that I didn't know his daughter,
that we'd become friendly only just now. If the music hadn't
stopped me I would have said that I hadn't come to hear her
sing but to collect my dead husband, who was impatient with
opera and was waiting outside. It was a horrible moment. All of

my confidence from earlier in the day was gone, all of my sense of conclusion washed away with the rising sound.

But I didn't speak, of course, and such thoughts only served to make me late in paying attention to the opening scene of the opera's first act. An American sailor was in a garden, anticipating the arrival of his bride, a young Japanese geisha girl. The sailor's love was of the cynical kind—we knew it because he was singing and carrying on, telling a friend who was with him that he'd keep this Japanese girl, but only for a while, that though she was really quite lovely, what he looked forward to in his deepest heart was the day when he would return to America and find a real American wife.

Until Miro came on stage I let my attention wander away from the awful attitude of the American sailor and the dark admonitions of his friend. They were both good singers, I suppose, but they reminded me of my father and Dr Zir: imperial England and its loyal Asian confidant. Still, the sailor's tenor and the friend's baritone worked together pretty well to cover up their limitations of power and range. Everyone in the opera was local. The sailor was a music teacher at the German school, his friend a Kimeru businessman, president of a company that imported engine parts and tyres.

When I first met Jules in London I think our courtship was a lot like the one taking place on stage. I didn't have the innocence or the youth of Madam Butterfly, but it was nevertheless I who fell in love first and hardest, I who most clearly heard that inner whisper telling me that Jules was the one. I believe Jules loved me during his life, I'm sure of it even now, but he loved the idea of Africa, the idea of high savannah, of elephants on the open range, at least as well. Since Jules was a ro-

mantic he thought of life in Kenya as romantic too, and he believed I shared his sense of adventure, whereas in fact elephants on the open range were for me a common girlhood
memory, farming above Narok a prescription for season after
season of unending toil. I'm not saying that I didn't love our
farm, that I don't love it still, but that during our first year or
two of marriage I altered my idea of what I loved until it became the farm, until I could see the world only through Jules's
eyes. That's what love does, I guess, that's what a woman does,
I know. Since I loved my husband with all my heart, I simply
quickened that heart, making it beat like his, until it loved
what he did too.

When Miro made her entrance there was a perceptible
change in everything. I could feel it in the attentiveness of the
audience and see it on stage in the postures of the American
sailor and his friend, in all the extras who played members of
her Japanese family and the citizens of the town. Even the orchestra seemed improved. When Miro sang her first notes they
were plaintive and strong and haunting, and easy in their
range. It was like the introduction of the world's finest wine
into a glass that still contained a sip or two of something poor.
Next to Miro's, the American sailor's voice, which had to wind
around it in the wedding song, seemed a stringy vine, and the
friend's baritone, though it held up better, made the friend
seem slow. Who could fail to love Madam Butterfly when she
could sing like that? And why couldn't she see the duplicity of
the American sailor when the rest of us could see it so well?

I sat up straighter in my chair, then chanced a look at
Miro's father sitting by my side. He was crying, shiny dark tear
tracks ran all the way from his eyes to the corners of his

mouth, but his face was such a picture of pure love and con-
centration that I couldn't look away. Miro's voice was not
strictly soprano, I know it because she told me it leaned a little
bit toward mezzo. She had a voice with body, a voice with
depth and flavour, like a wine again, though Miro had also said
it was ultimately the pure sopranos who got the best parts, the
high voices that garnered the greatest fame.

Miro was perfection, but otherwise Act One of the opera
contained too much busy stage movement, people shouting
and marching around. I had paid spotty attention and when
the act ended I was surprised. Madam Butterfly's uncle had dis-
owned her, not so much for marrying a foreigner but for casting her religion aside in order to embrace the American's, for
taking her sense of everything from her husband, just as I had,
including her sense of God. I could easily understand why it
angered her uncle so. It angered me too. Why couldn't she be
herself with this man? Why couldn't the American love her for
what she was and leave all these alterations alone?

The performance had two intermissions, and when the
people near us started to stand, I stood too, looked around one
time, and then quickly sat back down. I had glimpsed Mr
Smith with his own sad father, sitting behind us and off to the
side. Mr Smith hadn't seen me, but his expression was nevertheless sallow and mean. It wasn't a look of victory or defeat,
but a public reflection of his soul.

"There are drinks in the lobby," said Ralph. "Shall we get
you one? I could choose something for you and bring it back
down."

"I want a cup of coffee," I said.

When Ralph asked Miro's father the same question he said

he would like coffee too, with hot milk. Miro's father seemed a wonderful man, gentle and kind, but why were there so many men and so few women in the world I occupied? Had Miro's mother, and Mr Smith's too, died young, like my own, had they both departed life early, like Ralph's wife and Dr Zir's, leaving all these men to carry on? Was it the job of my generation to begin a change of emphasis, so that for the next thirty years only the women survived?

I touched Miro's father's arm and said, "She really is marvellous. I knew she'd be good but I had no idea."

That was true enough. Miro had talked about succeeding as a singer in the outside world, about her father's calling her back just as her reputation was starting to grow, but when she said those things I'd listened lightly, with barely half an ear. I, too, had wanted the outside world—that's why I'd gone to Oxford—yet both Miro and I had come back home. Now, however, though I would surely stay, it seemed impossible that Miro would remain here, impossible that she would not be lifted onto the shoulders of the real opera world, wildly celebrated and swept away.

"She is God's gift," Miro's father told me, "her voice is God's instrument for us to behold."

Ralph came back just as the lights dimmed once more. He was carrying three glasses of wine.

"The coffee is finished," he said. "Your father bought these and insisted I bring them to you with his compliments."

When the curtain came up on Act Two, the American sailor, now Madam Butterfly's husband, had apparently been gone for quite some time, and Madam Butterfly was waiting on a hillside, gazing out to sea. Her maid sat with her, and Madam

Butterfly listened while the maid sang her own sad song. The maid's devotion to Madam Butterfly was clear, but she was forlorn, sure the American sailor would never return. Miro's father had refused the wine, so while we watched I had two glasses in my hands. The maid was a pretty good singer too, better than either of the principal men, but when she finished her song and Miro leaned forward, about to admonish the maid for her lack of faith, Miro's father leaned forward too. "I love this part," he said. He wasn't speaking to me, I realised, but was uttering a little prayer, and just then Miro's voice came slowly up. Like a magnificent wind off the sea of Japan, a single note floated from the stage and, filling the theatre, lifted me out of my self.

> *"Un bel dì, vedremo*
> *Levarsi un fil de fumo sull'estremo*
> *Con fin del mare,*
> *E poi la nave appare."*

That a human voice could have such properties in the face of a crumbling world, that it could combine so with grief and longing and steadfastness of spirit, was suddenly enough to make me wild. I had followed the English libretto during the first act, but the wine in my hands and the music in the air made me forget it now. Miro's father was crying again and I was too. It was 1904, it was Japan, and somehow my new and only friend had found a way to touch and heal me far more profoundly than the switching of the tusks had done. Miro's voice was the one I'd been digging for, the one locked in my heart for so long.

The rest of the second act was an unhappy affair. It was

clear to everyone but Madam Butterfly that the American sailor
would never return. He had no steadfastness of spirit, no sense
of longing, so the real tragedy was that she, Miro, Madam
Butterfly, had fallen in love with the wrong man.

But what hope it gave me sitting there. I had not loved the
wrong man but had loved the right man, who had acted
wrongly, and what a difference there was in that, what power
it gave me, what renewed strength. Jules hadn't betrayed me,
as the American sailor had Miro, but had betrayed, instead, an
aspect of himself. And, oh, how he'd grieved for it, oh, how
clearly he'd known what he had done.

I was set free by Miro, though for poor Madam Butterfly
there could be no freedom short of death. There was a second
intermission, but all I did was drink my wine. I think my father
and Dr Zir came down, I know they did, to greet Miro's father
and to stand with Ralph, posing and grimly staring across the
room at poor Mr N'chele with his deplorable son. All these
men casting their eyes about aggressively, like bulls in tuxedos
snorting across an open field: my own father, so culpable once
and so untethered now, especially if the day grew long; Mr
N'chele, his mind clear but his son a blemish on his heart; and
Mr Smith, using the echo of that slap as a reason to spend his
time on earth in evil ways. These were the men in my life, and
they were just like Madam Butterfly's uncle in the world on
stage, raving and walking this way and that, in Japan and in
Kenya, years ago and now and in untold years to come.

In the third act a child came out, a boy of about three years
of age, and my first impulse was to be critical of the structure
of the play, of Puccini's decision to hide this child from us for
so long. But he was a beautiful boy, with hair of a colour no

Japanese child's could be and a way of walking across the stage that beguiled me with its innocence and its unselfconsciousness. The American sailor came back after all, not for Miro, whose wretchedness had compelled her to sleep at the very moment of his return, but with his big American wife, and in order to take the child away, in order to claim the boy so that he could grow up in a wider and more profitable world.

When Miro awoke and sang her final aria, a farewell to her beautiful child and to her awful existence as well, I thought she would sing *"Un bel dì"* one more time. I wanted her to, I wanted once again to feel it soar from my heart, but she did not. The orchestra let the slightest strain of it seep into the song she did sing, a glorious echo, but that high and golden note did not come out to waft across the room and torture us again. It couldn't, of course, because it had been a note of hope, and Madam Butterfly's hope was gone. And when she died, at her own hand, the audience sat stunned as the final curtain came down.

Dear God, I had not expected anything like this. I hadn't known that anything like this was possible in the world, that something like this could happen on a stage and before the naked eyes of ordinary humankind. I hadn't even wanted to come. Before the opera I had been lost—small of heart and grousing on about the scandal that my presence in the theatre would bring—but now I was at home again. It seemed to me that Miro had given the absolute performance of a lifetime and that it was directed only at me, a gift from my friend, a gift from her father's God, and, if you like, perhaps a gift from Julius Grant as well: the tragedy and drama of Madam Butterfly's life and my own life, there on the stage for everyone to see.

It took the audience a long time to begin to applaud, but once it started it simply wouldn't stop. When the American sailor and his friend came out there was a surge in the clapping and when Madam Butterfly's maid came out there was more, but when Miro reappeared, gorgeous and exhausted, such a roar went up from the throats of the people behind me that I nearly turned to see if something else had happened that was causing it. Miro bowed and stood and bowed again, and as I watched her, I could see Madam Butterfly leaving through the room's thin air. Flowers came from everywhere, falling across the entire stage floor, and when Miro's father went forward with a bundle of his own, who knows where he got them, the audience went wild again, one last adoring surge, before it re-membered itself and stood and filled up the aisles and headed for the doors.

/   /   /

Because we had front-row seats and were in the middle, it took us a long time to reach the foyer, where Mr Smith and I would attempt to exchange the keys we didn't have. I was languid and fulfilled. I didn't want to talk, I didn't want to see the man. From the opera I had learned that it was truly over, this hideous duel between Mr Smith and me, that human conflict in a temporal world has a natural end. I even somehow knew that Jules would be satisfied with the new lorry—I no longer needed to read his letter again to know that. I had managed to put the real tusks back where they belonged, and I knew he'd be pleased at the value put on his bones, at the fact that the lorry Mr Smith was giving us was the best that money could buy. It was strange, but when I saw the character of Madam Butterfly float away from Miro's brow, it was as if Jules had finally gone too, a thinned-out spirit, ever near me since he'd died, but too tired to stay around anymore.

So when I finally got up and followed Ralph into the foyer, I was tranquil. We had stayed so long in the theatre, however, that the rest of the audience was gone. Mr Smith and his father, in fact, faced my father and me in an almost empty room; only Dr Zir and Ralph stood a little bit off to the side. I was of a mind to remind him that the keys he wanted were waiting outside and then to pass him by, but Mr Smith's demeanour was peculiar to behold. The mood he'd affected in that morning's telephone call seemed completely gone.

"There has been another development," he said.

I could understand his words well enough, but the voice he used to say them was so choked that he had to stop almost as soon as he began. His emotions were strewn like driftwood, causing havoc all over his face, his eyes were up and his lips were down. I knew the opera hadn't done that to him, and the only other thought I could find was that he was planning on keeping what he'd said he'd give away, that he wanted to change boxes but take home the new Mercedes-Benz.

"I want my husband and I want the new lorry he's on top of," I said. "I want my pistol and my husband's letter too." I spoke quietly and with the deadly calm of that orchard snake. The opera had perhaps put me in a philosophical mood, but it hadn't made me an easy mark. I would end this thing tonight, but not on any terms other than those already agreed upon.

Mr Smith seemed to understand, and waved his hand impatiently, as if to say that what I was thinking did not compare with what he had to say, if only he could get it out. But whatever it was, a long time went by and he didn't say another word. He was choking on the air in the foyer, so finally his father stepped in.

"I have recently discovered the entire truth," Mr N'chele said, "not only about the big tusks on your lorry outside, but about the little ones that have been smuggled out of our country for a year and a half." Mr N'chele stopped and looked at his son to see if his son would take over, but his son would not.

"My son has decided that in order for him properly to rectify everything he has done, or at least as much of it as he can, you must not only take the new lorry, with its priceless cargo, but you must allow me to deliver, right now, the contents of the old lorry to the National Museum. You may come with me if you like, personally to view the exchange. It is what I was insisting that he do before your husband took the tusks away. I informed the museum before the opera, and people are standing by. Everything must go back where it belongs, my dear, then this whole thing can end. This is what I insist upon. Order first, and then all the trouble will be undone."

Madama Butterfly still had me under its spell, but could I believe my ears? As his father spoke Mr Smith's demeanour got worse. He couldn't stand it. He looked ready to explode. In his face I could see not only the man who had put Detective Mubia's legs to the fire, the man with whom I'd done battle over the dominion of my husband's body, but also the child with whom I had played so many years before. As I watched him I could see all those faces passing by, so it surprised me when he somehow did manage to mutter a few words.

"I concede that the lorries and their contents are both out of my control," he said, "given by me freely for the mistakes I have made."

Those words seemed to cause Mr Smith as much agony as giving up her son caused Madam Butterfly, and as I listened I understood that they were memorised words, words dictated to him by his father, words he had practised on the way to the opera or during an earlier part of the day. Speaking them out loud was the final part of the price his father had extracted for once again coming to his aid.

"I see," I said.

I had to think fast. I had to decide right now what I was going to do. Could I tell the truth to Mr N'chele in the presence of his son? Could I tell him not to worry, that Ahmed's authentic tusks were in Ahmed's authentic skull even as we spoke, or at worst still lying before him on the museum's floor? Should I admit to the switch I'd made or let the switch be made again? Though I looked for a second over at Ralph and Dr Zir and my dad, I could see nothing in those three faces that would begin to help me decide.

"There is no hope for us if we don't stop now," Mr N'chele added. "I believe you know it as clearly as I do. The tragedy of your husband's death cannot be undone, but the past is the past and the very distant past, the particular past in question here, is like something awful we have read in a book. That it was your father who wrote the book, that will have to be your own cross to bear."

Mr N'chele was looking at me in a kindly way, speaking from his heart.

"What will you do with the other tusks?" I asked softly. "What will you do with the artificial ones? Is it your position that they should be returned to your son?"

"What would you have me do with them?" Mr N'chele

asked. "Surely you don't want them for yourself. You will have your husband to take home, enough to handle without the extra burden to bear."

"Send them back to Marsabit," I said. "Send them up to Ahmed's own hometown. Build an exhibition hall up there for them. Then I will be satisfied."

I'd had no idea I would say such a thing, and Mr N'chele was so surprised that for a minute he couldn't speak at all. Mr Smith made another strangled sound, but his father looked only at me, steadily and for a good long time. After I had spoken I wouldn't take the words back again. I could not, however, either fathom where the idea had come from or sustain this old man's gaze, so I looked over at my own father once again. My father hadn't recognised Mr N'chele earlier, and I could immediately see that he was daydreaming now. This was the story of his life we were telling here, but he had missed it because he'd been thinking of something else, of an ancient delusion or maybe a move in the chess game he'd been playing only an hour before the opera began. The muscles of my father's face were as slack as Mr Smith's were contorted, and his mouth was slightly open, pulled down by nothing but the constant weight of his jaw.

"Very well," Mr N'chele finally said. "You have my word on it. We will take the artificial tusks to Marsabit and build them a home, find some appropriate place so that they can be displayed for the people who knew Ahmed best when he was alive."

"That's all I ask," I said. "If that happens, of course, this means an end to everything, an absolute end to it all. Only keep your son away from me from this day on."

What I was saying with such words, what I was reminding him of, was that we both had our crosses to bear, but Mr N'chele only nodded one last time.

Since there were no keys to exchange, we didn't have to worry about doing anything more, and no one spoke again as the six of us headed out the door. In the car park there were still a few operagoers standing by their cars, and somehow, from seeing these casual groups, I understood that the truth of the matter, the secret of where Ahmed's authentic tusks really were, was known by far more people than I would have felt comfortable trusting before. Miro and Ralph and I shared the secret of the first exchange, and though my father was forgetting quickly, for today at least, he knew, and Dr Zir knew, and perhaps even Miro's dad. That made five people whom I would have to trust where before I had trusted only one. Was it too much to hope for, the idea of trust and reliability, when the number of people was large? Could I go back to such an old proposition, could I begin to believe in it again at this late date, now that Julius Grant was gone?

Mr N'chele had a big black sedan parked in the main lot, ready to drive his defeated son away, and he had another driver waiting to take my farm lorry to the museum, to make the last exchange. I was about to insist on going too, that was my intention, but when we got to the area of the official cars and the lorries, I seemed to remember a little of what I had learned from Madam Butterfly. And when I saw Jules's coffin on the back of that Mercedes-Benz, I knew that my real job, my truest last job on this last and longest day, had to be to drive my husband home again. I could ask Ralph to go with Mr N'chele. Ralph could be my emissary, making sure that the final exchange was done, or I could even let Mr N'chele go alone.

It was just then, just as I had made my best decision of the night, that I saw Miro standing by the door of my old dance studio, her face perspiring and tired. And my final surprise was that Detective Mubia was there too, safe and standing by her side. Earlier, at the opera's end, I had wanted to find Miro and embrace her, but engagement with Mr Smith kept me from it, and I guess I believed also that after her spectacular performance she would need solitude for a while. But when I saw her at the studio door, when I rushed to kiss her and tell her what a glorious job she had done, it was the look of Detective Mubia that stopped me halfway up the stairs. The detective's face was composed and serious and calm, its muscles sculpted once again into their old mould. And incredible as it was to see, his red corduroy suit was still on him, over a clean white shirt and tie. His jacket was straight and his trousers were whole, washed where they'd been dirty, patched where they'd been burned, mended where they'd been torn.

Detective Mubia walked in front of us all, his head up high, and as he did so I realised that it was he who'd been responsible for what Mr N'chele said inside. Mr N'chele had come to his words not so much out of shame over his son or from his own ethical code, but because, after returning from my farm burned and broken and soiled, Detective Mubia had found Mr N'chele and told him that he must. In a word, Mr N'chele had once more done what he had to do to keep his awful son out of jail.

Detective Mubia left without speaking, and when he was gone Mr N'chele opened the door to his car and pushed his son inside. The parking attendant then gave Mr N'chele and me our lorry keys and we exchanged them, just as we were supposed to do in the foyer, after _Madama Butterfly_. I asked Ralph to ride with Mr N'chele in the old farm lorry and I asked Dr Zir to take my father home in a taxi.

So this is how it was when I walked across the car park and unlocked the door to the Mercedes-Benz. I was alone. Once inside the cab I looked at the gleaming knobs and the buttons and the windows that were so spotlessly clean. When I started the engine the sound was calm and low, and when I turned to look at Jules, to make sure he was securely tied, I saw my .380 automatic pistol and my husband's last letter on the seat beside me. The pistol was dirty and the letter was ripped apart; several pieces of it had fallen to the floor.

As I drove out of the car park the sky was clear and the moon was bright, and by the time I got to Kijabe Street no one else was on the road. As I passed the big roundabout, driving with one hand, I leaned down to pick up the pieces of Jules's letter, to smooth them out on the seat beside me, even before I got home.

That is the first stage of mending.

Matching up the pieces that are torn.

Act Three

22

Ahmed's Revenge

 I could go on, I think, writing until I caught up with my present life—writing each day as I've lived it these last five years, a summary hour each night, before allowing myself to sleep. It's a strange addiction, always telling what you know, always writing it down.

But let me forgo all that and just say that in view of what happened after the opera, Jules's wake was a sad and short affair. I reintroduced him to his skeletal left arm, putting it up the sleeve of his new black jacket, so he had a fleshy hand and a boney one, reminding everyone who looked at him that life was short. After the wake we buried him back on the farm, simple as that. And Mr N'chele was true to his word—he exchanged the tusks again, proving, I guess, that ivory and irony are anagrams, only a letter apart.

As for me, I haven't returned to the National Museum to see the place where Ahmed's bones still stand, but it's given me pleasure, all these years, to think of visitors from all over the world reaching across the cordon to touch Ahmed's tusks in awe, to marvel at their length and circumference and the numerous scars that they have, evidence of Ahmed's life and the battles that he won. That's Ahmed's own revenge, don't you think, that the tusks they touch aren't real?

The real tusks truly are up in Marsabit, though. Six months or so after the final exchange Mr N'chele supervised the building of a museum up there, out at the edge of the park where Ahmed lived. The entire museum is a single stone room, very simple, but it's got Ahmed standing at its centre, and around the outer walls it's got photographs of Ahmed as he lived before the guards were posted, and photographs of the Rendille Children's Choir singing "Greensleeves" with their Ahmed badges on. Ahmed's Marsabit skeleton, I should say, is nothing like the one in Nairobi. In Marsabit his skeleton is abstract and angular, deeply primitive and made of black wood. It is unlike any elephant who ever lived, and in that it is superb. How stark and beautiful to see his authentic tusks coming out of it the way they do. Ebony and ivory—it's extraordinary. I've been there many times. When Miro comes from New York, as a matter of fact, visiting Ahmed is the first thing she wants to do. Detective Mubia is back on the police force, by the way. I know it because Miro tells me. For five years now she has been the one sending money home, to pay his children's school fees.

One last thing. I want to tell you just in closing that Juliet is outside, playing in the orchard or down on the nearest side of the pond. As in the third act of *Madama Butterfly*, I'm bringing her to you late, at the end of my story, and with no hints of her before. I remember thinking that was a structural weakness in Puccini's opera, but I don't mind doing it myself, I don't mind doing it at all. Today is Juliet's fifth birthday, February 4, 1980, so it's a red-letter day in more ways than one, for it is also the day I had told myself I would finish this memoir, the day I would finally stop spending my mornings in the office and would step out onto the land, taking up real life once more.

My farm has changed a little bit over the years. Part of it is a tent camp now, like Cottar's, where Ralph brings his tourists for a night or two, where he can see Juliet and me on his way to the Mara or on his way home. The tent camp is where the orchard used to be, with a view of the pond on one side, and a full view of the Mara plains on the other. It isn't very far from Jules's grave.

When Juliet starts school in September we will have to move to my father's house in town. Ralph will take over the entire farm, managing the coffee and the tent camp and living in the house. Juliet and I will come occasionally to visit her father's grave, but eventually we will both turn into town people again, with full town lives to live. Already Juliet is talking about ballet lessons. Can you guess where those will be?

When Juliet comes into the house in a minute she will have her daily job to do. She will take the lunch tray from my hands and walk with it to the dormitory and give it to Beatrice, who will feed my father, who spends his days staring at the pond, sitting on the dormitory porch on that same old bench. The evil that men do lives after them, the good is oft interred with their bones. Is that it or is it the other way around?

There are more twists and turns to the story of one's life than one realises—that's something I've learned from writing all this down. We live our lives in three acts: the first, to know we are alive; the second, to try to understand; the third, to work and grow. That's what I'll teach Juliet, that's her legacy from Jules and me, that is what she has to know.

And when Juliet is grown up, who knows, maybe she will have her own tale to tell and will find her starting point in mine. That would be good. In this family we are into the women's generation now, and I think that kind of continuation would be fine. I like to imagine that Juliet will feel a certain peaceful recognition when she sits on the porch of her farm-house, watches the animals at her pond, and lets her eyes wander down to the words her mother wrote so many years ago.

I had a farm in Africa too. My farm was not in the Ngong Hills but on even richer land about eighty miles west of Nairobi. To get to my farm you drive down off what is called "the escarpment," into the Great Rift Valley and then up again, forty minutes or so north of the dusty Maasai town of Narok.

> January 1976–February 1980
> Grant's Coffee Farm
> Wildebeest Road, Kenya

About the Author

RICHARD WILEY is the author of four previous novels and a recipient of the PEN/Faulkner Award for *Soldiers in Hiding*. He has lived and worked in Japan, Korea, Nigeria, and Kenya and, with the publication of *Ahmed's Revenge*, has set a novel in each of those locales. Recently he has received grants from the NEA/Japan–United States Friendship Commission and the Japan Foundation, for work on a forthcoming novel, *Commodore Perry's Minstrel Show*.

About the Type

This book was set in Weiss, a typeface designed by a German artist, Emil Rudolf Weiss (1875–1942). The designs of the roman and italic were completed in 1928 and 1931 respectively. The Weiss types are rich, well-balanced, and even in color, and they reflect the subtle skill of a fine calligrapher.